THE MISTAKE

AJ CAMPBELL

The Mistake

by

AJ Campbell

Cover design © Tim Barber, Dissect Designs 2025

ALSO BY AJ CAMPBELL

Leave Well Alone

Don't Come Looking

Search No Further

The Phone Call

The Wrong Key

Her Missing Husband

My Perfect Marriage

Did I Kill My Husband?

First-Time Mother

All books are available at Amazon and are in Kindle Unlimited

A FREE GIFT FOR YOU

Warning signs presented themselves from the start. Flashing like the neon displays in Piccadilly Circus, they couldn't have advertised things more clearly.

But Abbie was too troubled to see clearly. Too damaged to see the dangers Tony Sharpe brought into her life. Until the day he pushed her too far.

See the back of the book for details on how to get your copy.

For my beautiful sister, Sally.
Thank you for your continued support with my writing.
Love always.
Amanda X

PROLOGUE

FundMeToday
GRACE'S APPEAL

Help Grace Hamilton get the treatment she desperately needs.
Mia Hamilton is organising this fundraising appeal on behalf of her niece, Grace.

Friends, family, and colleagues.
Earlier this year, my family's world was turned upside down when my baby niece, my
goddaughter, was diagnosed with a rare lung disease that was deemed incurable.
However, after carrying out extensive research, my brother and I discovered ground-breaking treatment in the USA, which will give Grace a second chance at life.
Sadly, this treatment isn't available under the NHS, but other children who have received it over the past year are making remarkable recoveries and leading normal lives. This

treatment comes at a considerable cost and will involve a lengthy stay in the USA for Grace and my sister, Ruby. Every penny you can give will go towards funding this treatment.

Thank you in advance for your support.

Mia x

£181,716 raised of £300,000 goal

598 donations

Recently donated:

Anthony Berg £10

Anonymous £500

Sonny Merritt £25

1

I knew I was making a mistake when I agreed to become part of Kat's little enterprise.

'You'll be fine.' Kat twirled a clump of her highlighted blonde hair around her forefinger. 'Think of the money. Ninety per cent of the proceeds will be yours.'

I fiddled with the hem of her short black dress I was wearing, picking at a loose thread.

'Think about your niece.' She certainly knew which buttons to press with me. That was how I became ensnared in her wretched plan. It hadn't taken her long, either. We met six months ago when I joined the KM Group, a boutique PR company. She was the owner's personal assistant, and I worked in the finance and admin team. Within three months, I'd moved in with her, soon realising Katherine West was the type of person you just went along with.

She sneezed into the crook of her arm. I recoiled at the deafening noise. My nerves were shot to pieces. She swiped a tissue from the box on the coffee table and wiped her nose.

'Damn cold.' Her nail varnish was peeling, which was

unlike her, and her blue-grey eyes were streaming. She prodded my elbow. 'Come on, drink up. Dutch courage and all that.'

I swallowed hard to lose the ball of apprehension stuck in my throat. It had been there since she'd first mentioned this idea. Mum crept into my thoughts. I missed living with her, even though I popped in to see her after work most days. I batted the thoughts away. I couldn't stomach thinking of Mum's reaction if she ever found out what I'd signed up for. It would break her heart. And that would break mine.

Instead, I filled my thoughts with images of my beautiful baby niece, my goddaughter, Grace. I thought about the future for our family if she didn't get the treatment she desperately needed.

A life without her.

And I thought of my sister, Ruby, a baby herself, really. I pictured the darkness blemishing the skin below her eyes these days. My mum, my brother, and I thought she'd made a big mistake last year when she'd decided to go ahead with the pregnancy. She was only seventeen and barely knew the father. My baby sister with a baby of her own was a burden she was far too young to bear, I'd thought. Until the night Grace exploded into our lives, and we all realised how wrong we'd been.

A life without her was one not worth considering.

I downed the remaining vodka and tonic Kat had poured earlier for me. 'What if he's not there?'

'Oh, he'll be there, alright. Don't you worry.' I wondered how she could be so sure. But typical of her whole persona, she remained convincing and forthright. She stood, coughed hard, and pulled me up. Swiping the empty tumbler from my hand, she ushered me towards the front door.

Further what-ifs slipped off my tongue. What if this Henry guy didn't go along with it? What if I got cold feet? What if I got caught? My heart was racing. The alcohol had heightened my anxiety levels, failing to numb them as Kat had convinced me it would.

'Life is full of what-ifs, Mia Hamilton. If we spend our lives questioning everything, we'd never do anything. Just get on with it.' She opened the apartment door and hurried me along like a mother seeing her child off to school. 'In less than an hour, it'll all be over. Follow my instructions, and it'll be fine. Remember, you're doing this for Grace.' She winked at me and grinned. 'Good luck. See you soon, Hazel.'

2

I perched on a stool in the hotel bar, the hem of Kat's little black dress sitting mid-thigh. My heart was beating as fast as the pianist's fingers dancing along the ivories of the mini-grand in the far corner of the dimly lit room. I was more uncomfortable than I could ever have imagined.

Taking a deep breath, I slowly let it out, unable to believe I'd signed up for this. But that was Kat for you. From the moment I met her, she seemed to have had the knack of getting me under her spell when it suited her. But this was it. I'd only do this once.

I stared across the bar, out of place, watching the fiery-orange-haired woman commanding the piano, treating the hotel guests to a piece of classical music with an elegance I deeply admired. The harmony amplified the elegance of the venue. The woman appeared to be young – way younger even than my twenty-two years – as if she should've been sitting in her bedroom doing homework, not entertaining guests with her mesmerising skills in one of the city's larger hotels. If only things had turned out differently, and Dad had hung around. Perhaps I could've been earning an income worthy of such sophistication. I'd always fancied learning to play the piano.

I turned my attention to the target, sitting two stools away. A tall man named Henry Robertson, early forties, with receding dark hair. He was drinking a bottle of Peroni. I caught his eye and quickly looked away, flicking my hair, long and platinum blonde with a hint of a curl, over my shoulder. I liked that wig. I'd always admired girls with hair down to their waist. It was Kat's favourite wig, too. She kept a bunch of them in a plastic box under her bed, which she used for such "jobs" and for the nights out when she wanted to be someone else, which was often. Soon after I moved in with her, renting her spare room for a sum far less than others I'd seen advertised in the city, she'd dragged that box into the living area. I was mesmerised. She'd donned each wig, parading around the room like an actress on a stage.

The transformation a simple prop could achieve was astonishing. Each wig came with a different accent, a different character and personality. That was part of the appeal, the fun. She poured shots – usually tequila, sometimes Jägermeister – every time she put on a different wig. Blonde, brunette, black, red, ginger, she had them all. Once she'd plied me with a couple of shots, she'd throw one of the wigs over to me and insist I took the stage alongside her.

When I agreed to that job – after weeks of nurturing from Kat that had become more compelling each time she broached the subject – she told me about the persona she'd built to make it even more fun.

She named her persona Tallulah, a travelling cosmetics saleswoman from the West Country. For me, she conjured up

Hazel, an Irish woman from Donegal, because, if nothing else, like Kat, I was good at impersonating different accents.

I engaged my Hazel personality, pursed my lips, and threw Henry another look.

He smiled.

I coyly returned the gesture like Kat had taught me.

The bartender appeared and slapped a square coaster on the bar. 'Good evening, ma'am. Would you like to see a menu?'

I shook my head. 'A vodka and tonic, please.'

'Coming right up.' He grabbed a glass. Not taking his eyes off me, he tossed it towards the ceiling.

I lowered my head, pretending to be busy on the phone Kat had given me. She'd warned me about not drawing attention to myself other than to the man in my sights. Out of the corner of my eye, I saw the bartender spin the glass three-sixty in the air and catch it in his waiting hand. He poured my drink and carefully placed it on the bar mat.

'A vodka and tonic water for the lady.'

Lady.

I'd never been called a lady before. I liked it. There was a unique ring to it. A ring of respect.

A small bowl of nuts appeared. Not peanuts. Not in a place like that. No, places like that served shelled pistachios, macadamias, and gourmet almonds.

The bartender held his hands behind his back. 'Would you like to settle the bill now or have it charged to your room?'

I tried to control my shaking voice. 'I'll settle it now, please.'

The bartender presented the bill on a dinky silver tray. I dug about in my large tote bag to find my phone. My real phone. But then I remembered. I didn't have it. Kat insisted I leave it at the apartment. She told me only to use cash and shoved a twenty-pound note in my hand when I said I didn't have any. I pulled the note from the inside pocket of my bag and left it on the silver tray.

I sipped my drink and returned to the phone Kat had given me for the night, working out my next move. From her experience, Kat said some targets proved easier than others. Sometimes the man approached her. Other times, it proved much harder, and she had to do all the leg work. 'Give it one drink,' she'd advised. 'Then you should know.' I asked her how many men she'd done this to. 'I've lost count,' came her reply with an insipid giggle. 'The first was the worst. It becomes a lot easier after that.'

Thankfully, luck appeared to be on my side. Henry slid along one stool to sit beside me. The pianist launched into a jazz piece. I clenched my teeth. I hated Nat King Cole. It reminded me of Dad.

The bartender returned my change on the silver tray. I scooped up the coins and threw them into the side pocket of my bag.

'Great music,' Henry said. There was a cocky lilt to his voice as if he could well own the place. 'Can I get you another drink?' he casually asked.

A strong, musky odour caught the back of my throat. He smelled like he'd drowned himself in a bottle of aftershave.

I lifted my glass and found Hazel and her well-practised Irish accent. 'I haven't finished this one yet.' I had to be careful. My voice was shaking. I gave him a close-lipped smile, not wanting to bare my teeth. One less clue to my identity, the better.

He swivelled on the stool until his body faced me, legs parted wide. 'Do I know you from somewhere?'

'I don't think so.' I took another sip of the drink and then another to calm my nerves.

'What's an attractive woman like you doing in a place like this?'

Oh, for heaven's sake. I smirked. 'Can't you do better than that?'

'Sorry.' He blushed. 'That was bad. Real bad. What's your name?'

Something about the initial exchange suggested he wasn't as well versed in chatting up women as Kat had led me to believe.

'Hazel.'

'Nice to meet you, Hazel. I'm Henry.'

Henry Robertson. Forty-two years old, Kat had told me earlier when she'd summarised my mission for the evening.

'What are you doing here?' I asked.

'I was meant to meet someone and they haven't turned up. Nice hotel, isn't it?'

'Very nice.' I lifted my glass but took a gulp that time.

'So what are you doing here?' he asked.

I racked my brain, momentarily forgetting what Kat told me to say. Oh, yes. Air hostess. The alcohol warmed my body and finally began to calm my nerves. I commenced the spiel. 'I'm an air hostess and have a free night in London. I'm trying to decide whether to call it a day and head to bed or hit a few bars, perhaps a club?'

'Sounds fun.'

'Fancy joining me?' I twiddled a strand of hair, unable to believe I was there saying those things.

He smiled and paused, as if deliberating my offer, making

his decision, questioning his morals. 'I need to go back to my room first.'

How perfect. That made my life a whole lot easier. I wasn't sure how successful I'd have been, trying to get him back to his room. I glanced down at my trembling hands. My stomach was tied in knots. Kat would tell me to get a grip, banish my fears, and throw myself into character. It was as if her voice was hissing in my ear: "Toughen up, Mia. You're not in a drama lesson now, practising for the school play. This is the real deal."

'Why?' I forged a pout. Another expression Kat insisted I practise when she'd pranced up and down the living area earlier, parading her different wigs.

'I need to make a call.' He downed the rest of his beer. 'I'll meet you back here in ten minutes.'

'How about I come with you?' I couldn't believe how easily the words were slipping from my mouth. It was no longer me sitting there conversing with a stranger. Hazel had taken full control. 'I could make us a drink while you make your call.'

He smiled. An "it's wrong but yes" boyish grin that made him look like a naughty kid.

Boy, was he going to regret meeting Hazel tonight.

3

I tottered in Kat's black stilettos back to room four-nine-three
on the fourth floor, pretending to be interested in what Henry
did for a living. Something about an all-singing, all-dancing,
technical breakthrough gadget that, apparently, was about to
change the world. I wondered if that was true or if he was
simply trying to impress me.

I was struggling to walk. I'd never owned a pair of stilettos. They were another accessory I'd borrowed from Kat.
Following him inside his room, I passed a bathroom and
proceeded to the living space, where a metal-framed bed, a
long leather sofa, and a mahogany desk with a swivel chair
framed the room. Henry pulled the heavy curtains across the
floor-to-ceiling glass doors leading to a balcony with river
views.

I clutched the wall to steady myself. My nerves had really
kicked in. A what-if occurred to me. One I hadn't thought of
asking Kat. What if he turned out to be a weirdo? I know how
she would've answered that. Just get the drink into him, and
I'd be away. Her self-assured, poised voice would say: "Do

what you have to do and get the hell out of there as soon as you can."

'I'll make drinks while I'm waiting,' I said.

Henry pointed to a black built-in unit. 'The minibar's in there. Indulge yourself. I need to make a call. I'll be back in a couple of minutes.'

'What's your favourite drink?'

'I'll have what you were having at the bar.'

I winked at him. 'A vodka and tonic coming straight up.' Give him lots of winks, Kat had told me. Men like him relish it. It was strange. I seemed to be flitting between utter terror and radiating Hazel's confident character. Hazel's Irish accent was coming through loud and clear. I couldn't believe how well I adopted her persona when I was in full flow.

I licked my red-glossed lips. Another action Kat told me to keep repeating. 'Don't be long.'

He smiled nervously and disappeared into the bathroom.

Poor guy. Despite Kat's insistence that men like him "do this sort of thing all the time", I found it hard to believe he'd done it before. But Kat often mocked me for being so unworldly. She would taunt me: "How warm and comfy is that rock you live under?"

I breathed in the cocktail of scents, from the waft of expensive aftershave Henry had left in his wake to the tinge of lime and basil from the reed diffuser on the desk.

On top of the minibar sat a silver tray with a selection of glasses and a pile of white napkins beside a blue lanyard with the initials KM in white. He must have forgotten to give it back when he left the office today. Pulling open the double doors to the minibar, I spotted two miniature bottles of champagne. Henry's voice intensified through the walls. The sound of frustration and anger. He was arguing with someone. I picked a mini bottle of champagne and popped the cork, catching the fizz in a crystal glass. Inhaling a large lungful of air, I slowly released it and sipped the drink.

I grabbed a bottle of vodka and a can of tonic and prepared Henry's drink. I found the small drawstring pouch Kat had given me earlier and dropped its contents into the waiting glass. The concoction fizzed. Bubbles rose. Using my index finger, I gave it a good stir.

Henry appeared from the bathroom. 'Sorry about that, Hazel.' He fiddled with the TV remote control. The news switched to a music channel. He raised the volume. Classical music filled the room. It was an odd choice for the occasion.

'It sounded like you were angry with someone,' I said. 'Was it the person who didn't turn up?'

'Just some business to sort out.'

'Have a sip of your drink. I've poured you a special one.' My Irish accent faltered. Hazel was slipping from my control. That couldn't happen.

He frowned. 'A special one?'

I held out the glass of vodka and tonic. 'It's a good brand. My favourite.'

'You've gone for champagne,' he observed.

'I fancied some bubbles.'

He raised his eyebrows. 'Expensive tastes, eh?'

'I'll have a vodka afterwards.'

'A real party girl?'

He couldn't be further from the truth. I was a million miles from being a party girl. True, I'd gone out more since moving in with Kat, but only on the occasions she'd invited me. I was more of the stay-at-home type, watching movies with my family or playing board games. Although we didn't play games much anymore. Grace drained everyone's energy to such an extent that when my sister finally got her to sleep, we had little else left in us.

'I sure am a party girl.' That line always worked, Kat told me.

Although they'd deny it if questioned, men like Henry Robertson were bored with their wives. That's not to say they didn't love them, and they certainly had no intention of ever leaving them. They simply needed an air of excitement pumped back into their monotonous lives.

He laughed and sipped his drink.

I struggled to remember what Kat had told me to do next. Oh, yes. The race. 'I'll tell you what.'

He raised an eyebrow like my brother, Callum, when questioning what someone had told him. I winced, thinking about Callum and what he'd say if he ever found out what I was up to and the dire consequences for him if I was caught. He'd be so ashamed of me.

'Let's have a race,' I said.

'A race?'

I grabbed another glass and fixed myself a vodka and tonic, going sparingly on the vodka. 'We down our drinks in one. The last to finish removes an item of clothing. Then we can finish the champers.'

He almost choked on his drink. 'Steady on.'

'You in or not?'

His jaw dropped. He gave a nervous laugh. 'You *are* a party girl.'

Kat's instructions pumped through my head. I raised my glass. 'Cheers, Henry. We're going to have the best night.' I couldn't believe what was coming out of my mouth. Hazel was far more brazen than I'd ever been – a different persona entirely.

Hesitantly, he allowed me to clink my glass against his. 'Cheers.'

'After three. Ready? One, two, three...' Lifting my glass, I parted my lips and downed my drink, my eyes not leaving his. He copied me.

I won. There was no way I was removing a single item of clothing. I wasn't wearing enough as it was.

The drink caught in the back of his throat. He coughed. 'Sorry.' He spluttered, wiping the spilt liquid from his chin.

He slipped into a one-sided conversation about how he'd worked his way up from nothing to owning his own business. I pretended to listen, nodding intently, while silently urging the drugs to hurry up around his system. Eventually, his shoulders twitched. He took an unsteady step backwards. And another one.

I clenched my fists in anticipation.

There we go. The moment Kat had told me about.

Show time.

He squeezed his eyes shut, grimacing, before snapping them open again. Sweat glistened on his forehead. He fumbled with a shirt button, his body swaying. 'Christ. How much vodka did you put in that drink?' His words came out low and slow. 'I feel like I've drunk ten of them.' He wiped his forehead with the back of his hand. 'Hell.'

'Only one. You're rather pale.'

Kat's directions echoed in my thoughts: "Make sure you encourage him to sit down before he falls. And make sure you appear to look as if you give a damn."

I reached to take his glass. 'Why don't you sit down, Henry?'

He stumbled, grabbing the arm of the leather sofa. 'I don't feel too good.'

'Let me call a doctor.'

He clumsily removed his wallet from his pocket, chucked it on the table, and fell onto the sofa, his face as red as the scarlet cushions. 'No. No.' He was struggling to squeeze out his words. 'I'll be fine in a moment.'

My heart was racing, my legs shaky. I waited for his eyes to close and for him to fall into unconsciousness.

But I gave it a minute – just to be on the safe side.

Then I moved on to the next stage.

4

———————

Speed was essential at that point – another piece of advice from Kat.

I reached into my bag and pulled out the pair of blue surgical gloves and a packet of wipes Kat had given me. Snapping the gloves onto my shaking hands, I cleaned up, wiping the glasses and everything I'd touched. 'Make sure you're thorough,' Kat said. 'Just to be sure.'

There was no way I could ever go through that again.

I dragged Henry's shirtsleeve up his arm. My heart was beating fast. There it was – the Hublot watch. It looked like any other men's watch, but Kat told me it was worth over thirty grand. It wouldn't fetch her anywhere near such a sum, but her contact always gave her a good cut, which she promised to give to me minus her ten per cent for arranging the deal. 'Think of how much it'll boost Grace's fundraising page,' she said. 'Another large step closer to getting her the treatment she needs.'

I needed to be quick. I'd never been so out of my depth. I set to work, arranging Henry's body in an uncompromising position on the sofa the way Kat had instructed, parting his legs and tilting his head backwards slightly. He was a big bloke. It was an effort, especially for a small woman like me.

I stepped away and checked my endeavours. It should be OK. The camera lens wouldn't capture his face, so his closed eyes wouldn't appear in the photo. I rearranged the sofa cushions, plumping them up under his arms. I tipped his head backwards a fraction more and spread his legs wider apart. As quickly as I could, I removed the Fuji Instax Mini camera that Kat had given me from my bag. I squatted between his legs, ruffled the hair of the blonde wig and spread it across my shoulders. Further commands from Kat rang in my head: "Get two photos in case the first doesn't come out."

The music on the TV turned dark, a sombre-sounding piece fitting for a funeral march. It was unsettling. I clicked the button. A clear and unflattering photo of poor Henry Robertson appeared from the body of the camera. I grabbed a pen from my bag and wrote a message on the back of the photo. The short pitch Kat made me learn by heart.

> *Dear Henry*
> *You keep quiet, and so will I.*
> *Kindest regards*
> *Hazel*

It was time to go.

The sombre music was grating on me. I pulled out the soft cream-coloured cloth Kat had given me earlier from my bag. Unclasping the strap of Henry's watch, I slipped it off his limp wrist and wrapped it inside the cloth. I'd never held an item of such value. And I never would again. There was no way I'd let Kat coerce me into any kind of crime again. No way. She'd try. Oh, my, would she. She was that kind of person – persuasive and demanding.

Quickly, I gathered my things and threw them inside my bag, checking around me to ensure I hadn't left anything incriminating behind. I snatched his wallet from the table. I don't know why. Kat had insisted I never touch any other personal belongings of the victim. Only the watch. 'You can't risk having anything else remotely traceable,' I remembered her saying.

Victim. I disliked labelling Henry in those terms, but I guessed that was what the men Kat targeted were — what Tallulah and Hazel turned them into.

I flipped open the wallet. My heart jolted at the picture of a dark-haired woman with two children. I bit my lip. It must've been his wife and kids. Poor woman. Poor kids. My guilt hit new levels. I wasn't cut out for any of it. They were real people.

Expanding the notes section, I found a wad of money. I removed it and fanned the twenty-pound notes. They were crisp, fresh from a cashpoint. I quickly counted them. Two hundred quid. Who carried that kind of cash around with them these days?

A powerful knock at the door startled me.

A low male voice called out, 'Housekeeping. Are you there, sir?'

I momentarily froze. Damn, I'd forgotten to hang the do-not-disturb sign on the door when we arrived, even though Kat had insisted it was a must.

Another knock shocked me into action.

'I'm coming in, sir.'

I picked up the photo I'd taken with Kat's camera and squashed it into the wallet.

The door clicked open.

I didn't know what to do. It was too late to tell them to go away. Still holding the wallet, I grabbed my bag, dived into the bathroom, and hid behind the door, hoping to hell the housekeeper couldn't hear my heart exploding like a firework.

The main door to the room quietly closed. Footsteps strode along the hallway. I willed myself to stay calm. The housekeeper would see the state of the guest and, not wanting to disturb him, would slip quietly away.

How wrong could I have been?

The smell of imminent danger hung heavy in the air.

I peered through the gap in the door. It wasn't a house-keeper at all. But a unit of a guy dressed entirely in black, including a balaclava which, apart from his eyes, hid most of his face, marched boldly into the room, pushing a laundry trolley.

Discarding the trolley, the guy confidently paced up to the sprawled Henry and stood in front of his comatose body.

I blinked several times as if my brain thought my eyes were deceiving me.

Five or so seconds passed before the guy pulled a gun from the inside pocket of his jacket and calmly fired it point-blank at the centre of Henry's glistening forehead.

5

Terror bolted through me like a flash of lightning. I'd expected a boom and was confused. All I heard was a crack, accompanied by the burning waft of gunpowder that intensified the smell of danger.

I placed my hand over my mouth to stifle a scream. My bag dropped to the floor. The intruder turned, peering in my direction. The taste of champagne burned the back of my throat. I thought I was going to throw up. That couldn't happen. I willed myself to take stock and take charge. Otherwise, I'd never make it out of there alive.

It was difficult to tell if he could see me, despite the sensation he was staring directly at me. I sidestepped away from the doorframe, deliberating my options. But there was only one firm choice if I was to make it out of there alive. I needed to make a sharp exit, quickly and quietly. I glanced through the gap in the door again.

Evidently, the intruder hadn't seen me because he was dragging what appeared to be a piece of black material out of the laundry basket. I glimpsed at Henry's lifeless body still sprawled on the sofa. My gaze moved to the hole in his forehead. What the hell had he done to deserve such a brutal end? He was an idiot to have engaged with a person like Hazel and have her in his room, yes. But that?

I gasped. I was still clutching Henry's wallet. I peered through the gap again.

The intruder was rifling through the pockets of Henry's suit jacket.

I yanked the handles of my bag and threw the wallet inside, shooting another look through the gap in the door. The drumbeat of my hammering heart exacerbated. I couldn't risk staying there another second.

It was a case of now or never.

I removed the stilettos and took a final peep. I was as safe as I'd ever be, so I slipped out of the bathroom and lunged for the main door. With a trembling hand, I pulled the handle. It squeaked. I peered over my shoulder.

There was no mistake.

The balaclava guy seemed to be staring straight at me. He raised his gun, his forefinger wrapped around the trigger guard.

And he pointed it in my direction.

His eyes appeared to bore into mine, but I don't think we'd have recognised each other without his balaclava and my wig and the ton of make-up I had plastered on my face.

Fear tightened its hold, digging its claws deep into my flesh. I slipped into the air-conditioned corridor, and a low, gravelly voice demanded, 'Stop right there.'

6

My breaths came short and sharp. I fled the hotel room and crashed into another large laundry trolley waiting outside the door. I shoved it from my path and ran for my life.

I was in trouble – deep, deep trouble.

Blasts of adrenaline propelled me along the carpeted hallway. My bag, slung over my shoulder, bounced against my side. Five doors down, I passed a cleaner's room. A fleeting thought of hiding in there passed through my mind, and for a split second, I considered it as a possible place of safety, but my best option was to get the hell out of there.

A door opened and banged shut. I gazed over my shoulder. He was coming for me.

The meaning of fear took on a new definition.

I turned the corner to a landing with three lifts. One of them had its doors open. The white digital buttons above the other two indicated they were in transit. I dashed for the open doors, but stopped. I couldn't chance it.

Without a nanosecond to spare, I darted towards the stairwell and pushed open the door. At school, I had been fast and lithe, earning the nickname Speedy, because I'd always won the running races on sports day. But that had been on a grass track with gym shoes. Nevertheless, I was sure I'd never moved so fast in my life.

My cold, clammy hands grasped the railings, and I took the steps three at a time. My body took off as I flew around the corners between the flights of stairs. I gasped for air. Halfway down the second flight, a door from a floor above swung open. It crashed against the wall. I peered upwards.

He was coming for me.

I darted away from the railings, ducking from his line of vision. Trailing the wall, I continued racing downwards. The sound of footsteps advanced rapidly, catching up with me like he was an animal chasing its prey. At the bottom floor, I forced open the bar of the exit and blasted through into the rare heat of a late September evening.

I was disoriented. I'd entered the hotel via the front, which faced the river, and the sun had been shining. Then I was in a dark backstreet and dusk was approaching, the sun slowly dipping below the horizon. I ran along the street, constantly peering behind me. The guy was nowhere to be seen. I begged above for mercy, hoping I'd lost him.

Desperation pushed me forward, while the dread of capture frightened me to death. I stopped to chuck the stilettos in my bag and took out my ballet pumps. My go-to shoes when I wasn't in trainers. I quickly slipped them onto my feet, debating whether to ditch the wig now or later. Time wasn't on my side. I had to run for my life.

The street led me into a burst of people enjoying an evening outside. The hum of chatter and laughter filled the air. It should have been a night to enjoy, one to savour before the chill of autumn arrived. I couldn't believe I was being chased by a criminal with a gun and fleeing the scene of a terrible crime. All I could think about was Mum. The thought of her finding out what I'd done was mortifying.

A trail of people was heading for the river; others were hanging around the park or swarming towards a pop-up market selling street food. I stopped for a moment to catch my breath and consider my options. The outcome of that showdown could mean life or death.

People. I had to lose myself among the throng of people. I'd be safe in the thick of the crowds congregating in the backstreets behind the river. And I needed to get changed. What little there was of the black dress stuck to my back, and my scalp was itchy beneath the uncomfortable blonde wig. I needed to ditch them at the first opportunity. It would aid my escape. The gunman would be searching for a woman with long blonde hair, not one with a shoulder-length, layered bob.

Dipping into the park, I passed a group of students lazing on the grass playing a drinking game. They were sipping cider from bottles and beer from cans, laughing and squealing. It should've been me, lost in the joy of a carefree evening. Instead, my pulse was racing like a speed train, and I was running for my life. I ducked behind an oak tree and peered around the trunk.

There he was. Unsurprisingly, he'd ditched his disguise, the balaclava replaced by a baseball cap with an extra-large brim. But I recognised his lightweight jacket: the gun, no doubt, hidden inside the pocket. To anybody else, he appeared a regular guy. Six feet, perhaps. Broad. He held a hand to his forehead, and although his animal eyes continued to scan for its prey, I was unable to make out any more of his features. He dropped his hand and purposefully strode towards me. I ducked behind the tree trunk, praying he hadn't seen me. Panic gripped my throat. I started hyper-ventilating, my breaths coming thick and fast. I was not only way out of my depth, but I was also quickly sinking.

I made a snap decision and darted towards the opposite entrance to the park adjoining a road. Loud rap music sounded from a passing car that had all its windows down. The driver beeped the horn. The backseat passenger leaned out of the window – a drunken youth with a vocal volume much louder than the music, who said, 'Want to party, blondie?' His hollering attracted attention I couldn't afford. 'Party at eighty-nine South Street. Come and join us.' If I were Kat, I'd have given him a mouthful and told him exactly where he could shove his unwanted invitation. But I wasn't Kat. I quickly turned in the other direction. The driver tooted the horn again, and his passengers cheered as he sped away.

Turning back on myself, I joined the merriment of people enjoying an innocent summer's evening. I glanced left and right. A group of lively businessmen were congregated outside a bar to the left, steering me to stay on the path. That was my best bet. The gunman would never take a shot at me with so many people around. But I couldn't forget how brutal he'd proved himself to be. A dangerous maniac. I'd seen it first-hand. He'd slid that gun out of his jacket and shot Henry Robertson as calmly as if he'd walked into a bar, ordered a pint of beer, and slipped his phone out of his pocket to pay.

I glanced behind me again. He was marching steadfastly in my direction, staring straight at me.

Dodging between people wandering without purpose, attracting the occasional curse, I headed for the main market. I could lose him among the stalls. I wondered if he'd dare take a shot. My fear intensified. I couldn't die. I still had so much I needed and wanted to do. And baby Grace needed me. I couldn't fail her.

I turned my head. He'd broken into a jog. I considered stopping an unsuspecting bystander and asking for help. But I'd lose valuable time. And no one would want anything to do with a crazy, half-dressed woman running the streets like a lunatic. Where were the police when you needed them? I was kidding myself. What would I say? I'd drugged and fleeced an unsuspecting man. And in his unconscious state, he'd been shot. That wasn't a clever idea.

I peered over my shoulder again.

A fresh wave of terror reared within me.

The gunman was gaining on me.

7

I fled along the uneven cobbled road and stumbled. My ankle rolled. Pain pierced through me, but the adrenalin pumping through my veins forced me onwards.

A late-night event was being held at the market square tonight – something to do with the city mayor. When I'd stopped by at Mum's place the previous night, she'd told Ruby and me about it and proposed we go together as a family.

'It'll be a good opportunity to get Grace out in the fresh air. And you, too, Ruby,' she'd said.

I'd faked a stream of positivity, hoping Ruby would agree despite knowing full well it wouldn't happen. Apart from when needs must with Grace, Ruby had barely left the flat in seven months.

The gunman's determined stride was gaining on me. A group of drunken youngsters had blocked his way, giving me the much-needed time to launch myself into the packed market and lose myself among the crowds.

The different blends of smells from international food mingled into a melting pot of aromatic scents. I wove in and out of the meandering concourse, people savouring an assortment of flavours from takeaway boxes, tubs, and cones. Dodging a horde of customers perusing a display of dried fruit, nuts, and nibbles, I came to a cheese stall. Usually, I loved cheese – any sort, any way. But tonight, the ammonia stench of Stilton was too much.

Blood seeped through a run in my stockinged foot. But there wasn't time. I'd have to deal with the pain, the blood, and the mental torture of the horrific ordeal later. If fate had a "later" in store for me.

Right then, I needed to concentrate on staying alive.

I left the food area, which had morphed into an expanse of stalls selling an array of goods and services. A few stall-holders had started to pack up. A Chinese man was giving a woman a massage in a seated chair beside a lively couple running a stall selling hats, scarves, bags, and handmade shawls. I glanced behind me. The gunman was not in sight.

I took my chance.

Worming my way between the tarpaulin separating the stalls, I ducked behind the canvas backing of the couple's stall where they stored boxes of stock. I grabbed a metal pole, cold to my clammy palm, and dropped my head, trying to calm my breathing. The effects of the alcohol had long gone, washed away by the overdose of adrenaline rushing through me.

I grabbed the blonde wig and ripped it off, discarding it around the side of the boxes. That was a brainless move. People would be seeking a blonde woman in a black dress crazily running around the city when they connected me to the murder in that hotel room.

Because it was sure to happen.

CCTV would've caught me at the hotel at some point and perhaps along the way. I wasn't that stupid. Despite what Kat had taught me, and how careful I'd been, I wasn't sharp enough to have bypassed it all. Witnesses were bound to come forward saying they'd seen the blonde with the victim only minutes before he was brutally murdered. There had been the suited man who exited the lift when Henry and I headed to his room. And the elderly couple strolling arm in arm we had passed in the corridor. And the barman. Of course, the barman.

I shoved the wig into my bag. My heart was beating so fast that I thought I was going to pass out.

Grace entered my thoughts. The baby I'd treated as my own before she was even born. I remembered the excitement when she'd first kicked inside Ruby. Every subsequent time, my sister had grabbed my hand and laid it across her expanding belly, and we'd giggled together at each prod and poke. All I wanted was to give my beautiful goddaughter hope.

My hands shook uncontrollably. I caught the blonde strands trying to escape from the bag and forced them back inside. Fishing through my make-up bag, I removed the mirror. My naturally strawberry-blonde hair was stuck to my scalp and appeared darker from the sweat. I fluffed the layers and found a tissue to wipe the overdone blusher from my cheeks, the red gloss from my lips, and the concealer masking the beauty spot below my left eye. I'd been scrolling through TikTok one night and came across a woman who claimed moles gave away personality traits. I was an introvert with money problems, according to her. She hadn't been far wrong.

'I might have a large around the back,' hollered a throaty male voice.

A stout man swiped aside the canvas curtain separating the front of the stall from his stock of items out the back. I ducked behind a stack of boxes. He entered the area, literally only a few metres from where I was peering through a gap in the boxes. He rooted through piles of stock on the foldable trestle table, discarding items as he searched for the size he needed. He stopped.

My heart missed a beat.

I muttered a silent prayer. I wasn't a religious person. Not in the sense of attending church every Sunday morning. Life had never steered me in that direction. But I was a believer. God lived somewhere. I silently said my third prayer of the night: please don't let this man see me. I wouldn't be able to explain what I was doing hiding amongst his livelihood. I continued staring at him, swallowing hard.

He snatched up an item of clothing. 'Definitely, large, luv?' he called out to his potential customer. 'Here we go. I've got it in the navy. But not purple...'

He disappeared. I breathed a sigh of relief and tugged a rolled-up pair of leggings and a T-shirt from my bag, grateful for the mild weather. The black dress was as tight as a strait-jacket and a pain to escape from. The small space wasn't helping. I shimmied and writhed until I was free, thankful for the freedom the leggings and T-shirt allowed.

A waist-high stack of marked boxes caught my attention. I opened the top one packed with shawls wrapped in plastic. Removing a dark-purple one, I unsealed the packaging and draped the shawl over my shoulders. It wasn't an item of clothing I'd usually be seen in, but it wasn't a fashion show.

The box beneath was labelled "small RS". I pushed the top box aside until a large enough gap allowed me to grab an army-green rucksack. It was ideal. Exactly what I needed to blend in and stay under the radar of ruthless men with guns. It was unreal. It was like I was watching myself in an action movie, not living the nightmare in person.

I emptied the contents of my tote bag into the rucksack, stuffing in the flowing strands of hair from the wig. I shoved the tote inside, too, and slipped the rucksack on my back.

The box at the bottom was labelled "hats". But there was no way I could reach it without disturbing the others. I stepped to the gap in the tarpaulin. On second thought, what had happened wasn't the stallholder's fault. I removed the rucksack and dug inside my tote until I found Henry's wallet. Snapping it open, I snatched two twenty-pound notes and dropped them into the box of shawls.

I found Kat's phone. There were three missed calls from her and a text.

> I've been trying to get hold of you. Why haven't you called? Phone me ASAP. K

I pressed the call button, only to be put straight through to her voicemail. I cut the call and sent a text instead.

> Disaster. Don't call me. On my way back.

I left the market, my chin dropped to my chest. I needed to get back to her apartment. Fast. Because even if the gunman was no longer looking for me, the police soon would be.

8

I arrived at Kat's block of apartments, sweating. I banged on the door, too frazzled to search for my keys.

It wasn't the most impressive block of apartments in the neighbourhood. The façade could have done with a good lick of paint, the hallway, too, but what did that matter when you were a short stroll from the river, and in under twenty minutes, you could journey to the pumping heart of the city by foot?

It was time to find somewhere else to rent. "You never know someone until you live with them," Mum always told us. I never realised until I moved in with Kat that this advice applied equally to friends as it did lovers.

Kat appeared in her fluffy pink bathrobe that matched her slippers. Her blonde hair was tied up into a messy pineapple on top of her head, and the end of her nose was as red as her flushed cheeks. 'Why haven't you called?' Her voice was raspy and scratchy as if she'd smoked a hundred cigarettes.

Her presence sent waves of emotion crashing through me. I'd held it together all the way back. Now I was scared and confused. But I was mainly angry. I barged past her. The front door banged closed. I didn't realise how much I'd been holding back. My voice trembled. 'You're not going to believe what happened.'

Kat trailed me, trying to grab my shoulder. I shook her off, unable to bear her touch.

'What the hell's wrong?' she snapped. 'Calm down.'

I stumbled over my words in my haste to get them out. 'I can't calm down.' I slapped my hands on my cheeks and dragged them down my face, stretching my lower eyelids. 'I saw a man get shot tonight.'

Her eyes widened. 'What? Who?'

I removed the rucksack from my back. 'Henry.'

'Henry Robertson?'

'Correct. The man you set me up with tonight. And whoever killed him chased me.'

Kat let out one of her posh laughs as if she thought I'd fabricated the drama I claimed to have played out. Until she realised from my frenzied expression and how much I was shaking that there was no way I could've fabricated such a story. 'OK. Calm down.' She took my flailing arms and steadied them.

I turned away from her cigarette-infused breath. I couldn't calm down. The gravity of the situation hit me like a speeding car veering into the wrong lane. My body shook uncontrollably.

'You need a drink.' Kat led me into the open-plan living space, where the smell of eucalyptus oil wafted in the air. A floor lamp at the side of the sofa shone a dim light across the room.

Marching over to the window, I parted the closed curtains an inch and examined the shadowy street below. But only the usual evening scene played out: people on their way home late from work, on their way into town, or walking their dogs.

'Did he follow you?'

I continued staring outside. 'I think I lost him at the market.'

'You think?'

I left the window. 'I never saw him again after that.' I grimaced at *Love Island* playing on the TV. 'Turn that off, can you?' I was never normally so demanding, so outspoken towards Kat – towards anyone. But it wasn't a usual night.

Kat snatched the TV remote control from the arm of the sofa and pressed pause. Scooping the large patchwork blanket from the sofa, she discarded it on a banana-yellow plastic chair not meant for sitting, but as more of an accessory she'd bought on a whim from a trendy store in town one Saturday afternoon. It was the day I began to wonder where she got her money from, because the chair had come with a price tag exceeding my monthly salary.

She ordered me to sit down. 'Now tell me exactly what's happened.'

I couldn't speak, and I couldn't stop shaking.

Striding to the other side of the room, Kat slid open the door of the 1950s sideboard, removed a bottle of whisky, and took it to the small kitchen area. She opened a kitchen cupboard. Glasses clinked. She removed two and placed them on the worktop.

I stared at the TV screen, paused on two girls dressed in skimpy bikinis, who were lounging on sunbeds and sipping pina coladas. How had my life turned into such a dreadful mess? I was twenty-two years old. I should've been sipping cocktails by a pool in a sunny climate, not witnessing a brutal murder.

9

Kat returned to the sofa with generous measures of the brown liquid in two tumblers. 'Get this down you.' She dropped back down beside me.

I raised the glass to my lips. The toxic smell was overpowering, a warning the drink was bound to rot my insides and mess with my head, but I was past caring. I swigged it in one. The fiery liquid burned the back of my throat and slid down to my stomach. I grimaced. 'That was rank.'

'It's the cheap stuff that loser I dated over the summer brought around the night I dumped him. I knew it'd come in handy at some point.' She picked up a packet of cigarettes from the table, removed one, and stuffed it between my lips. Grabbing a lighter, she lit the cigarette. 'Have a puff on that and talk to me.' She removed another cigarette, lit it and took a drag, coughing but not letting that stop her taking another.

I'd never smoked until I met her. I took a long, hard drag. My hands gripped the glass resting in my lap. 'It all went to plan.' My voice wavered. 'I did exactly what you told me.' I cast a sideways glance at her.

She was staring at me intently, her gaze lingering. It was eerie.

'But someone knocked on the door. I never expected that.'

The memory backpedalled into my mind. I let out a low moan and delivered my recollection of the evening in a whisper. 'I thought it was housekeeping, so I hid in the bathroom. A guy in a balaclava marched straight up to Henry and then... then... he pulled out a gun and shot him in the head.'

Kat's mouth opened wide. 'You're not joking, are you?' She stared at me in horror, not expecting me to answer her remark. 'What did you do?'

I took another drag on the cigarette and continued. 'What could I do?' My voice adopted a high-pitched squeal. Words shot out fast and furiously. 'I was petrified he was going to see me and murder me as well. It was terrifying. I got away, but he must've heard me. He followed me.'

Kat spluttered and coughed, but still she continued smoking. 'What, in a balaclava?'

I shook my head vigorously. 'No, he ditched it. I managed to lose him. Thank goodness that market was on tonight.' I glared at her. 'Who the hell was Henry Robertson, Kat?'

She smirked as if she was taking some macabre pleasure in my plight. 'Just someone who came into the office for a meeting with Kelly at lunchtime today.' Kat covered reception when the receptionist took her lunchbreak. 'I was chatting with him. That's when I noticed his watch and thought he'd be a perfect target. He was quite flirty.'

'Was he a new client?'

Kat sniffed. 'I don't know.'

'You're Kelly's PA. How can you not know who she's seeing?'

'She must've put the meeting in her diary herself.' She

scoffed and grabbed a tissue from the box on the coffee table that was littered with unopened mail, dirty cups, discarded, sodden tissues, and an empty box of Lindt chocolate balls. 'She sometimes does that without me knowing.'

'How long did Kelly meet him for?'

'I don't know. I came home sick. What's with all the questions?' She paused. 'Christ.' She sucked in air, making a screeching whistling sound, which grated on my already frayed nerves. 'It should've been me. If I hadn't been sick.'

Typical Kat! She always thought of herself.

'They're going to be looking for me,' I said. 'When they find the body, the police will search CCTV.'

'Calm down. You were in disguise.' Kat extinguished her cigarette, leaned backwards, and threw me a questioning glare. 'Please tell me you were.'

'Obviously I was. But what about my fingerprints?'

'You cleaned up like I told you to, didn't you?'

I couldn't believe I was sitting there discussing such criminal behaviour. When she'd first told me about her side hustle and suggested I join her on the grounds my niece needed me to, I'd told her no way. It wasn't for me. I didn't have the guts. And I'd only screw it up somehow. Besides, I was too honest. The nearest I'd got to breaking the law was stealing a bag of sweets when I was eight years old for Ruby who wanted them so badly, she'd cried and screamed when Mum had said she didn't have the money for them. Mum had cried, too, although she'd tried to hide it. It was the first time I'd realised how poor we were.

'Of course I cleaned up. But what if I missed something? They'll find my fibres in the room. On his clothes.'

'You don't have a criminal record, so they can't trace it

back to you.' She paused. 'You don't, do you? You were telling me the truth.'

I rolled my eyes.

'Did you stay away from CCTV like I told you to?'

I nodded. 'I think so. As best I could.'

'Well, stop stressing.'

'Let's not be naive, Kat. I'd have been caught on camera at some point.'

I stared at her incredulously, wondering how she could be so flippant.

She sneezed. Her eyes were streaming as if she'd been chopping an onion. 'Make sure you stay out of trouble. Then they can't trace it all to you.'

'Once they catch me on CCTV, do you think they'll be able to tell I was wearing a wig? Don't they have technology now to tell this kind of stuff?'

'Stop going on, will you? I've seen you with your make-up on. You're a totally different person. And with the wig, there's no way you're recognisable.'

My teeth were chattering. 'I wonder if they've found him yet? They could've done. My picture could be all over the news any time now.' I picked up the TV remote control.

She snatched it back from me. 'He was staying there the night. You said there was no noise. So no one has reason to go in that room.'

I couldn't understand how she could appear so calm. 'What if he was due to meet someone? His wife?'

'For fuck's sake, Mia. I told you to stop stressing. He lives up north somewhere. The earliest someone will realise he's missing is tomorrow when he doesn't check out and they go to clean his room. Chill.'

'Chill? You don't get it, do you, Kat? A man was murdered,

and I was the last one to see him alive. And what's more, I witnessed the murder! And before he died, I drugged him.'

She stretched her arms above her head, yawned, and stood. 'You're talking in riddles. Technically you weren't the last person to see him alive. It was the dude who pulled the trigger.' She snatched my glass. 'I'll get you another one of these.'

I got up and went to the window, scanning the streets below but still noticed nothing out of the ordinary. If that gun man had followed me back, he was staying out of view. With a trembling hand, I picked up my phone from the small table by the window where I'd left it before going out.

I googled the local news. Nothing had broken about the incident yet.

I was safe... for the time being.

Returning to the sofa, I stared again at the two women on the TV dressed in bikinis. Their perfect bodies and perfect lives shone through the screen like the sunshine from the blue skies overlooking the plush resort they were staying in.

I bent my upper body forwards and dropped my head in my hands. A sick sensation of dread pooled in my stomach.

From the moment I met Kat, I should've known our acquaintance could only end in disaster.

10

Three months ago

Halfway through my first day working at the KM Group, a slim woman a few years older than me approached my desk. She was sporting the casual corporate look: a satin blouse, grey wide-legged trousers, and loafers. She had the same hairstyle as me: a layered shoulder-length bob. Her large eyes were the same colour as mine: a deep, velvety brown that Mum always said reminded her of a deer.

There was something entrancing about that woman. It took me a while to realise it was her mouth – her full lips and the gap between her two front teeth.

'Hi, Mia. I'm Kat, Kelly's personal assistant. Have you had lunch yet? I usually grab something from Pret. You can come with me today.'

From the get-go, she rolled me around in her manipulative little hands like a piece of soft putty.

'Sure.' I locked my computer. I was nervous. But not for

long. From that first meeting, it was as if Kat West had already calculated how she was going to deal with me.

'It's raining. Have you got an umbrella?' she asked, smacking the button to call the lift.

I shook my head.

She shook a bright-pink umbrella in my face. 'You can share mine.'

With a sharp jerk, she burst it open and held it over our heads when we left the glass-fronted building and stepped into the rain. It was awkward at first, our bodies of equal height touching as we huddled to keep dry from the unrelenting rain. She chatted incessantly like we were old school friends. I intermittently nodded, hopping from side to side trying to dodge the puddles and crevices in the pavement.

Arriving at Pret, we stamped our feet to shake off the water seeping through our shoes. The place was busy, full of lunchtime workers grabbing a bite to eat and people drinking coffee trying to dodge the grim weather.

'Let's go for something hot. It'll warm us up.' She pointed to the hot shelf display. 'They do the best Thai vegetable curry soup.' She picked up two cartons without even asking me.

And I let her.

I followed the enchanting woman to a spare table in the corner of the seating area. She placed the tray on the table and dished out the two cartons of soup and two bottles of orange juice. I didn't even like soup. And I'd have chosen Diet Coke over orange juice any day.

'This is a treat.' She removed the lid from her carton of soup. Steam rose from the top. She dug her wooden spoon into the thick mixture and slurped a mouthful. 'I usually eat a sandwich at my desk.'

45

'Why?' I asked.

'Kelly works me to the bone. It's OK, though. She compensates me well.' She fired questions like bullets from a gun the whole time we were there, starting with, 'Who do you live with?'

I remember thinking it was a strange question to ask someone who you'd only recently met. 'I'm still at home with my mum, sister, and niece.' I took a mouthful of soup. It burnt my tongue, but I swallowed it anyway.

'Doesn't your sister have a partner?' she asked, twisting the lid off the bottle of juice and glugging a mouthful.

I shook my head. 'Her pregnancy was a mistake.' I told her the bare bones of Ruby's one-night stand, who she'd met on a girlie night out.

Kat pulled a face of distaste. 'How old is she?'

'Seventeen.'

'Christ. Didn't she consider abortion?' she said bluntly.

I sat back in the chair, shocked at her suggestion. 'No.'

'How old's your niece?'

'Seven months.' It was unlike me to open up to a stranger about my personal life. I was normally much more reserved, but there was something about Kat that allowed me to tell her about Grace's illness, the problems it had caused, and how my brother and I had spent hours researching treatment options. And the extortionate amount of money we needed to raise to get the treatment Grace needed to save her life.

'What a story!' Kat tapped her recyclable spoon on the plastic tray. 'You know what? I can help.'

Her words exuded such confidence that I leaned forward closer to her as if she had a secret I wanted to hear. 'How?'

'I'll speak to Kelly. She's great at supporting charitable causes. She'll get behind this. I know she will.'

'Wow!' I said. 'Really?'

'Consider it done. Have you got a FundMeToday page?'

I shook my head.

'You need one. As soon as I've finished work tonight, we'll set one up.' She always referred to us as *we*. It was as if we were a team from that first meeting. She paused, deep in thought. 'Isn't it hard living with a baby?'

It was. Although I adored my niece, living with her was difficult. I told Kat about the disturbed sleep and how I struggled to get out of bed most mornings. Mum said it was because Grace was born early. Due to her prematurity, she still needed frequent night feeds. 'It's crowded, too,' I said. 'I never realised how much stuff a baby needs.'

Callum moved out when we discovered Ruby's pregnancy, which she had kept hidden from us for four months. I agreed to a room swap. Ruby took the biggest, and Mum took the one Ruby and I used to share, leaving me with Callum's box room, which was barely bigger than a walk-in closet.

Kat's brown eyes lit up. 'Why don't you get your own place?'

'I can't afford it.' When Callum moved out, I explored finding somewhere of my own, but the deposit that landlords demanded was way out of my reach, let alone the month's rent in advance.

Kat shot me a look I couldn't decipher at the time. And that was that. We struck up a relationship. I was going to say, a friendship. But it wasn't. She took me under – what I at first thought was – her protective wing, showing me who was who in the office and introducing me to bars after work that I'd never come across. By the end of that first day she'd taken me to Pret, she had Grace's Appeal up and running, and had persuaded Kelly to back it. Kat reached out to clients, pulling in significant funds my family could never have achieved. And she was the one who came up with the idea of the charity ball she was helping to organise that was set to raise a hefty sum with the advance tickets, raffle, and silent auction.

I liked Kat at first. I more than liked her. I was in awe of her. And I was grateful for what she'd done for Grace. She was the kind of person I'd always wanted to be. Strong, determined, and outside of work, a lot of fun to be around. She introduced me to her Friday Frolickers, as she called them. A group of party animals who went on a bender at the end of the working week that rolled into Saturday morning and often started again in the evening.

Two weeks after I'd started my job, she told me her flat-mate was moving out and I should consider moving in. I was flattered. Wasting no time, she invited me to her home – a modern and spacious apartment in a prime location south of the river. It all seemed perfect. Her spare room was four times the size of the box room at home, and the apartment was only a twenty-minute walk from work in one direction and the same distance from Mum's place in the other. I could easily visit my family whenever I wanted to.

On reflection, it was ignorant of me not to question how she could afford such a place on a PA's salary. I mean, it should've been obvious. But I was too blinded by the daily pouring of compliments she showered upon me. In my eyes, she was glamorous and fun. She was pretty, had a wardrobe packed with beautiful clothes, and was everything I'd always wanted to be.

But the cover only ever tells part of the story.

11

FundMeToday
GRACE'S APPEAL

£207,300 raised of £300,000 goal
727 donations
Recently donated:
Mr & Mrs Percival £1000
Sally Arthur £5
Kay Aitkin £40

Another generous donation had come in from Kelly's friends in the USA she'd told me about. I clicked the calculator app on my phone, computing we were still short of our target by nearly ninety-three thousand pounds. Funds were still due in from the fun run Callum had arranged for the following Sunday and from the casino-themed ball taking place in ten days' time.

But time was running out. In twelve days, the opportunity to secure the treatment for Grace would no longer be possible. The reality filled me with utter despair.

My phone beeped with a message from my sister.

> We're nearly out of formula. Can you grab a tin, please, on your way over? And a loaf of bread. Rx

Damn. She'd forgotten I'd said I wasn't dropping in there that evening.

Kat returned to the sofa with another measure of the cheap whisky. 'Did you get his watch?'

Her callousness took me by surprise. Not that it should've. Deep down, I knew what she was like by then. 'Is that all you care about?'

She raised her eyebrows in surprise.

I'd hit a nerve.

She took a sip of her drink. 'We don't want this all to be for nothing.'

She talked to me like I was a child, and it suddenly dawned on me: she'd always used that tone with me. I just hadn't noticed. When I first moved in with her, I felt sorry for her. One night, in a drunken stupor, she'd told me about the abuse she'd suffered as a child at the hands of her stepfather.

But finally the blinkered eyes I'd been seeing her through had been shown the light.

'Well, did you?' she repeated.

If I wasn't mistaken, the slightest note of venom tinged her tone.

I went to take a sip of the whisky but stopped. My stomach convulsed at the smell. I placed the glass on the table and dragged my tote bag from the rucksack. Reaching inside, I found the cloth holding Henry's watch and tossed it into her lap, plagued by a morbid sense of wrongness.

Kat carefully unwrapped the cloth, avoiding touching the watch. Her lips formed a wry smile. 'Nice.' She studied the face, expertly twirling the gold bracelet on the bed of soft velvet with the cloth so her fingers never touched the watch. She caressed the clasp through the fabric. 'What a beauty. This'll fetch a nice sum.'

I had to look away. Her indifference to how the night had ended was too much. I clutched Henry's wallet in my bag and was about to take it out but stopped. What was I thinking? She'd told me never to take anything other than the watch. It wasn't worth it, she said. It could lead to all kinds of trouble. My finger stroked the smooth leather. I needed to destroy it. It was another piece of evidence the police would track down.

She nudged my elbow. 'Think of all the money you'll get and how much you've helped your niece.' She wrapped the watch back inside the cloth and placed it on the lamp table alongside the sofa. 'I'll give it a thorough clean in the morning and get it sold.'

A low moan escaped me. 'I feel so guilty.'

Kat slapped my knee. 'I've told you before. Guilt doesn't come into it. If he's enough of a dick to cheat on his wife, he doesn't deserve your shame.'

'No one deserves to be shot, Kat.' I was incredulous at her blasé attitude. 'It was brutal.'

'I wonder what he did to end up in such a state.' Kat

grabbed a handful of tissues and blew her nose. 'I mean, he seemed like your average bloke. There was nothing to suggest he was involved in anything to warrant getting a bullet through his head.' She picked up her glass of whisky and took a sip. 'You're right. It was brutal.'

'I can't live with myself.'

'Now you can stop right there.' She held up her hand. 'You need to get a grip.'

I strained to hear her over the cold or flu bug, or whatever was wrong with her.

'You're not going to get caught.' Her nose ran. She grabbed another tissue and wiped it, discarding it with the pile of others at the foot of the sofa. 'Bloody cold. It's a nightmare.' With another fresh tissue, she dabbed her eyes.

'I would've been caught on CCTV at some point.'

'But you won't be recognised.' She rolled her eyes, gritting her teeth. 'How many more times do I have to tell you?' She stood, picked up the watch, and walked to the small desk built into the alcove in the corner of the room. Opening the bottom drawer, she placed the watch inside.

I let out another groan, long and low.

'Stop. Now,' she demanded. 'You're beginning to get on my nerves.'

I picked up the rucksack and my bag. 'I need to get going. My mum's at work, and I need to drop in on Ruby.'

'You're not in a fit state to go out.'

'My sister needs me.'

'That family of yours is so demanding.'

I shivered. 'I'm going to get changed.'

I left her blowing her nose and headed to my room. Perching on the edge of my bed, I covered my face with my hands. I couldn't get my head around what I'd done. My phone rang. It was Ruby. I let the call ring into voicemail and chucked the phone across the bed.

I kicked off my pumps, stripped down to my underwear, and changed into jeans, a sweatshirt, and a pair of trainers. Kat turned the TV up. The sound of the hip-hop music she loved bellowed out. I opened my bag, drawing out Kat's black dress and shoes. She'd encouraged me to get that dress because she said it suited me. But she had been, in reality, grooming me for the part she wanted me to play in her side hustle. I couldn't afford it. I was broke until payday at the end of the month, so she'd paid for it on the understanding I'd pay her back. I hadn't, so in effect it was her dress. She could have it. I scrunched a handful of the polyester, hating myself.

The enormity of what I'd done overcame me. Fishing Henry's wallet from my bag, I opened it and lifted the flap as if I needed to punish myself with the photo of his wife and kids. Shame descended in two thick tears that fell down my face. I grabbed my phone and googled the neighbourhood news, scrolling past the stories about the local MP involved in another expenses scandal and a police raid where they seized stolen cars from a warehouse on the edge of the city; but I found nothing about a shooting at the Parkside Hotel.

A noise disturbed me. I dropped the wallet back into my bag.

Kat was standing at my bedroom door. 'I've organised an Uber for you. There's one in seven minutes.'

'Leave it. I'll walk. I need to stop off at the supermarket.'

'You can't, Mia.' Her voice was firm. 'You're in too much of a state.'

I'd had enough of that woman telling me what to do. I snatched the wig, dress, shoes, and camera, stormed over to her, and shoved them in her chest. 'I said, leave it!' I pushed the door to and yanked my denim jacket from a hook on the back.

Kat was prancing around in the hallway. The blonde wig sat crooked on her head. I stared at her, astounded. 'Come on. Lighten up,' she said. 'Take the cab. I'll pay.'

I pushed her out of the way. 'Taking a cab isn't going to get me out of this mess.' My strained voice was a cry for help.

But it was as clear as day.

There was no one to help me.

I was on my own.

12

I regretted not taking a cab. My ankle ached from rolling it earlier, and the sense of dread that someone was following me didn't let up the whole way to the small supermarket on the main road leading to Mum's flat. They sold baby formula, albeit at a ridiculously exorbitant price compared to the main store, but Grace needed it.

The evening was still warm. I constantly checked over my shoulder. At one point, I thought I saw someone in a balaclava only to realise it was a guy with a beard and long hair.

A dishevelled man with hair as matted as a bird's nest was sitting in the alcove beside the entrance to the shop. He held a sign between his yellow-stained fingers and thumb, muttering for a contribution towards his dinner. His old trench coat reminded me of Dad. A cold pang of sadness mushroomed through my heart, thinking about the man who had abandoned us seventeen years ago, when Mum fell pregnant with Ruby, because he couldn't cope. Ruby had never met him. Callum refused to have anything to do with him. I visited him about five years ago, but the last I'd heard, he'd moved into shared accommodation in a town between Edinburgh and Glasgow. He stopped texting, and, eventually, so did I.

'I don't have any change.' I nodded towards the shop door. 'Hold tight. I'll get some for you.'

The store was busy. Swinging a right, I headed to the aisle stocking baby products and found a tin of formula. After stopping for a loaf of bread, I hurried to the till, gritting my teeth. A long queue snaked around the aisle and into the next. I joined the end at the magazine stand where a copy of *OK!* magazine welcomed readers into a couple's enviable country home. I picked up a copy, trying to distract myself, flicking through the glossy pages jammed with stunning homes and beautiful people.

A gruff voice breathed into my neck. 'Are you in the queue or what?'

I turned around and did a double-take. With his receding dark hair, I briefly thought the man was Henry Robertson. I steadied myself on the shelf beside me. I didn't believe in ghosts. But it was as if Henry's troubled spirit was lingering at my heel, waiting to trip me up.

The taste of rotten whisky shot up my throat. 'Sorry.' I replaced the magazine on the stand and shuffled along the queue, reliving the evening in my mind. I wondered how long it'd be before the police started looking for blonde Hazel.

I removed my phone from my bag and refreshed the page for the local news but learnt nothing. I searched the national news while the queue crawled to the checkout, but I couldn't find any mention of the incident anywhere online. But as Kat said, there was no reason why anyone would've ventured into room four-nine-three of the Parkside Hotel yet.

When I reached the front of the queue, the cashier scanned my items. It was painfully slow. When I tried to pay, a beeping noise sounded above the hustle and bustle of shoppers filling their baskets. The card reader had declined my payment. I tried again, but the same thing happened. I searched through my virtual wallet. My credit card was maxed out, but it was worth a shot. I changed payment options, praying for a fraction of luck at least to show up tonight. The machine declined the payment again.

Leaving the store without formula wasn't an option. Grace couldn't go without a feed.

'Hurry up, can you?' the man behind me muttered. 'I've got a train to catch.'

I took a deep breath, opened my bag and fished for Henry's wallet. I peered around. CCTV cameras loomed over the tills. I found the wallet but didn't remove it from the bag. 'I'll pay by cash,' I told the cashier. Flipping open the wallet, I removed one of the twenty-pound notes, handed it to her, and chucked the goods into my bag. I collected my change and rushed out of the shop.

A warm breeze had reduced the temperature a little, taking the edge off the evening heat. I shivered. The drunk, reeking of alcohol, raised his cardboard cup, shaking the few pennies inside. He grinned at me. His yellow teeth made me want to pop back into the shop to buy a toothbrush and a tube of Colgate. I dug into my jacket pocket, found the change I'd just been given, and dropped it into his cup. The coins jingled. Another frightening thought edged into my mind. When the police started the investigation into Henry's death, and it would happen – very soon, if it hadn't already – would they be able to tell that the twenty-pound note I'd used came from the money Henry had recently withdrawn from the cashpoint?

I was being paranoid.

But it wasn't the time for reckless actions.

One foot wrong, and I'd find myself behind bars.

13

I fumbled with the key to Mum's flat, struggling to get it into the lock as if I was holding it in my left hand. My nerves had overtaken my coordination. It took me three attempts to open the door. My heart thudded relentlessly. And it wasn't from the three floors I'd climbed.

All the way there, I'd considered handing myself in – walking into the local police station across the river and confessing my crime. Despite Kat's assurances, I was way out of my depth. But every time I considered how confessing my crime would play out, my family's distraught faces crawled into my thoughts. I couldn't do it to them.

The lock clicked. Pushing open the door, I glanced behind me and quickly slipped inside. I grimaced at the faint smell of baby sick.

'That you, Mia?' Ruby called. 'Did you get my texts? I've been trying to get hold of you.'

'I've got everything.' I kicked off my shoes and took a deep breath, trying to calm my racing pulse.

Callum appeared from the living area, dressed in his uniform.

'What are you doing here?' I asked. The sight of a police officer heightened my unease. Even if that person was my brother. My heart sank as I once again considered the consequences for him of handing myself in.

'Nice to see you, too, sis.'

He was fit, my brother. Four mornings a week, he ran two laps of the park – four miles – even when he was working nights. On the other three mornings, he worked out at the gym. His unwavering dedication had rewarded him with toned biceps and washboard abs. Add that to his boyish blond curls and intense blue eyes, although he'd deny it, girls flocked after him. Not that he'd ever had a serious relationship. Not that I knew of, anyway. He always jested that Mum, Ruby, and I kept him far too busy. And then Grace came along.

'What's up with you?' he asked.

I found a fake smile. 'Nothing.'

He eyed me suspiciously. I could get away with lying to Mum. Not that I ever seriously lied; just white lies to save people's feelings. But there was never the chance of pulling the wool of deceit over my brother's circumspect eyes. That's what made him such a good police officer.

'I'm tired.'

He slung his rucksack over his shoulder. 'You stink of booze. Where've you been?'

'I had a drink with Kat.'

'I need to get back to work.' He pecked my cheek and opened the door. 'Catch you later.'

Ruby appeared, jiggling a moaning baby Grace in her arms. Her taut midriff was on display between her black leggings and white crop top. It was hard to believe she'd given birth that year. 'You were meant to be here ages ago.'

'I'm sorry. I got held up. I'm here now.'

'What's happened to you?'

'What do you mean?'

She smirked. 'Did you drag yourself through a hedge backwards getting here?'

I fluffed my hair. 'I'm fine.' I pulled the tin of baby formula and the loaf of bread from my bag. 'You can't let levels run so low, Rue. What if I wasn't around to get this for you?'

I studied the telltale signs my sister was still so young: her drawn face, braced teeth, and the unsightly outbreak of spots on her forehead.

'I'm sorry.' Ruby traded Grace for the tin of formula. 'I'll go and make her a bottle. I've got everything ready.'

Given no choice in the exchange, I replaced the pink dummy that had fallen on my niece's tummy. I kissed the smooth, thin skin on her forehead, careful not to dislodge the nasal gastric tube she'd had for medication and fortified feeds since she was a few weeks old, when the professionals were trying to work out why she was failing to thrive. She was doing a little better – drinking more milk and eating bird-like quantities – but she still couldn't consume enough to meet her needs.

She spat out the dummy and grinned at me. A smile as weak as her body, but still she managed it. I held her frail bones to my chest, stroking her back.

How I adored that bundle of perfection. I briefly closed my eyes and whispered in her ear, 'I did it for you, darling girl. All for you.'

She cooed, low bubbling sounds that brought tears to my eyes. But there was no time for tears.

Following my sister into the kitchen, I tripped over a wooden activity cube on the linoleum floor. I held Grace tighter to my chest and slammed my hand on the kitchen counter to break my fall. 'Rue, you need to pick up her toys. I could've broken my neck on that thing.'

She tutted. 'You sound like Mum. What's wrong with you tonight? Why are you so touchy?'

'I've had a bad day.' I opened the back door to let some fresh air into the kitchen. The smoky smell of gunpowder was still coating my nostrils. 'Where's Mum?'

'She's going to be late. She texted something about two night staff ringing in sick, and they'd had two emergency admissions, so she's had to stay late.' She filled one of Grace's bottles with water from the kettle. 'Did you see that anonymous donation on the FundMeToday page? Five hundred pounds! Do you know who it's from?'

I shrugged. 'Probably a client from work.'

Frequent large donations came in from my work's wealthy client base. I stepped onto the small balcony cluttered with laundry folded over a collapsible airer, jiggling Grace in my arms. I glanced over the railings at a group of youngsters hanging around the dated kids' playground equipment on the grass below, vaping and swigging from cans of lager. I sighed, thinking about the balconies of the duplex apartments overlooking the river that showed up on my Instagram feed. The ones with integrated kitchen appliances and underfloor heating throughout.

Ruby came to the door, holding out a bottle. 'Give this a shake and give it to her, would you? I haven't showered yet today.'

She'd reached the kitchen door before I could protest. 'Be quick!' I called. 'I can't stay long.'

Grace reached for the bottle with her tiny hands, drawing it to her mouth. I pulled it back. She clenched her tiny fists and let out a piercing scream. I vigorously shook the bottle. 'Calm down, sweet girl. I won't be a second.' I sat at the kitchen table, and, removing the cap, tested the milk on my wrist. The temperature was fine. I gave the bottle to her.

The pipes creaked from the pressure of the shower. I needed a shower, too. The chance to remove any proof of what I'd done that might be clinging to my clammy body.

Who was I kidding?

However hard I scrubbed, the memory of what had happened would never go away.

It was going to stay with me forever.

14

Grace's blue eyes drooped. I waited until they slowly closed and the teat slipped from her mouth along with a dribble. The bottle was still half-empty. I gently tapped her cheek, trying to rouse her so she could drink some more, but her eyes remained closed. Ruby needed to give her the rest of the feed via her gastric tube later. I could do it. I'd been trained, but it was a job I'd rather avoid.

I carried Grace to her cot, squashed into the corner of Ruby's bedroom. My sister was never the tidiest or cleanest of people. I used to moan at her for the state of her half of the room we shared, and for the empty cups she let pile up on her bedside cabinet, and when there was no room left on there, under the bed. But she changed when Grace was born, and the room couldn't have been tidier.

Carefully, I laid Grace down as if she were a delicate piece of china I was scared of breaking. I kissed her forehead with the same heart-wrenching pang that always troubled me when she slept. I stayed for a few minutes, savouring my time with her. There was an unspoken saying in our family: spend as much time with Grace as you can, because she might not be there tomorrow.

I checked the baby monitor on the bookcase. When Ruby and I shared the room, the bookcase was stacked with books, which were all mine because Ruby hadn't picked up a book since she'd left primary school. There wasn't room in the box room for the bookcase when we switched rooms, so all my books were now in boxes under my bed. The bookcase was full of baby photos and Grace's toys. And piles of medical records that I kept in order, because Ruby couldn't face them.

I picked up the beige teddy bear I'd bought when Grace was born. It was still way bigger than her, which was why it lived on the bookcase. Ruby was paranoid it would suffocate Grace if she left it in the cot. It had a zip down the back that opened to an area to store the pair of Minnie Mouse pyjamas I'd bought at the same time. I loved those pyjamas. I couldn't wait for her to grow big enough to wear them. Mum had told me to buy them aged six-to-nine months to give her some clothes to grow into. But they were still too big, and it was daunting knowing she might never wear them. It was another harsh reminder that raising the funds for her treatment was more urgent than ever.

Time was running out.

I wandered to my room. It was how I'd left it with the few belongings I hadn't taken to Kat's as if Mum knew I'd be back one day. Over the top of the small wardrobe door hung the red off-the-shoulder ball gown with a full skirt and imitation diamond beading to the waist that I'd bought for the ball. I'd found it in a second-hand shop on one of the posh roads in town. It wasn't my style, the skirt too puffy, the top too revealing, and it was a little on the tight side, but it was cheap.

Sitting on my bed, I opened my bag and took out Henry's

wallet, slapping it repeatedly in the palm of my shaking hand. I needed to dispose of it. The police would search for it when they found his body. I tossed it on the bed and found the phone Kat gave me for the evening. I wanted to scream. I'd been such a fool. I threw it on the floor and stamped on it. An act so out of character, but I couldn't help it. I continued tramping on it in a silent fit of rage until it shattered into several pieces like broken glass.

The shower turned off in the bathroom. I came to my senses, bent down and retrieved the SIM card. Finding a pair of scissors from my bedside cabinet, I cut it up into the smallest pieces possible and wrapped them in a tissue. I had to get rid of it all. Kat would kill me. It was her phone. But I was past caring. I grabbed a sock from the chest of drawers and funnelled everything inside.

I picked up the wallet. I needed a hiding place until I could think more clearly. There was a closet by the front door where we kept coats and shoes. It wasn't a large space, but it was messy and cluttered. I took the wallet and sock to find a hiding space among the coats and shoes. But Mum must've had a massive clear-out. It was tidier than I'd ever seen it.

I closed the door. I needed to find another hiding place. Passing Ruby's room, I stopped. Grace was moaning. I went to comfort her. Even when she was cranky, she was beautiful. I threw the sock and wallet on the edge of the mattress, placed a hand on her chest and gently rocked her.

'Go to sleep, baby girl.'

Within seconds, she closed her eyes. I'd always been the one who could easily coax her back to sleep.

I was about to pick up the wallet and sock when her teddy bear caught my eye. That was a possibility for a couple of days until I worked out what to do. I grabbed it and unzipped the back, not giving my actions a second thought as I stuffed the wallet and sock inside with the Minnie Mouse pyjamas. No one was going to find them in there.

15

I returned to the living area to wait for Ruby. One of Mum's favourite cookery shows was on the TV. Ruby appeared from the shower with a towel wrapped around her head. Her eyes were red and swollen.

'What's happened?' I asked.

She sat beside me, her shoulders hunched in defeat. 'I'm so scared.'

I didn't need to ask her why. We had that conversation often. 'We're going to get the money, Rue.'

'But what if we don't?'

It was hard to stomach seeing my baby sister like that. Motherhood had changed her. When we were growing up, as far as I could remember, she'd been a tomboy, a real tough cookie, confident and outspoken, preferring being outside on her bike with her friends than at home with me cooking or watching a film with Mum. The childhood Ruby was the complete opposite of the wreck of a teenager with a face as white as a cloud sitting beside me.

I squeezed her knee. 'We will.'

I don't know how many times I'd repeated those words to her over the past few months. In my darker moments, faced alone, I had visions of failing Grace and my sister. But the thought of that happening was so frightening, it spurred me on to try harder. Each day I searched for opportunities to reach the sum of money we needed. It was exhausting.

I gave her knee another hard squeeze. 'Never give up hope.'

The sound of Grace stirring in her cot sounded through the baby monitor. Ruby jumped up and ran to her.

I dug my phone from the back pocket of my jeans and checked the news, but there'd been no update since I last looked.

A selfie Ruby had taken of the four of us popped up on the screen. It was from before Grace was born, and Ruby was heavily pregnant. Little did we know how much our lives were about to change. Callum had taken us out to dinner – a rare treat – for pizza at our favourite Italian restaurant along the river. I stared at Mum. It was hard to believe she was only fifty-two years old. Underneath the tiredness, she was an attractive woman. She'd modelled for a kids' clothing company as a child. But, year by year, life had chipped away at her beauty. I thought of my boss, Kelly. She was two years older than Mum but looked years younger than the woman staring back at me. Poor Mum. She'd had it tough raising the three of us alone. She'd be beside herself if I told her I'd drugged a man for financial gain and then witnessed someone blow his brains out.

I ran my finger over the glossy image of Callum's face, considering the impact my possible arrest would have on his career prospects. It didn't bear thinking about. All of them would be so disappointed in me, especially Mum. She could never find out. Never.

Waves of shame and regret continued surging through me. My shoulders slumped. I was sweating despite the cool breeze flowing through the open window. I glanced at the time. It was only nine o'clock. It felt like a week had passed since I was sitting in that hotel bar listening to the pianist elegantly strumming chords on the mini-grand. I watched a news summary, dread gripping my stomach at the turn of each new story. But the unfortunate events in the Parkside Hotel never got a mention. But as Kat had said, Henry's body wouldn't be found until tomorrow when he didn't check out of the hotel.

I opened Facebook and typed "Henry Robertson" into the search bar. Pages of profiles appeared. I squinted at the screen, studying each picture and clicking the ones who could've been the man I was looking for. A flat door slamming somewhere from within the block startled me. I was constantly on edge.

Several clicks later, I found him. His profile picture was not a photo of his face, but it was definitely Henry's page. The photo was the same as the one in his wallet – the one of his wife and two sons.

Clicking the page, I browsed through his account. Pictures of his wife and kids were sprinkled amongst memes about the cost-of-living crisis and the disgraceful antics of British MPs. His wife had dark hair with vivid green eyes, and his sons were miniature versions of him. My heart contracted. He'd loved his family, that was for sure.

But not enough, Kat would say, to ward off women like Hazel or Tallulah.

I located his wife's page. Charlene Robertson. It was disappointing to find it set to private.

I continued stalking his page, stopping at a picture of him playing football, striking the ball into a goal. He lived up north, in a town west of Sheffield, but there was no suggestion he came to the city yesterday, and nothing to suggest why he had met with Kelly.

16

When I arrived back at Kat's apartment I was fuming to find she'd already gone to bed. I needed someone to talk to, and she was the only person. But waking her up was out of the question. Beware the person who tried. Kat was a woman who needed her sleep.

Fully clothed, I threw myself onto my bed and fell into a fitful sleep of my own, plagued with nightmares featuring men in balaclavas lurking in the shadows.

In the morning, I found her sitting at the small table by the window, holding a bottle of cleaning fluid. A glass of water and Henry's watch were on the table. Usually, at that time of the day, she was fully made up and dressed in smart clothes, ready for the working day ahead. But today she was in her bathrobe. Her hair was still tied up on top of her head from the previous night, and loose strands trailed messily around her ashen face.

I sometimes sat at that table alone when eating my dinner, absently staring out onto the people below hurrying along the river path. I was lonely living there. Kat was always out. Monday to Thursday, she went to the gym after work and often met up with friends afterwards. And, on the weekends, she spent more time out than in.

'Eleven o'clock,' was the first thing she said, above the sound from the kitchen of the washing machine spinning on full speed.

'Sorry?'

'Check-out time at the Parkside Hotel. That's when the shit is going to hit the fan.'

I gulped, standing by her side. My whole body oozed the dread that had been expanding inside me all night as I'd tossed and turned, alternating staring at the leopard-print wallpaper and the IKEA wardrobe in the room in which I no longer belonged. 'We need a plan.' My voice wavered. 'Because I'm going out of my mind here.' I lifted my hands and dropped them heavily by my sides.

'I wonder how much this beauty is going to fetch.' Kat removed the cap from the bottle of cleaning fluid and poured a few drops onto a microfibre cloth she whipped from her bathrobe pocket, as if she was a magician magicking a hankie from a hat. She picked up the watch and rubbed the cloth over it, hard and furiously.

'We need a plan,' I repeated.

'What do I keep saying? You've got to act normal.' She coughed. 'Carry on as if nothing has happened.'

'Act normal? I've hardly slept. I was checking the news all night.' I bit my fingernail. Not that there was much left to bite. 'Have you heard anything? Read anything online?' There was no doubting the pleading tone of my voice.

'Nothing.' She leaned across to the windowsill, picked up a half-smoked joint and slipped it between her lips. Taking a lighter from her other bathrobe pocket, she lit the joint and took a long drag. She sucked in the smoke which she held in her lungs before slowly letting it out. 'Forget Henry Robertson. What happened to him would've happened if you'd been there or not.' She took another puff on the joint and offered it to me. 'Have some. It'll calm you down.'

I waved her offer away.

'He wasn't a good man. He cheated on his wife,' she said.

'But he didn't deserve to die. No one deserves to die in that way.'

'We all have to die someday.'

'But not like that,' I repeated. I wasn't getting through to her. Or was she so pig-headed, so full of her own self-importance, that she didn't give a damn about anyone other than herself?

'You don't know what he'd done. And whatever it was, it must've been something real bad to end up with a bullet through his head.' Coughing uncontrollably, she took a sip of water from the glass on the table. 'I'm not going to make it to work today. I'm so disappointed. A client is coming in who I wanted to see. Billy Brookes, the footballer. Remember me telling you about him? He came in a few months ago.'

I shook my head. I was hidden out in the back of the KM Group offices, tucked in the corner with the small finance and admin team. A glass partition separated us from the main office, so I had little to do with the clients.

'He's loaded, that guy. I overheard Alex telling Kelly he earns a fortune.'

Alex was Kelly's brother and my line manager.

'Seven figures,' Kat continued. 'Seven! Can you imagine. I think we could have some fun with him.' She continued rubbing Henry's watch with the cloth. 'The last time he came in, he was wearing a Rolex. But not your run-of-the-mill

74

Rolex. No! That baby was a Cosmograph. A real beauty. The same as I got from that other footballer I told you about. Remember? They can fetch thousands. I'm telling you... thousands.' She waved Henry's watch in my face. 'Much more than this! He's staying in town for the night. I booked him a room. I'm wondering if he could be our next target.'

I stared at her incredulously. 'You're not seriously considering asking me to do this again.'

'Think of the money.'

I gritted my teeth. It had taken me so long to see through the façade that woman displayed to the world. I couldn't believe I'd wanted to be her.

'Think of your niece. You're nearly there. One more job could secure the final funds to get her the treatment she needs.'

'I'm hoping the ball will do that.'

'Oh, Mia. Mia. Mia. You're so innocent, aren't you? The ball's not going to secure the amount you need.' She sighed deeply, shaking her head.

I couldn't work out if she was lying or not – suckering me into doing another one of her *jobs*. 'I'm going to call in sick, too.' I couldn't face anyone. 'I'll say I've caught your flu bug.'

'You can't.' Another cough, another splutter. 'You have to go in.'

I held out my trembling hands. 'I can't stop shaking.'

She stood, tightening her bathrobe belt. Turning to face me, she pressed her hands on my shoulders. 'For heaven's sake, Mia. You've got to calm down.'

'How can I?'

'Look at me.' She roughly shook me into submission. 'Look at me, I said.'

I stared into her eyes, red from her rubbing them or from

all the weed she'd smoked, I couldn't tell. 'How can you be so calm?'

'I'm in it as deep as you.'

'What do you take me for?' I wriggled free from her grip. 'I'd never snitch on you.'

'Oh, Mia. You're so fricking naive. Don't you see? If the police find out what you did, it'll only be a matter of time before they trace it back to me.'

'How?'

'I know you. You're weak.'

I balled my fingers into clenched fists.

'They'll want to know how you decided to target him and grill you until you tell them everything.'

I dropped down onto the sofa, groaning loudly. 'I'm more worried about that fricking balaclava guy than the police at the moment. All the way to my mum's place last night and back here, I thought someone was following me. It freaked me out.'

'I've been thinking about that guy, too. I wonder what Henry did to upset him. He didn't seem the type of man. Flirty, yes. A little creepy, definitely. But not a gangster or anything like that.' The gleam in her eyes suggested she was taking some kind of perverted pleasure from all the drama.

'You were wrong. He must've been involved in some real deep trouble to be on the receiving end of that. The balaclava guy was so calm, it was terrifying.'

'Where's my phone, by the way?' she asked.

'Phone?'

'The one I gave you for the job.'

The one I stamped on and was in pieces in a sock in my niece's teddy bear. 'At my mum's place. I left it there last night.'

'Could you bring it back for me?'

My heart sank. 'Sure.'

She coughed again. 'Listen, there's something I want you to do for me today.'

I crossed my arms.

'It's OK. It doesn't involve hotel rooms or watches.' She grinned.

I shook my head, unable to hide the raging disgust I felt for her. 'That's not even nearly funny.'

'I left my gym kit at the office. I doubt I'll be going in tomorrow, either. But if I'm better, I might want it at the weekend. It's under my desk. Bring it back for me tonight, can you?'

'I don't want to go in.'

'You have to. You've already had a day off this week for your niece. Come on, don't wreck your chances of getting a permanent position there. I told you what I overheard Alex saying to Kelly last week. He's impressed with you. He wants to make you permanent.'

She's right. I took Monday off work to help Ruby. Grace had two hospital appointments, and Ruby had begged me to go with her because Mum had to work. My position was only temporary at the KM Group, so I was paid by the hour. If I didn't turn up, I didn't get paid. And I needed every penny I could get.

'Listen, Mia. You've got to hold your nerve. Nothing can pin you to that hotel room last night.'

I held her stare.

The admiration I'd held for her finally diminished to nothing.

17

The KM Group operated from a large glass-fronted office block in a cobbled side street south of the city centre. Owned and headed by Kelly Meyers, a level-headed, ambitious woman, the PR company was renowned for reshaping and transforming a colourful cast of shady characters. They included celebrities, footballers, politicians, and the like. Some of whom were guilty of a vast array of misdemeanours and had endured the wrath of the nation. Individuals who Kelly and her team had brushed down and turned around, and in some cases even revolutionised into national treasures.

It was a brisk walk from Kat's apartment. Usually, Kat caught a bus. I always walked, listening to music, headphones slotted in my ears, oblivious to other commuters rushing by. But today, I needed to be on full alert. I crossed the bridge over the river with the hum of the city keeping me company.

The sun was out again, but thunderous clouds of fear and shame hung over me, zapping my energy and slowing my step. As I turned every street corner, I glanced over my shoulder, paranoid the guy in the balaclava was following me. I kept reminding myself I'd lost him at the market, but the devil of dread lurking in my ear continued asking: But what if you didn't? He could've followed me back to Kat's apartment with the intention of returning to get me. I was being irrational. But still, the fear was real. I could taste it in the bitterness of the bile repeatedly shooting up my throat.

The glass of the office block rebounded the morning sun. I glanced at my watch when I entered the opulent marble-floored lobby. It was eight-thirty and less than three hours until Henry Robertson was meant to check out of the Parkside Hotel. I'd been counting down the hours all night.

I made for the lifts to the right of the lobby. The ones to the left led to the private wealth management arm of the company. On the second floor, I exited into the reception area. As expected of a company of KM's standing, it was luxurious in every regard. I'd temped in several offices before I landed that job, but nowhere as plush as there.

The receptionist, Lauren, who doubled as the office manager, greeted me from behind a toughened-glass curved reception desk. 'Morning, Mia.'

She was a sunny soul, pristinely turned out – every bit the corporate face of the KM Group. She'd been with the company for so long, she was an intricate part of the fabric, and everyone loved her. A dedicated employee, she balanced the art of toeing the company line while still being open to the odd bit of frivolity. If you needed anything delicately pushed up the line of command, a quiet word with Lauren normally did the trick. Not that I'd witnessed that first-hand. It was what Kat had told me on my first day. Lauren used to be Kelly's personal assistant until the job became too stressful. It had been hindering her chances of falling pregnant, so Kat took over the role.

'Morning!' I tried my best to sound upbeat.

'No Kat again today?'

'She's got a lousy cold.' I hope she couldn't notice how uneven and shaky my voice was.

'She sounded dreadful when I spoke to her. Tom from Media has called in sick, too.' She coughed. 'I'm not feeling great myself, either. This bug is doing the rounds.' She stared into my eyes. It was unnerving. It was like she could see into my soul as it begged for forgiveness for my unpardonable sins. 'You're a little pale yourself.'

I dug deep to fix a fake smile on my face. 'All good, thanks.'

A set of double doors swished apart, leading to a long corridor. I passed Kelly's glass-fronted office. The smell of expensive perfume clogged in my throat, making me cough, the same as Henry Robertson's aftershave in that hotel room. The vanes of the stylish slatted blinds were closed, indicating the boss didn't want to be disturbed, but she called my name.

I turned around.

She was standing in the doorway to her office. 'Come in. Come in.'

She waved her hand, beckoning me inside. She was a tall woman with thick, wavy hair she dyed a chestnut brown, and she had a Mediterranean appearance, her skin an olive tone. Kat liked working for her. She described her as demanding but fair.

I entered the office where luxury screamed its presence from all four corners. Everything about the large space – the desk and chair, custom-built shelving and modern pendant lighting – was stylish and expensive. It even smelled of opulence: a blend of Kelly's sophisticated perfume and the rich leather of the sofa. I thought of Henry lying on a similar sofa in that hotel room last night. My stomach turned.

Kelly's directness interrupted my thoughts. 'How's your niece?'

'She's doing OK at the moment. Thanks for asking.'

'Not long until the ball now.'

'Nine days.'

'That's what I wanted to talk to you about.' Her eyes, a striking green, lit up. 'I've managed to get one of our clients to donate a weekend in London. Two nights at The Savoy. As you know, it's one of the best hotels in London.'

Her support for Grace's Appeal had been unwavering ever since I'd joined the company. Kat told me Kelly had lost a baby to a genetic disease when she was much younger, which was why she'd taken a particular interest in Grace's Appeal. She'd organised a silent auction, collecting items to be auctioned off on the night of the ball. Details of the items were going to be displayed around the venue for guests to bid on. And in some cases – a signed football shirt from a premier league team, a Fortnum & Mason luxury gift basket, and a painting by a famous artist – the physical items were going on display.

She clasped her hands together. Her fingernails were painted burnt red, perfectly matching her wrapover dress. 'And I'm working on one of my acquaintances in the industry to donate another piece of artwork. Matty Goodall, a collector in his spare time. You know him?'

I shook my head. Those were circles I'd never heard of, let alone mixed in. 'That's wonderful. Thank you. I'm truly grateful for everything you're doing for my family.'

'It's my pleasure. Now. I'd like you to do a job for me, if that's alright.'

AJ CAMPBELL

I tried to inject enthusiasm into my voice. 'Sure.'

'With Kat off sick, I've been left short, so I need some help. Normally, I'd ask Lauren but I have other work I need to give to her. We have a new client coming in next week, Paul Blake. I've booked out Tuesday and Wednesday in my diary to spend with him. Please could you book him a hotel for Tuesday night?' The authoritative air of her demeanour was impressive. It was no wonder she'd found herself heading a company as impressive as the KM Group.

I'd never booked a hotel for a client. It was part of Kat's job role. I didn't even know where to start. But one positive about Kat was that she'd taught me to be resourceful. 'Any hotel in particular?'

'Kat keeps a list of the ones we use for clients. The Avon, or the Parkside, or the River Hotel spring to mind.'

I fiddled with the bottom button of my blouse. The last place I wanted any contact with was the Parkside Hotel.

'Ask Alex to give you a company credit card to sort it out.'

I faked enthusiasm. 'Sure.'

She sat at her desk, a silent act of dismissal.

I hesitated. The need to ask why Henry Robertson was there yesterday and why she'd met with him was overwhelming. But of course, I couldn't. First, I needed to wait until his body had been found.

18

I left Kelly's office and passed Kat's and two smaller unoccupied rooms, heading into the open-plan space where most of the company's thirty staff were already engrossed in their work. They always were. High standards were expected at the KM Group.

I made for my workspace in the corner, pretending to text so I didn't have to speak to anybody. Tossing my bag under my desk, I swapped my trainers for my ballerina pumps, yet another reminder of last night.

I switched on my computer. I shouldn't have been there; the nausea was overwhelming. I tidied the desk, straightening the keyboard and placing pens into the plastic holder. Alex ended a phone call and swung his chair around to face me.

Alex and Kelly jointly owned the company. Kelly ran the core business, and Alex was mainly in charge of the back office, including the small accounts department comprised of him, Shari, and me, although he also had a handful of clients he serviced. Shari was currently on maternity leave, which was how I got a job there.

Alex had his own office but sometimes worked from Shari's desk beside me. He was a good-looking guy, in his early forties, with high cheekbones that were the envy of all the women in the office. He had the same Mediterranean appearance as his sister; although, Kat told me, they were as British as the King. Alex's sleek buzzcut hairstyle accentuating his dark eyes probably added to the image.

I liked Alex. He was professional and efficient, but sometimes I felt sorry for him. Although Kat told me he and Kelly jointly owned the company, at times, Alex seemed to operate in the shadow of Kelly's upper hand.

Very much like Kat had the upper hand with me.

But not anymore.

'Earth to Mia, did you hear me?' Alex's raised voice broke my trance.

'Sorry, what did you say?'

'Are you ready for Sunday?'

'Sunday?'

'The run?'

'Yes. Sure.' I inwardly groaned. Six staff members, including Alex and I, were participating in a 10k fun run on Sunday. My brother had arranged it and was joining in, too, with a group of his friends from work. Fourteen of us in total, all raising funds for Grace's Appeal. I'd been training for weeks. But all I could think of was making it to Sunday alive and avoiding police custody.

Alex rubbed his trimmed beard, which was patchy in places, as if he couldn't quite grow a full one. 'I've been promised a donation from one of my clients. It should be a good one.'

Everyone in the company had been so supportive since Kat started spreading the word about Grace shortly after I started there. Many had generously donated to her appeal and often asked how the fundraising was going.

Alex waved his hand at me. 'Did you hear me?'

'Sorry?' I was miles away. My thoughts were in room four-nine-three of the Parkside Hotel and with the poor cleaners who were about to have the shock of their lives.

'How did you get on with those expense reports I gave you yesterday? I'll need them by the end of the day.'

'I've nearly finished them. I'll get them to you before I go home.' Home time was a distant dream. The day was going to drag big time.

'Elodie is coming in later,' he said.

Elodie was his wife. She often popped in with their daughter, Savannah, and he took them to lunch. I liked Elodie. She emanated calmness, whereas Alex could sometimes be slightly angsty, especially when he was stressed. Elodie had been instrumental in securing a signed baseball shirt for the silent auction for the ball from her cousin, who played for one of the big teams in the States.

'So I'll be going out to lunch,' Alex continued. 'Could we work on the presentation another time? After work, perhaps? Or tomorrow?'

He'd kindly been helping me prepare a presentation and a speech for Ruby and me to deliver at the upcoming ball. I'd initially planned on doing it on my own, but he said it'd help encourage donations if Ruby and I took the stage together as a united front. I was dreading it. Being the centre of attention had never sat comfortably with me. But if it helped Grace, I'd do it.

The presentation was all the better for his input. He knew

his stuff. 'You need to appeal equally to hearts and minds,' he'd said when he'd transformed the rough draft I'd put together. 'Don't litter it with bullet points. You need photos that hit hard and pivotal words that deliver the key message.' Within a few days, he'd crafted a compelling story, which simply needed, as he put it, 'tweaking to perfection.'

'Also, I'd like you to join a meeting this afternoon. I have an important client coming in, Billy Brookes and his team. And I need someone to take the minutes, seeing as Kat isn't here. Join us upstairs at two o'clock, please.'

Billy Brookes was the guy Kat had mentioned last night. The one with the expensive watch. I'd never taken minutes of a meeting. Kat was responsible for organising all the meet-and-greets and note-taking for client meetings.

'Client room A. Bring a notepad and pen.'

Logging in to my computer, I set to work, but I struggled to concentrate fully. I steeled myself to focus but couldn't stop checking the digital clock at the top of the screen, moving slower than a snail towards eleven o'clock.

I fetched a coffee to pass the time. Not that it made it pass any faster. I checked the local news channels for the umpteenth time.

Eleven o'clock came, and then twelve.

My nerves were fraying more by the hour.

The sound of Alex's baby preceded Elodie appearing with her. Savannah cried like Grace, with the breathy sobs and raw vulnerability of a baby.

Elodie waved a bag at me. 'It arrived this morning.' She placed the bag on my desk while jigging Savannah on her hip. 'The right person will pay a fortune for this.' She flicked her long hair, which was as shiny as a pearl, over her slight shoulder.

Savannah's cries grew louder.

Elodie kissed the top of the child's head. 'Teething. Terrible times. How's your niece?' Ever since she and Alex had found out about Grace, they had been sympathetic to her cause. 'Teething, too?'

'She's got her two bottom teeth now.' I opened the bag. 'The shirt! Thanks, Elodie. I can't tell you how grateful my family is for your help.'

Alex appeared from a meeting. He kissed his wife and whisked his daughter from her arms. Savannah immediately stopped crying.

'Perhaps we need to swap places?' Elodie said.

Alex winked at her, and they both laughed. He shrugged into his jacket while still holding his daughter, shuffling her from one arm to the other.

As they left, I wondered what it'd be like to have a special person in your life like they had.

I turned to my phone and checked the news again but found nothing about the dead man lying in the room at the Parkside Hotel.

It was hell.

19

With frayed nerves, at two o'clock, I headed to the top floor. I'd spent the last hour researching the most effective way of taking minutes of a meeting as a beginner from the wealth of information on the internet. I'd downloaded a template. Key goal: keep it as simple as possible without omitting any important details.

I'd only ventured up to the top floor once – on my induction day when Alex had given me a tour of the building. And the closest I'd come to meeting one of the KM Group clients was by accident when I'd been leaving work one day. Kelly was shaking hands with the toothpick-thin woman clad in a designer all-in-one in the lobby.

Four plush meeting rooms spanned the top floor, positioned around a seating area with four armchairs and a designer coffee table comprising a round piece of glass laid upon three large silver balls. The rooms were shared with the private wealth management arm of the company.

I knocked on the door. A commanding voice ordered me to enter. The room was light and airy with a round boardroom table and five chairs. Alex gestured for me to take the seat next to him and introduced me to Billy Brookes, followed by his agent, a heavyset guy in his late forties, who resembled more of a bouncer rather than a businessman. He constantly played with his shirt collar which bit into the overflowing rolls of his neck flesh. Billy had a clean-cut, pale complexion. His hair was slicked back in a side parting. His eyes fixed on me when I sat. It was unnerving.

Within seconds, Alex had the meeting underway. As I took notes, I couldn't stop looking at the digital clock on the wall, my thoughts consumed with the news of Henry's murder about to break and wondering if CCTV pictures of the blonde woman with him had yet been plastered on every online news channel across the country.

The afternoon passed even more slowly than the morning. I repeatedly checked the news. At three-thirty, there was still no update. I couldn't understand it. I struggled to concentrate. I was as good as useless, but however hard I tried, I couldn't help it.

'I've got a spare half-hour. Let's work on tweaking that presentation,' Alex said. 'Get it up on your computer, and I'll be there in a second.'

Five minutes later, he propelled his chair around to my desk, bringing the sweet, resinous waft of his aftershave. 'I've been thinking about it. We want one big cute photo of Grace – in hospital if possible. Do you have some?'

I sighed heavily. 'I've got lots.' I picked up my phone, clicking from the news to my photo app.

He politely asked to take over my keyboard, while I searched in the folder for my niece. I found a few suitable photos and showed them to him.

'That one,' he said of the picture of Grace propped up in

her hospital cot when she was admitted last month. She was half-heartedly smiling, but pain flashed from her eyes like the beam from a bright light. 'Definitely that one. Airdrop it to your computer, and I'll slot it in.'

He clicked and typed, sitting upright, his back straight and head held high. He always carried himself with a quiet confidence. Before long, he slid the keyboard back towards me. 'Done! I think we're good to go. All you and your sister need to do now is practice your lines. You need to impress people on the night, so it's important you're as flawless as possible.'

By the time I was ready to leave for the day, there was still no news on Henry.

It didn't make sense. The cleaners must have found his body.

By six o'clock, when I was crossing the river back to Kat's apartment, there was still no update. I felt like I was in a boat on rough seas heading to shore, knowing the police were waiting to arrest me when we docked. My phone rang. I thought it was Kat. I hadn't heard from her all day, but Ruby's name flashed across the screen.

She delivered her message between sobs. 'Grace... stop... stopped breathing.'

I stood still, my racing heart at odds with the boats meandering under the bridge.

Ruby continued. 'Mum did CPR. She's breathing again now, but we're in an ambulance on the way to hospital. They don't know what's wrong with her. I'm really scared she's not... she's not going to make it.'

20

Mum met me at the doors to the Accident and Emergency department. The strain was engrained in the lines of her weathered face. She never could hide her emotions.

'How is she?' Sweat poured down my back from where I'd raced across the city.

'Not good. They're doing tests.' Mum's voice broke. 'You should've seen the colour of her. Grey, she was. Grey. Only one other person's allowed in with them. Go and get a cup of tea, and we'll take turns to support them. I'll come out again in half an hour.'

'Do you want anything?'

She shook her head. 'I'll get a coffee when you take over.'

'Text me if there's any change.'

I headed to the café, checking my phone. The frustration was growing with the lack of updates about Henry. Every minute felt like an hour. Grabbing a packet of crisps, I dropped it on a tray and ordered a cup of tea from the server. I wasn't hungry. But I had to eat. All I'd consumed all day was a biscuit in the meeting Alex had summoned me to. And even that I'd had to force down.

I found a table in the corner, sat, and opened the packet of crisps, reluctantly eating a handful. My throat was tight with anxiety. A tall man approached the table. I flinched. Every stranger felt like a threat. He asked if he could take the spare chair opposite me.

I forced a smile. 'Sure. Go ahead.'

I looked around, twitchy, paranoid someone had followed me, or was spying on me. But people were either glued to their phones or watching a quiz show playing on a giant TV attached to the wall a few tables down, biting into burgers and munching on chips.

I checked my phone again. There was still nothing. It was torture. I opened Facebook and found Henry's account. It was as if I couldn't help tormenting myself. Perhaps, subconsciously, I was trying to punish myself for what I'd done. Someone had to. Henry had been tagged in a post his wife had put up only an hour ago. I clicked on her name, surprised Charlene Robertson's page was no longer set to private. She'd pinned a picture of Henry. It was there at the top of her page for every visitor to see. I read the attached message beginning with the word MISSING.

It was about to kick off.

My eyes widened in alarm. I read her post, two heartfelt paragraphs summarising her desperate plea for help. Henry had told her he was staying with friends a few miles outside the city for the night, but he'd never turned up. She'd been to the police, but after carrying out a risk assessment, they hadn't deemed Henry a priority case. He was of sane mind. He wasn't vulnerable. He'd never gone missing before.

I called Kat and explained where I was, relaying what I'd

found. 'She says it's so out of character for him not to come home when he says he's going to. And also, for him not to contact her or answer her calls.' My voice rose in volume with each breath.

'Chill out, Mia. People will hear you.'

'Reading the comments, her friends agree. And get this—' I touched the screen and scrolled through Charlene's emotional words. 'He told her he was staying with a friend last night. Not at the Parkside Hotel. So he lied to her. Why did he do that?'

Kat hissed down the phone. 'Because, like I told you, Mia, he was a cheating liar. All men are.'

21

When the results from blood tests and a chest X-ray came back, Grace was immediately whisked off to the paediatric intensive care unit. Midnight was fast approaching, but it was hard to distinguish between night and day with all the erratic comings and goings of the nurses and doctors seeing to the many sick children on the ward.

Mum had insisted on taking Ruby for a coffee, despite my sister's reluctance, leaving me to sit by Grace's small cot, watching her nestled amid the tangled wires joining her body to the various monitors and machines beeping and humming in robotic symphony. High-pitched alarms constantly beeped, screwing with my head. It took me back to the time she was born and was taken to the neonatal intensive care unit, where she spent the first month of her life. The joy that overcame me when I first set eyes on her had been explosive. Pure unconditional love. I slotted my pinky finger inside her fragile fist, watching her take tiny breaths.

A hand landed on my shoulder. I jumped out of my skin.

Callum moved to my side and patted my arm, his voice a

whisper. 'Sorry. I didn't mean to scare you. I got here as soon as I could.'

'I didn't know you were coming.' Seeing my brother made me want to cry. He'd always been my rock. A strong urge to open up to him overcame me. Tell him everything. Get his advice. He would've known what to do.

He bent over the cot and repositioned the cellular blanket over Grace's legs. 'How's our little girl?'

I forced a smile. 'They're talking about ventilating her.'

'Ruby told me.' His eyes glassed over. He was a big softy when it came to Grace. We all were. 'God. I hate seeing her like this.' He took the chair next to me. 'How's Ruby bearing up?'

'Not great, as you can imagine. She's insisting on staying the night. We tried to get one of the parents' rooms along the corridor so she could at least get some sleep but be nearby if anything happened. But we live too close. Some parents live out of the city and need the rooms more.'

'Fair enough. The uncle of one of the guys from work has promised to make a donation to the FundMeToday page. I reckon we're on to raise nearly ten grand this weekend. That's not bad going, is it? A grand for every kilometre run.'

I updated him on the items for the silent auction Kelly had mentioned earlier.

'How's work?' he asked. 'Has the mighty KM Group sold any more souls to the Devil lately?'

I managed a laugh and gently punched his arm. Callum used to know a client of the KM Group. She was a former police officer turned popular novelist, who he'd claimed wasn't the cleanest of characters when she was in the force. Her publicist had hired the KM Group to shake up her image, which, according to Callum, had been a farce. She was rotten through and through.

'It's not that bad,' I said. 'Besides, we'd never have raised what we have for Grace without them. And there's still the ball to come.'

'I know. We've got a lot to thank them for.'

Ruby appeared. It was hard to believe my baby sister was a mum. She wasn't old enough to vote, buy alcohol, or get a tattoo, yet she had a vulnerable baby's life in her young hands.

I stood. 'I'll get going,' I said, abiding by the rule of only two per bedside at one time. How strange that I was a stickler for rules but had broken so many in the past thirty hours.

Ruby's voice broke. 'I'm scared she's going to die.'

Callum told her to stop. 'It's pneumonia. Kids get it all the time. A course of IV antibiotics and oxygen therapy, and she'll be back home in a few days.'

'It's not, though, is it?' Ruby replied flatly.

'What do you mean?' I said.

'It's part of her illness. If she doesn't get this treatment, she'll spend her short miserable life in and out of hospital with these kinds of problems.'

I dipped my head, unable to argue with the stark reality of the situation.

She removed her phone from her pocket, tapped the screen, and turned it to Callum and me. 'We had a five-hundred-pound donation this evening from that charity I approached. We're now at nearly two hundred and ten thousand.'

'And we've got plans for the rest.' My tone was upbeat. I was trying to disguise the anxiety in my voice.

'I reckon the fun run will pull in ten grand on Sunday,' Callum added.

I shifted in my chair. 'And the ball is set to bring in close to the rest.'

'Close!' Ruby touched the side of the cot. 'But there's no guarantee it'll be enough. We're running out of time.' Two tears cascaded down her face. She brushed her hand across her cheeks to sweep them away. 'I've got to get that money. She has to have this treatment. If she doesn't, we're going to lose her...' Her voice gave way to a flood of tears. 'Very soon.'

22

The TV was blaring out when I got back to Kat's apartment, despite the time approaching one a.m. My head spun as if I'd just stepped off a roller coaster.

Kat was huddled under her patchwork blanket on the sofa, watching a late-night chat show on catch-up. Her nose was bright red, but the rest of her face was as white as the mound of tissues growing on the floor.

The place reeked of weed. I couldn't understand how she could smoke so much when she was so full of cold.

The first thing she said was, 'Did you get my gym bag?'

'Sorry, I forgot.'

'You're useless sometimes, you know.' She laughed, but there was a serious undertone to her voice.

I took a cigarette from her packet on the table and lit it. 'That was the second-worst day of my life.'

She raised her eyebrows and pulled them together. 'And the first was?'

'What do you think?'

She pointed the remote control at the TV. 'I've been checking the news all night. There's still nothing.'

'It doesn't make sense. He should've checked out more than twelve hours ago. Surely they would've found his body by now?'

'It appears not.' She wiped her nose with a fresh tissue from the box on the arm of the sofa. 'Maybe the cleaners haven't got to his room yet.'

I tilted my head to the side. 'Really? In a busy hotel like that? You'd think they'd want to get it ready for the next guests as soon as possible.' I paused and took a long drag of the cigarette. 'I want to go there.'

'Don't be so stupid.'

I swallowed another ball of unease that had constantly appeared in my throat throughout the day. 'I'm going out of my mind. I'm going to have to hand myself in, aren't I?'

'What? Why?'

'Because someone's bound to recognise me when they find a picture of me on CCTV.'

'For fuck's sake, Mia. You're going to do nothing of the sort. I keep telling you. You were in disguise and plastered in make-up. I'd never have known it was you. Besides, those CCTV pictures are often grainy. No one is going to recognise you. Hold your nerve. You can be so weak at times. You need to toughen up.' Her words echoed in my mind. She often told me I needed to toughen up. 'You can't fall apart every time there's a development.'

Her words grated on me. 'How can you act so cool?'

She ignored my question. She had a habit of doing that.

'I'm off to bed.' I stubbed out the cigarette and headed to the kitchen to get a glass of water. She hadn't even asked how Grace was.

As I turned on the kitchen tap, she shrieked, 'Mia! Get in here.'

I left the glass in the sink and rushed over to her. She edged to the front of the sofa and wielded her phone at me.

My heart sank. 'What is it?'

I squinted, expecting a picture of a blonde me dominating the screen. But all I could make out was a Facebook post. She flipped her wrist and turned the screen back to face her.

She mumbled a summary of the words she was reading. 'The police are now taking Henry's disappearance seriously.' She glanced at me, her eyebrows raised, and returned her attention to the screen. 'His office has been broken into and ransacked. CCTV cameras were tampered with, so they have nothing to go on. They believe it was a targeted burglary. They've now begun a full investigation into his disappearance.'

My breath came thick and fast. I snatched the phone from her and read the post, praying somehow she'd got it wrong. But she hadn't. Police were urging anyone who saw anything suspicious to come forward. Fear pulsed through me as my raw nerves took yet another shredding.

Kat snatched the phone back, shaking her head. 'That's kinda weird, you know.' She slowly turned to me. 'Henry's murder and his office break-in!' Her lips twisted to the side. 'They must be somehow connected.'

23

Friday morning passed in a blur, with still no news of Henry's body being found and nothing more on the break-in at his office. I was going out of my mind. His wife had shared a further appeal on her Facebook page, posting a picture of him and their two sons and asking for help to find him. *Please help me share this post far and wide*, she'd written. *Someone must know where he is.*

I swallowed hard. I was that someone who could help her.

Alex appeared, waving his car keys. 'Are you ready?'

I glanced at the clock on my computer. It was midday. 'Sorry?' I racked my brain for what I was meant to be ready for.

'Moorlands. Remember our conversation this morning?'

'Sorry. I was miles away.'

Kat and I were meant to visit Moorlands, the venue for the ball next weekend, today, but as she was off sick, Alex had kindly agreed to go in her place.

I locked my computer and picked up my bag. 'Let's go.'

Alex drove us to Moorlands, a substantial Edwardian house across town that had been turned into a hotel. It was a stunning stone building, massive, like one of those giant houses from the period dramas Mum liked to watch. It was one of the poshest places I'd ever seen. When we'd been searching for a venue to hold the ball, Kelly had taken me and Kat there. The manager was a friend of hers. It ticked all the right boxes.

'What a beautiful building,' Alex said.

Our shoes crunched along the gravel driveway which was bordered by lush gardens and imposing trees. Fountains flanked the grand portico entrance. It was the perfect venue to hold a ball, but I couldn't help feeling like a pauper at the opera.

Susan Trice, who owned the events management company Kelly had commissioned to organise the ball, was waiting for us at a table in the expansive reception area filled with antique furnishings. I'd spoken to her a few times, but I hadn't been able to make the meeting when Kat and Kelly had first met her.

'You must be Mia.' She held out her hand for a fist bump. 'Nice to meet you at last.' She was a short, chatty woman, slightly shorter than my five foot four inches, but her heeled court shoes made her tower over me. She fist-bumped Alex, too. 'I've spoken to the hotel manager. We can pop into the Eddison Suite, but, of course, it won't be set up as it will be for the ball. Come with me.'

Alex and I followed her along a hallway with wood-panelled walls and ornamental cornices. It led to an open space with several doors leading to surrounding rooms.

'We're in there.' Susan pointed to a cream door with a silver placard announcing the *Eddison Suite*.

The door opened into the grand ballroom. 'Let me summarise how it's going to look on the night.' Susan's strong voice echoed around the large, grand room as she told us how she planned to arrange the thirty tables around the stage where Ruby and I would give our speeches. 'And over there...' She pointed to a set of double doors. 'They lead to two large rooms where the silent auction items will be displayed, and the other room will be dedicated to roulette, blackjack, and poker tables. I've sourced everything for that. It's all under control. You don't need to worry about a thing.'

Alex gestured towards the stage. 'Go and stand up there,' he said to me. 'It'll give you a feel for how it'll be on the night when you and your sister make your speeches. You can pretend we're the audience.'

I hesitated. I wasn't in the mood.

'Come on. Don't be shy,' Susan said.

'I'm not ready,' I said. 'I still need to learn the speech.'

'It doesn't matter.' Alex nudged me towards the stage. 'It's good to be pushed out of your comfort zone.'

He had no idea how far I'd already been pushed out of my comfort zone. I was close to snapping. But I couldn't refuse. He was doing it all for me and my family.

'Go on!' Like Kat, he could be very persuasive.

Begrudgingly, I stepped up to the stage and turned to face them.

'Say something,' Alex said. 'Anything.'

Uncomfortable, I rattled off some spiel about the weather.

'You need to project your voice more,' Alex said. 'I'll give you some pointers when we get back to the office, and you can practise again before the night.'

I tried to envision the venue next Saturday, but I was too on edge. I wanted to know how Henry's murder and his office break-in were connected. Perhaps that could lead to why his body had not yet been found. It was all I could think about.

24

After work, I went to Kat's to pick up an overnight bag. I wanted to stay at Mum's tonight. Afterwards, I headed straight to the hospital. Grace had deteriorated and was on a ventilator.

'Why don't you go home?' I suggested to Ruby.

She hadn't showered all day and looked like a wreck. But she flatly refused.

'At least go for something to eat.'

'I had a sandwich earlier.'

'I'll pay for your dinner,' I offered.

She didn't have a penny to her name. All her benefits went towards Grace.

I sat beside her, watching the fragile waif of a human lost in the rhythmic beat of the ventilator's wires and ghastly tubes. I fought back tears. There was no way I'd cry in front of my sister. Two nurses were busy around us, one typing on a computer resting on a portable stand, recording, I guessed, Grace's vital signs; the other administering a feed via Grace's NG tube.

My phone rang. It was Kat. I was about to send the call to voicemail but stopped. She might have had news about Henry. 'I need to take this.' I left Ruby and went to the family room at the end of the ward.

'I've not heard anything,' Kat said. 'You?'

'Nothing. I can't believe he hasn't been found. It's been forty-eight hours now. Wouldn't it be stinking in that room?'

'You'd have thought so. I can't understand it either. He must've decided to stay a few more days in the city and moved the checkout date.'

'It doesn't add up.'

'I'm better today,' she said, changing the subject, which she often did. I'd never realised how annoying it was until then. 'I could've gone into work, but I thought I might as well squeeze another day out of the situation. Do you fancy coming out tonight? I thought we could go to the pub.'

The woman had no morals.

'I'm fed up with being stuck here,' she continued. 'I need to sort this watch out, too.'

'I'm at the hospital.' I shook my head incredulously, wondering how she could be so brazen. 'Aren't you scared of bumping into someone from work?'

She let out a cackle. 'No one from there comes this side of the river on a Friday night. And especially not to the Old George.'

'I'm staying with my mum tonight.'

'Come back tomorrow. I want to talk to you about something.'

'What?' I asked, but she ended the call.

When I returned to Ruby, a consultant appeared. He was a gangly, strawberry-blond guy with whom Ruby and I'd had a number of conversations since Grace's diagnosis. He was fully conversant with our efforts to fund her treatment.

'I'm glad I caught you both.' He had what Ruby called a posh accent, the sort you acquired from a private school education. 'Could I have a word?' He pointed towards the nurses' station. 'There's a free room over there.'

'Sure,' Ruby and I said in unison.

We followed him into a room with a desk and two chairs and exchanged glances.

'I hate to deliver such news, but I'll cut to the chase.' He perched on the side of the desk.

Ruby and I sat in the chairs.

I gritted my teeth, preparing myself for the worse.

'I'm being candid here, but I need to tell you, with this deterioration, we're on borrowed time. I've spoken to my counterparts at the treatment centre in the US, and they're ready to receive Grace and commence treatment as soon as we have assurances of funding. But there is a finite amount of time, and the window is closing by the day. I hate to be frank, but that's where we are.' Each word was carefully articulated as if he'd practised his speech before meeting with us.

Ruby bowed her head and cracked her knuckles.

'Thank you for being so honest,' I said. 'At least we know where we stand.'

'I know it's not what you want to hear, but I must manage expectations.'

I tapped my phone and showed him the latest of our fundraising efforts. 'We have the ball next weekend. We're hoping that's going to crack it for us.'

The consultant crossed his fingers. 'Great. I'll be thinking of you.' He stood and placed his hands in his pockets. 'You have my secretary's details. Please keep me posted. I'll let you get back to Grace.'

'She's going to die, isn't she?' Ruby said when he left the room.

'No. No, she's not.' I shook my head. 'Never give up hope. We need to keep positive. We're going to get this money.'

'Isn't there anyone else we could try? Think of all the rich people out there with tons of money.'

'We're doing all we can. The ball should do it.'

We headed back to Grace's cot and sat in silence. Ruby's head fell on my shoulder, and we watched Grace's chest rise and fall with each mechanical breath of the ventilator.

It angered me how messed up the world was. Grace had suffered so much in her short life, yet there were so many criminals out there. Men like that animal who had pulled the trigger of that gun on Wednesday night. And women like Kat... and me.

I held Grace's floppy hand in mine. My emotions were overwhelming, confirming my thoughts. I'd have done anything for that tiny human being.

25

I considered taking a bus home, but they were often sporadic at night and rarely ran to the timetable. I quickened my pace, crossing the main road from the hospital to the quieter streets leading homewards. Every few steps, I peered over my shoulder. The sickening sense someone was following me was overwhelming. The slam of a car door, the backfiring of a car engine, the group of teenagers hanging out around a street corner, all heightened my unease.

Two streets from home, the door to a house suddenly opened. A tall man rushed out into my path.

I stepped back in fright.

'Sorry, luv. Didn't see you there.' He held up his hands and let me pass.

A clicking noise sounded. I glanced behind me. He darted across the street. Lights flashed, and he jumped into a car.

I ran the rest of the way home.

Mum was asleep with her feet on the coffee table. The TV was playing one of the soaps she loved. Removing the remote control from her limp hand, I switched channels to the news but learned nothing new. I pressed the off button.

Mum immediately woke up. She yawned, stretching her arms above her head. 'How is she?'

'Stable for now. Ruby wouldn't come home.'

'I tried to make her come back, as well.'

'I said I'll stay up there tomorrow night with Grace, so she can come home and get a proper night's sleep.' I relayed the conversation with the consultant. 'We're counting on this ball.'

'Talking of the ball, I've found a dress.' Mum shuffled forward to the edge of the sofa. 'Do you want to see it?'

I stifled a groan. Ball dresses were the last thing on my mind. 'Sure.'

'I got lucky.' She raised a hand. 'I know. I know. It doesn't happen often. I was telling a new nurse who recently joined the ward about Grace and the ball and how I was looking for something to wear. We're about the same size, it turns out, and she said she had a dress I could borrow. She brought it in for me today.' She hauled herself up from the sofa. 'Come and see.'

Reluctantly, I followed her into her bedroom. All I wanted to do was get to bed.

Mum flicked the light switch. 'Ta-da.' She held her hand out to a mint-green dress hanging from the doorframe of a small built-in cupboard she used as a wardrobe. It was a flattering Grecian style with a ruched pleated bodice and a large bow to the side. 'Whaddya think?'

'It's beautiful, Mum.'

'And it fits me perfectly. But the best news is the money I've been putting aside to buy a new dress can now go towards Grace's treatment. Win-win all round, hey?'

I touched the smooth but grainy material. 'Put it on.'

'Oh, no, not now.' She fingered her frowzy hair. 'I'm a mess. I'll do it tomorrow. I'm going to bed. I cooked a lasagne. It's out on the side. Help yourself and put the rest in the fridge.'

I shook my head. 'I picked up a burger at the hospital,' I lied. Food was the last thing on my mind.

'Oh, and get this,' she continued. 'There's a matching bag. She said I can have it, too, if the dress fits, which it does. More money I can give to Grace.' She paused and stared at me. 'Mia? Are you OK?'

The words shot out of my mouth before I could stop them. 'Can I move back in, Mum?'

'What brought this on?'

'I miss you all.'

'I knew something was up with you.' Delight shone in her eyes, as if I'd just told her she'd won the lottery.

She hugged me. My heart jolted. There was a part of Mum that always got to me. She was the most unselfish person on the planet and always so full of positivity, but Grace's disease had dragged her down. It had dragged us all down.

'Well, can I... move back in?'

'You don't even need to ask.'

Over the past year, I'd realised that life had weathered Mum. The stress of raising three children single-handedly while working full-time and taking extra shifts to make ends meet had given her more lines than her friends had.

Discovering what I had done would finish her off.

26

My legs were heavy, my body weary. The journey to Kat's apartment seemed to go on forever. It felt as if I'd already climbed a mountain today with a heavy sack tied on my back.

It was nearly seventy-two hours since I'd witnessed Henry getting shot, and there was still no news coming from the Parkside Hotel.

The thought of telling Kat I was moving out, among other things, had kept me up all night. She'd be angry. And she'd try to persuade me to stay. But I was ready.

The front door to the apartment left ajar first awakened my senses to something amiss. I stopped outside. Kat must've gone out and left it open. That was unlike her. She was always fastidious about security, like a stuck record, always telling me to ensure I locked the door on my way out. Often, we'd get halfway down the street when she'd tell me to wait while she returned to double-check. At first, I thought she was just overly security-conscious, until the night she opened up about her side hustle.

I pushed the door open wider. My sense of unease was

growing. I stepped inside. A foldable clothes airer stood in the hallway. The black dress I'd worn to meet Henry on Wednesday evening hung on a hanger among the other dark clothes drying. I shuddered. The cloth I'd wrapped his watch in was hanging over the top rack.

The silence was unnerving. Kat always had the TV on. Even if she wasn't watching anything, she had an expensive surround-sound system through which she played music that she left on when she went out. An unpleasant smell, like food that had passed its sell-by date, warned me not to venture further. But my rationality told me not to be so silly. Kat had probably left the door open on her way in and was in her bedroom. She'd texted earlier in the afternoon to say her cold had progressed to her chest.

'Kat, you here?' I called out.

I stood stock still, staring along the dark hallway. 'Kat.'

A beam of light from the window suddenly bounced off the mirror, sending particles flickering into the air. I quietly placed my keys in the dish on the console table by the door. The keyring containing a photo of me holding Grace on the day she was born clinked on the porcelain. A sound so light, yet so loud against the silent background. I sneaked towards the living area. The door was shut, which was odd in itself. It was usually wedged open by a rubber doorstop. Neither Kat nor I ever closed it.

The balaclava guy crept into my mind. I spun around, half expecting him to jump out on me. I opened the door. Panic flared in my chest. It looked as if a bomb had been dropped. 'What the hell?' I whispered, my sixth sense telling me not to draw attention to myself.

The sofa was upturned, and so was Kat's yellow chair, her patchwork blanket thrown to the side. The plants hanging from the ceiling had been ripped from their hooks, and their earth strewn across the floor. I spun around, stopping suddenly. The doors of Kat's 1950s sideboard had been unceremoniously yanked off their hinges and dumped on top of the unit. Someone had extracted the contents and randomly thrown everything across the floor. My attention turned to the kitchen area. Cups, plates, and bowls from the cupboards had been discarded on the breakfast bar. And every drawer had been pulled out, their contents strewn across the floor.

My breaths came short and fast. We'd been burgled. Kat had always told me no one else knew about her side hustle besides me and her dealer who flogged the watches and gave her a percentage of his gains. He never came here, she'd told me. I wondered if she'd opened up to the wrong person or had been overheard in conversation with someone about her shady secret set-up. The dreadful sense of unease turning my stomach intensified as I questioned whether the balaclava guy followed me there that night and had returned for Henry's watch.

Abandoning the chaos in the kitchen, I advanced through the disorder. I crept along the hallway. When I got to my bedroom, I opened the door. Whoever had been there didn't stop in the living area. My room was also a mess, my personal space savagely attacked. The contents of my wardrobe were scattered across the floor, as were those of the drawers and bedside cabinet. I trawled through the jungle of discarded clothes and spun around, panicked and overwhelmed from what I'd seen and for what could still be to come.

I glanced down the hallway towards Kat's room, wondering if she'd gone out before the intruder arrived. Or worse still, if someone was in there with her now. I didn't know what to do for the best. Telephoning for help seemed the sensible option, but facing the police was the last thing I needed.

I wanted to run – as far away from there as possible.

I crept along the hallway, my mouth dry, my heart racing, until I reached Kat's room. The door was ajar, a splinter of light slicing across the hallway.

Hesitantly, I nudged the handle. My breathing quickened.

I opened the door.

It squeaked.

I froze.

27

'Kat!' My voice was a faint whisper.

Her lifeless body was slumped on the bed against the wall.

A cruel sense of déjà vu hit me. Room four-nine-three at the Parkside Hotel, and Henry Robertson's body sprawled on the sofa.

But that time there was more blood.

A lot more.

I rushed to her. At first, I couldn't make out if she was alive or dead. Her face was bruised and swollen, her lip split, and her hair was matted with blood. She must've taken a blow to the head.

'Kat!' My hand hovered above her.

I gently shook her arm but stopped when she weakly cried out in pain. Her eyes were black and puffy. She could barely open them. Plum-coloured bruising spread across her cheekbones, and her clothes were ripped. A shallow breath rattled from between her lips.

I didn't know what to do. The shock was overwhelming –

like I was in a nightmare I couldn't wake up from. Stunned, I peered around the room. It was in the same state as mine, drawers open, doors ajar. Numerous items – clothes and the contents of her dressing table – were a jumble on the floor. Her bedside was upturned, the glass lamp in pieces. 'What the hell happened, Kat?'

She squinted through her engorged eyes. Her mouth opened. Her breath was ragged and shallow. A trickle of blood dribbled from her lips and dripped down her chin. She tried to lift her arm.

'Who did this to you, Kat? Did you know them?'

All she managed was another mumble.

'I need to get you help.' The panic in my voice was palpable. I didn't know what to do first. Call for assistance or try to help her myself. 'And we need to get the police here.'

Oh, hell! The police.

The grunting continued as if Kat was protesting. She tried to raise a hand but couldn't achieve the simplest of motions. The desperation in her eyes was gut-wrenching. She grunted again. Her eyes rolled back, and she lost consciousness.

I panicked, wondering if she was dead. A bang made me jump. At first I thought it was someone coming into the apartment. But it was the main door to the building slamming shut.

I fumbled for my phone in my pocket, groaning at Kat's collection of wigs half hanging from one of many boxes stored under her bed. I slammed my hand on my forehead. Think. I needed to think carefully. The police would find those wigs. And when the news story about Henry Robertson eventually broke, they'd trace the woman in the blonde wig with him that evening back to Kat. A terrible thought entered my head. The same maniac who shot Henry Robertson had followed me back. He could've returned to finish the job and mistaken Kat for me.

Was it supposed to be me lying there in a pool of blood?

I needed to get rid of the wigs. Burn the lot. But I couldn't be seen leaving the apartment to dispose of them. I'd be exposed once the police started their investigation into the brutal attack. And they'd ask me why I didn't report the incident straight away. I kicked the wigs under the bed.

I was in deeper trouble than I ever could've imagined.

28

I called 999, unable to stop shaking. The fear of where it all could lead was unbearable. But I had no choice. Kat needed help, and I had to get it for her fast.

'Emergency. Which service do you require?'

I tried to keep my voice steady. 'Ambulance and police.'

There was a clicking sound, and a woman calmly asked, 'What's the exact location of the emergency?'

The shock had disorientated me. I relayed the apartment number and the name of the street, but I couldn't recall the postcode.

'What's happened?'

I couldn't bring myself to say the words 'I think my flatmate is dead'. *Breathe.* I willed myself to take a deep breath. 'My flatmate's been beaten up. I'm scared she might be dead.'

'A vehicle is on its way. Is she breathing?'

'I don... don't know.'

'You need to check her pulse. Do that for me now, please.'

I was shaking so hard I dropped the phone onto the bed. I wrapped my fingers around Kat's slim wrist. It was difficult to determine if there was a pulse or not. I grabbed the phone. 'I can't tell.'

'Put your ear to her mouth and look for chest movements.' The woman was so calm and collected, like an old friend you could always rely upon. A stark contrast to the quivering wreck I'd turned into.

I followed her instructions. 'There's a faint breath.'

She continued. 'How bad are the injuries?'

I answered the best I could.

'Is anyone else present in the building?'

Her question stunned me. I couldn't remember if I'd shut the front door I'd found open. Someone could come back any minute. I ran into the hallway.

The door to the apartment was wide open.

The knot of fear in my stomach tightened. With the phone still in my hand, I raced down the hallway and slammed the door shut, only to regret it. Whoever did that to Kat could easily have slipped back in while I was seeing to her. I stood still, listening. Apart from the faint hum of traffic outside, there was silence.

The operator repeated her question.

I placed the phone to my ear. 'I don... don't know. I'm looking.' Tentatively, I crept from room to room, checking. I felt like a character in a Halloween movie, terrified someone was going to jump out at me. I was more scared than I was the night Henry died.

The bathroom door was closed. I went to open it but stopped. I hadn't yet checked in there. Whoever attacked Kat could still be in there. I pulled down the handle and pushed open the door. Chaos prevailed, the same as in the other rooms. The drawer in the unit built around the sink was open, its contents a mess, the same with the wall cabinet. Mine and Kat's bathrobes had been ripped from the hook on the back of the door and were in a pile on the floor.

'There's no... no one else,' I stuttered into my phone.

'Is there any immediate danger to yourself?'

'I don't think so.'

The woman kept me on the line. I couldn't remember what we discussed other than making sure Kat was OK. Before I knew it, sirens indicated the police had arrived. It all happened so quickly. There was a knock at the door. I went to open it, and two armed officers burst into the apartment.

They followed me to where Kat was lying out cold on the bed. One of them, a tall, lanky guy with arms as long as his legs, spoke into the radio attached to his shoulder. Words I couldn't make out. The other guided me away from the room. They needed to preserve the crime scene, the stocky guy with a goatee informed me.

But my fingerprints were all over it. Once they found Henry Robertson's body, they'd find my fingerprints in his room. Although I'd been careful to wipe down the surfaces as Kat had instructed me to, there was no way I would've got them all.

Two paramedics, a man and a woman, arrived, loaded with bags and equipment. The guy spoke into his radio; something about backup and a Scenes of Crime officer.

I walked out in a trance, my thoughts a carousel of deep concerns. Selfishly, I couldn't help but wonder what the implications were for me. I allowed the police officer to guide me along the hallway. 'It looks like a break-in,' were the only words I could find.

'You weren't here when it happened, I take it?' the officer asked.

I shook my head. 'I arrived back about a minute before I called for help.'

'And you are?'

'Kat's flatmate.' I pointed to my bedroom. 'I rent that room from her.' I couldn't believe I was standing there in such dire circumstances. 'My room's in just as much a mess.'

'Have you been in there?'

'Yes. Before I went into Kat's room. My door was open, which is strange because I always close it.' I was shaking.

'Can you tell me Kat's next of kin?'

I had to think hard. I knew little about the woman I'd lived with for the past three months. 'She has a mum. I don't know where she lives, though. What happens now?'

'We're going to need to take a statement from you. I'm waiting for my colleagues to arrive, and we'll take you to the station.'

Station? 'Do I have to? Can't we do it here?'

'This isn't the place. We need to get you away from here. You'll be able to think more clearly. You can make your own way there, but it's probably best we take you.'

He led me out of the front door while asking further questions. And before I knew it, I was being escorted to a waiting police car and told to mind my head as I climbed into the back seat.

29

They took my fingerprints. 'So we can distinguish between the occupants' and the intruder's prints,' the officer told me. He was a burly man, with thick arms that looked as if they wanted to burst out of his shirtsleeves.

Panic rose in me. My fingerprints were now on the national police database. When Henry's body was found, the police would link me to that room.

The officer led me to an interview room, where I sat on a plastic chair drinking a cup of sweet tea while waiting for the meeting to start. It was hot in there, but I'd already stripped down to my T-shirt.

I needed to make a decision. And I needed to make it fast. I could own up to what I knew about Kat's side hustle, ultimately revealing my own involvement, or I could keep quiet. But every time I considered the two options, it came back to the same question. If I came clean about my involvement, what would happen to Grace?

The ball was a week away. It had to go ahead.

I wanted to call Callum. My brother had always been the

one I'd turned to when I needed help. But I couldn't. As soon as I started talking to him, he'd know there was more than I was letting on.

That's what happens when you play with fire. You end up getting burnt.

A female officer entered the room. She was there to assess my needs, she told me, and asked if I required any psychological support. Hell, yes! What I'd experienced over the previous three days would haunt me for the rest of my life. But not yet. I needed to get away from there as soon as possible, and waiting for someone to arrive would only delay the process.

'I can put you in touch with someone if you change your mind.' She handed over a card with her details. 'Call me any time.'

When she left, a male and a female officer clutching tablets and a paper file entered the room. They took the chairs opposite me.

'I'm DI Prince,' the forty-something-year-old man said. He was heavy-set and appeared jaded, as if he lived off fast food and little sleep. His ill-fitting suit probably would've been flattering several years earlier. But he looked haggard. Tired. Worn out. The same as me.

'And this is DS Harrow.' He nodded to the female officer sitting beside him, who was dressed in smart trousers and a fashionable pale-blue, Crimplene blouse. Her auburn hair, tied in a single ponytail, trailed down to her lower back.

He cleared his throat and explained that I was there as a witness and that they simply wanted to ask a few questions to help them with their investigation.

For a brief moment, I considered asking for legal representation, thinking that was what you were meant to do when confronted by the police in that situation. But that'd surely make me look guilty. And it'd only delay things. All I wanted to do was answer their questions and get the hell out of there. 'How is she?' I asked. 'Do you know?'

'We've spoken briefly to Katherine, but she is heavily sedated, so we gained little from her,' DI Prince replied.

I sat on my hands to stop my fingers fiddling. 'Where is she?'

'Riverside Hospital. OK. Let's get going.' The DI scratched his bald head.

The initial questions were easy to answer. I met Kat through work and moved in with her three months ago.

'When did you last see her before the incident?'

'Yesterday evening I popped back after work to pick up some stuff as I'd planned to stay at my mum's place for the night.'

'And why is that?'

'My baby niece is in hospital.' I explained my complicated family set-up. 'I wanted to support my mum and sister.'

'What time was that?'

I shrugged. 'I can't remember exactly.'

'Think a little harder, if you can. This is important. Let's not make any bones about this. We're dealing with a case of attempted murder here, Mia. What time did you leave the apartment? We can probably find video footage of you leaving from somewhere in the vicinity. It'd make our jobs easier if you could remember.'

I fidgeted in the chair. It was only meant to be an informal chat, but he was making me feel as guilty as sin. I puffed out a large breath, thinking hard. It was a struggle. My thoughts were a muddled mess. I hadn't been able to think straight since Wednesday night. 'Around six.'

'And you say you were away all night?'

'That's right. I was at the hospital until maybe ten o'clock. My brother was there. He's a police officer, based at this station. So you can corroborate that with him.'

'Why would we need to corroborate anything?'

I needed to watch what I said. 'I don't know. This is the first time I've been in this situation. I'm not sure how it all works.'

'What's his name?'

'Callum Hamilton.'

Saying his name hurt. During the application process to join the police, he'd had to declare any criminal activity in which his family had been involved. I'd bring such shame to him if the truth came out. He didn't deserve that.

The same as Mum, he must never, ever find out what I'd done.

30

DI Prince scribbled a note and asked me, 'How do you consider Katherine?'

I frowned, not understanding the context of his question. 'What do you mean?'

'You rent a room from her. Do you consider her a land-lord, a flatmate, a friend?'

'A friend, I guess.' It was a lie. I inwardly winced. A few questions in, and I'd already lied. Kat had never been a friend. I could see that. She had used me. Love-bombed me to her advantage. But I had to take some responsibility. I was an adult, at the end of the day. To my shame, I went along with everything, even if it had taken heavy persuasion on Kat's part.

'Tell us a little more about your friendship.'

'What do you mean?'

'We need to understand more about Katherine's life and what she got up to on a daily basis. Was this a random burglary that went wrong, or was Kat involved in something that resulted in the attack?'

I considered how much to divulge. I was out of my depth. Way out of it. And I was sinking fast. I redirected thoughts of Grace and Mum into my mind. I needed to hold it together for their sakes. 'We work together, as I said. Not closely. She's the boss's PA, and I work in the admin team, so we have little to do with each other in the office. We sometimes go out for drinks after work with other staff.'

'What about the weekends? Do you spend time together?'

'Sometimes I go out with her and her friends on a Saturday night.'

'I'll need details of those friends.'

I bit my bottom lip. I didn't know those people. Not really. I could count on one hand how often I'd met them. I knew their names. But they weren't even their real names. Unless their parents had really christened them Popeye and Daisy Chain. That was about as far as it went. Kat always insisted on drinks and a line of coke before we went out. I'd never touched drugs until I'd moved in with her... and I'd never touch them again. So, on top of all the alcohol we consumed while getting ready, by the time we met her friends, I was on another planet. That was the truth of it. They were Kat's friends. Not mine.

I'd enjoyed those nights at first. Meeting exciting new people who wore clothes and hairstyles I'd seen on social media but didn't have the confidence to try myself. But it hadn't been until two Saturdays ago when I saw them through sober eyes. I'd been helping Ruby with Grace, who'd had one of her turns, and so I hadn't had the self-confidence-boosting cocktail of alcohol and cocaine before I'd met up with them. It was that night I learnt they weren't the nicest of people.

'Did you hear me, Mia?'

I glanced at the detective. 'Sorry?' My hands had made their way into my lap, and I was fiddling with the hem of my T-shirt.

'I said I'll need details of those friends.'

'I think it's best you speak to Drake.'

'Drake?'

'He works in the Orange Bush in the centre of town. That's where the evenings usually started when I went out with her. He knows most of her friends.'

DS Harrow made a note on her tablet. She was a pretty woman. People would've said the same about Kat. And so would I, once upon a time.

DI Prince dropped his head to the side and looked at me questioningly. 'Mia, do you know anyone who'd want to do this to your friend?'

A few months ago, I would've vehemently shouted no to that question. But where did I even start? I had no clue how many men Kat had fleeced over the years. I'd asked her when she'd first told me about her side hustle, but the reply had come coated in a bout of laughter as she'd shamelessly admitted she'd lost count.

Friend. I cringed at the word. Kat used me. She saw me as an easy target to manipulate to do her dirty work.

'Does Katherine have a mobile phone?'

That seemed a strange question. Everyone had a mobile phone. 'Yes.'

'It's just we can't locate it.'

I shrugged. 'She's always on her phone.'

'Her assailant must have taken it with them. We can get her phone records by other means.'

I panicked, wondering what past messages Kat and I had exchanged that could expose us. But she'd had strict rules about texting regarding anything to do with her side hustle. I was only allowed to use the phone she gave me – the one still in pieces in a sock with Henry's wallet in my niece's teddy bear. Hell! Another wave of panic struck me. I needed to get home fast and get rid of them.

I focused on the detective, trying to remain calm. I had to get through the ordeal.

The questioning lasted roughly an hour.

'Is there anyone else you think we should speak to?' DI Prince asked.

I shook my head, wondering if I was being too naive. What were the chances they'd find out about my involvement in Kat's illicit hustle? Grace's sunken features entered my thoughts. The frail baby fighting for her life in the PICU. I couldn't reveal the truth about Kat. Not yet.

The DI nodded at the DS, who formally ended the interview.

He stood. 'We'll get your witness statement printed for you to read and sign.'

'What happens next?' I asked. 'Can I go and get my stuff?'

'You won't be able to return to the apartment until the forensic examination has been completed. Do you have somewhere else you can stay? Can you go home to your family?'

I nodded.

'Do you have any reason to believe – and this is important – your life is in danger, Mia?'

I vigorously shook my head. Another lie. I was in more danger and more trouble than I could ever have imagined. 'How? Why?'

'I'm simply checking. If you're sure, then you're free to leave.' DI Prince dug his stumpy fingers into his jacket pocket and produced a business card. He pushed it across the table towards me. 'If you can think of anything else, please let me know. We'll be in touch about when you can return to the apartment or if we have any further questions for you.'

31

The waft of sizzling bacon drifted into my room, the signature smell of Sunday mornings. Callum said it was one of the things he missed most when he'd moved out. I had to agree.

I wanted to stay in bed. It was getting on for midnight by the time I left the police station. Thankfully, Mum had been asleep when I got home. There was no way I could have faced her. One look at me, and she'd have known something was wrong.

The late-September sun streamed in through the gap in the curtains. I picked up my phone and searched the local news. The break-in at Kat's apartment had made the front page of one of the local papers. I scanned the brief bulletin. The police continued to carry out door-to-door enquiries but had nothing to go on. They were appealing for witnesses in the area around the hours of the suspected break-in to come forward.

I continued searching the news for other stories.

And there it was.

I knew it'd come at some point.

The news about the missing Henry Robertson.

It was only a tiny piece, barely five succinct lines, in an online local newspaper from the town where he'd lived. I shuffled up the bed, hugging the covers around me, and continued reading. My eyes widened.

Henry hadn't contacted his wife since Wednesday morning, when he'd left for work. He'd told her he wouldn't be home until the following evening because he had a business meeting and was staying there overnight, which wasn't unusual. He often stayed away for business. Police were tracing his movements from the moment he'd left home, but he hadn't been seen since boarding a train. The police asked for anyone who had seen him to contact them on the number given.

But Kat saw him at the KM Group. He'd met with Kelly. Unless Kat had been lying.

I turned to Facebook and apprehensively searched for Henry's wife's page. The poor woman must be going through hell. Since I last looked, she'd posted several photos of Henry, with a simple one-liner: *Have you seen Henry?* And further images of him with their sons, with the plea: *Help us find our dad!*

It was gut-wrenching.

The woman's pain spilled in buckets from every post, morphing into guilt as it gushed through my veins. I could've ended that woman's and her family's suffering. But where would that leave my family? The ball was less than a week away.

I checked for any other news of Henry, still expecting the blonde woman seen with him the night he was killed to be plastered over the news. But, there was still nothing. I couldn't work it out. He simply must've been found by then. Or, perhaps, it was a professional hit followed by a professional cleanup operation. That could be the only conclusion. Rolling over, I hauled the duvet over my head. I wanted the world to go away and stay away; give me some peace from its relentless knocks and shocks for a while.

The smell from the kitchen intensified. Mum knocked on my door, opened it, and popped her head through the gap. 'I'm making bacon sandwiches.'

I took a deep breath. I needed to face her at some point. 'Give me a minute,' I mumbled.

'They'll be ready in five minutes. Come straight away.'

I typed a text to Callum, saying I couldn't make the Fun Run today because I'd pulled a muscle in my leg. My finger hovered over the send key, but I didn't press it. I couldn't let Grace down. There was money riding on me finishing that race today. Kelly had sponsored me, on behalf of the KM Group, one hundred pounds for every kilometre I completed.

I deleted the text and trudged into the kitchen in my pyjamas.

'Where were you last night?' Mum asked. 'I thought you were meant to come to the hospital.' Three plates of sandwiches and three cups of tea sat waiting on the table. She was ripping sheets of kitchen paper from the roll on the wall to use as napkins.

'I was busy. Is Callum here?' I pointed to the plates.

'No. Ruby came home for the night. She's going to eat with us then go straight back to the hospital.'

As if on cue, Ruby appeared, yawning. 'I've called the ward. She had a stable night.'

'That's good news,' Mum said. 'Now eat up.'

We sat in our nightwear, diving into the bacon sandwiches. It was an effort. I had to force the first half down, despite it being the most food I'd consumed for days.

'What happened to you last night?' Ruby asked through a mouthful of sandwich. 'I thought you said you wouldn't be long.' Ketchup squeezed from the side of her lips and dripped onto her fingers like a drop of blood.

Kat's smashed-up face swam before my eyes. I threw my half-eaten sandwich on the plate and took a sip of tea. 'Sorry. I'll stop by after the run today.'

'Do you promise?' she asked. The corners of her mouth dropped, expressing an air of vulnerability.

I sometimes forgot how young she was.

'I promise.' I sighed deeply. 'Something dreadful has happened.'

'What?' they asked in unison.

I scrunched the makeshift napkin into a ball. 'Kat got beaten up.'

Ruby had never met Kat, but Mum had on the day she'd helped me move. And on another occasion when she'd brought a bag of groceries around to the flat.

Mum gasped. 'That's dreadful. Where? Who? Why?'

'I found her at the apartment. There was a break-in.'

'What did they take?' Mum asked. 'What have two young women like you got to take?'

If only she knew.

'She wasn't in a fit state to talk, so I don't know. I had to go to the police station and make a witness statement.'

'That's awful.' Mum licked her lips. 'Why did you say in your text you were going out?'

'I didn't want you to worry.'

'How many times have I told you never to lie?'

I inwardly cringed for the lies that were sure to emerge

from my mouth in the coming days, weeks, and months. Years, even. And perhaps for the rest of my life.

Mum's worry lines were creasing her forehead more than I'd ever seen. Her thoughts were easy to read. I'd asked to move back home, and in the next breath, Kat's flat got burgled and she was beaten up.

Mum stretched her arm across the table. 'Are you OK?'

I took another sip of tea. My eyes were stinging with fatigue, and my body was weak from the stress and lack of food. The ringing sound of my phone from my bedroom saved me from having to answer her. It was a blessing. I wouldn't get away with dodging Mum's questions for long. I wasn't that verbally agile. I'd have to face them at some point, but I needed to get myself together first. I threw my balled napkin on the table and jumped up. 'I'd better get that.'

I rushed to the bedroom to catch the call. No Caller ID scrolled across the screen. I considered not answering it in case it was one of the detectives from last night, but something made me accept the call.

It was a nurse from the hospital where Kat was taken last night.

She informed me that Kat had regained consciousness.

And she was asking to see me.

32

I pressed the buzzer to the high-dependency ward, where visitors were welcome from ten a.m. until midday and for a few hours in the afternoon. I couldn't believe I'd found myself in that place again, with my niece on one floor and my ex-landlady on another.

A cranky voice crackled through the intercom. 'Can I help you?'

'I'm here to see Katherine West.' My stomach was turning at the thought of facing her.

'Who are you?'

'Mia Hamilton. A nurse called me earlier and said Katherine wanted to see me.'

The lock released. The doors clunked, followed by a loud squeak. They opened onto a corridor lined with beds and medical equipment. The smell of disinfectant wafted strongly in the air. I walked along, peering into the rooms flanking the corridor, searching for Kat.

When I reached the unmanned nurses' station, a health-

AJ CAMPBELL

care assistant pushing a blood pressure monitor hurried towards me.

'Can I help you?' Her cheeks were rosy, and her greying hair was pulled into a bun.

'I'm looking for Katherine West.'

'Let me get someone.' She pointed to the nurses' station, her face wrinkled but kind, her smile, too. She reminded me of Mum. 'Wait there, and I'll be back in a minute.'

The toing and froing of the hectic ward grabbed my attention. It was boiling in there. I removed my hoodie, stripping down to my running T-shirt Callum got printed especially for the Fun Run. It had a cute picture of Grace printed on the front and back, along with the name of her appeal, *Saving Baby Grace*, and a QR code to her FundMeToday page. A harassed nurse appeared, asking how she could help. She had a particular look about her. Weary and worn out. It's the same look Mum's face acquired at the end of one of her many stressful shifts.

'I'm here to see my flatmate, Katherine West.' There was a raspy edge to my voice from my dry throat.

'Sure. It was me who called you earlier. Come with me.' The nurse marched me further along the corridor until we arrived at another open ward with six beds and its own mini nursing station.

I didn't recognise Kat at first. A dressing covered most of her hairline. Her face was still puffy and swollen, and her eyes appeared blacker than yesterday. I swallowed the lump in the back of my throat. Her left arm was in plaster, and the fingers of her right hand were in splints as if they'd been broken.

'She's heavily sedated,' the nurse said. 'So I'm not sure how much you'll get out of her.'

'How is she?' My voice wavered. Despite the trouble Kat had got me into, I never would've wished that upon her.

'Well, let's say she won't be going home any time soon.' The nurse picked up a paper towel from the floor and placed it in the bin. 'We're still ascertaining the extent of her injuries. Some internal. She's a tough cookie, that's for sure. In the little time she's been awake, she's been quite insistent on seeing you.'

I gave the nurse a close-lipped smile and studied Kat's broken body. She was a shadow of the large character I'd got to know. 'She's going to be OK, isn't she?' I turned back to the nurse, but she'd already gone.

I sat in the high-backed armchair beside the bed, careful not to interfere with the drip stands and monitor wires attached to Kat's body. 'Hey, how ya doing?' I berated myself for asking such a silly question.

Flitting in and out of consciousness, Kat coughed. She tried to speak, but she was groggy. Spittle bubbled at the side of her mouth. Her face contorted. She let out a long, low moan.

'Who did this to you, Kat?' I whispered.

Her face twitched. She fought to open her eyes. When she finally did, urgency flooded them. She attempted to speak, but scarcely a whisper escaped her swollen lips. 'You.' Her words were slurred, barely audible.

'Me?' I leaned in closer, trying to decipher what she was trying to tell me.

'He... was... looking... f... f... for you.'

'What do you mean?' I sucked in an anguished sob. 'The man who did this to you?'

Her head moved up and down ever so slightly. If I hadn't been focused, I'd have missed the small motion.

'Who was he, Kat? Did you know him?'

'You say nothing,' Kat continued, her voice a vile cocktail of confusion and desperation. 'He was going to—' She strained to carry on. 'Kill me.'

'Who was he?'

'Don't know... Amazon delivery driver... disturbed him.'

'What did he want?'

One of the monitors alarmed. The screen flashed.

Kat's eyes closed.

I needed to know. The beeping sound seemed to grow louder, piercing. A nurse peered over from the bed opposite, where she was seeing to a patient. I placed a hand on Kat's shoulder and gently shook it.

'Kat,' I whispered. 'Kat! Wake up. You need to tell me. What did he want?'

It took all her effort, but she managed to open her eyes. The nurse appeared. 'Wallet. He want... wanted... a wallet.'

33

Kat had drifted back to sleep by the time the nurse came to silence the beeping monitor. I left the ward in a hurry and stood in the corridor, leaning against the cold wall, taking deep breaths to stop myself from hyperventilating. Kat's mumbled words whirled around my mind. I should never have taken Henry's wallet. She'd warned me not to touch his personal belongings, only his watch. I couldn't believe I'd been so stupid.

It should've been me lying in that hospital bed, not Kat.

The monitor alarms were still ringing in my head. My knees shuddered. The hospital corridor whirled about me. I was going to pass out. I stumbled along the rubber flooring, clutching the wall until I reached, thankfully, an empty stretch of chairs. I broke into a cold sweat. The wretched sensation was overwhelming. I dropped onto the end chair and leant my head in my hands.

I needed to get rid of the wallet and the phone Kat gave me to use that night. The phone that was in hundreds of pieces still in Grace's teddy. What an idiotic place to hide them! What had I been thinking?! I needed to go home and burn the lot of it... but I wondered if that was the right thing to do. Whoever had come to get it wanted it for a reason.

The doors to the ward opened. Two doctors appeared, deep in conversation as though they were discussing a life-or-death situation. They probably were. I took deep breaths to contain the emotions running through me, trying to work out why Kat's attacker wanted Henry's wallet so badly. Bad enough to kill for! The guy who shot Henry must've followed me back to Kat's apartment after the market and mistaken Kat for me when he returned to finish the job. That was the only explanation I could think of. I considered the implications. The fear bubbling away inside me was reaching boiling point.

Each deep breath I took accompanied a change of heart. I considered going back to the police station and confessing everything. Kat was a savvy woman. She must have worked out that I'd taken Henry's wallet. But she wouldn't want to reveal her side hustle, because she knew she'd end up in prison. No. I was safe on that score. Kat's lips were sealed.

My phone beeped. I slipped it out from the side pocket of my leggings. Ruby had sent a photo to our family WhatsApp group, a selfie of her with Grace who looked so pale but was at least awake. Another ping delivered another message to accompany the text.

Hello from hospital. Good luck with the run today. We're so proud of you both. Hugs.
Ruby & Grace x

Another message popped up on the screen from Mum.

> I'm here. I've seen Callum but can't see you.
> Where are you? I'm by the ice cream van
> near to the start line. Mum X

Closing my eyes, I dropped my head to my forearm, going over everything in my mind. I didn't know what to do for the best. I'd been a good person until I met Kat. And then I'd made a dreadful, stupid mistake. One I'd pay for as long as I lived. But I didn't want my family paying for it, too.

I turned back to my phone and googled the latest news, checking for anything about Henry Robertson, but there was nothing. I glanced at the time. The Fun Run started in an hour. I couldn't go. There were more pressing things I needed to deal with. I dropped a text in our family group.

> I'm not going to make it. I slipped down the
> stairs and have pulled a muscle in my leg.
> Sorry to let you down. Good luck. See you at
> the finishing line. Mia X

Mum had always warned us that lies breed lies.

34

I raced home, throwing uneasy glances over my shoulder when I turned every corner. I needed to calm down. Every person I encountered was a witness to my stress and agitation. If the police were watching me, they'd question why I was acting so suspiciously. I was being irrational. They had no reason to watch me. Unless they suspected I knew more than I was letting on.

Discarding my coat, I hurried to Ruby's bedroom, anxious to get to the wallet. I needed to know what Kat had nearly died for. I grabbed the teddy from the shelf and unzipped the back. My stomach was on fire, a boiling pot of emotions. I opened the wallet, the expensive leather smooth against my fingers. It smelled earthy. I lifted the front flap and let out a low moan at the picture of Henry's wife and his sons. A woman, unaware she was a widow, and two kids who were yet to discover their dad was dead. I couldn't help the small sobs escaping from my mouth.

I puffed out a large breath. I had to keep my wits about

me. I'd got myself into this trouble. And I was the only one who could get myself out of it.

I sat on Ruby's bed and fanned open the back section of the wallet, seeing the crisp notes, remembering the three I'd spent that night: two I left for the stall holder in exchange for depleting his stock, and the one I used to pay for the tin of formula and loaf of bread.

One by one, I opened each side section and scrutinised the cards: a debit and two credit cards, a membership card for English Heritage, and Henry's driving licence. I pulled out the licence, staring at the dead man. My stomach convulsed. The dead man I'd drugged. That kind of reckless behaviour was for other people. People my brother and his colleagues worked tirelessly every day and night to put behind bars. People like Kat. Not me. I should've known better than to allow her to suck me into her corrupt world.

I removed a credit card. An item dropped onto my lap. At first I thought it was another credit card. But it was too small and too thick. I picked up the piece of black plastic. It was an SD card, a portable device for storing data. Callum had one for his camera to store the gazillion photos he was always taking. I twiddled the compact piece of plastic between my fingers.

I'd found it.

The piece of plastic was what the balaclava guy was looking for. Of that, I was certain.

And it was what Kat was tortured and nearly killed for.

I needed a card reader. I thought of asking Callum to borrow his but immediately discarded the idea. He'd only ask what I wanted it for, and I'd have to lie to him again. I needed to get a card reader of my own.

I replaced the wallet and the sock into the back of the teddy and went to my bedroom. It smelled musty, and the bed was unmade due to my rushing out that morning. I picked up my phone, opened the Amazon app, and typed *SD card reader* into the search bar. Pages of possible purchases filled the screen with pictures and a sponsored video on how they worked. I considered which one to pick. Size. It appeared to go by size.

I reached down, opened the bottom drawer of my bedside cabinet and removed the pencil case from my school days. Unzipping it, I rolled the pens and pencils aside until I found my collapsible ruler which unfolded into thirty centimetres. School days flashed through my mind. When life was so much easier, despite me thinking it was so hard. I couldn't wait to leave school. I counted down the days for my final years, and Mum always said I'd regret it one day. It sometimes annoyed me how she was right so much of the time.

I held the ruler against the edge of the piece of black plastic and measured the length and width. Returning to the screen, I searched for a suitable card reader that would allow me to find out what data the card held. I was about to drop it in the shopping basket but stopped. I wasn't thinking straight. If the police started investigating me for whatever reason and discovered I'd bought an SD card reader, they could question why. And I couldn't for the life of me think of an excuse as to why I would.

I cleared my search history. I couldn't chance it. It wasn't the correct way to go about things. I had to use my brain. Then I remembered. I'd seen one of those card readers at work. There was one in the stationary cupboard between my desk and Alex's.

I had a plan.

I'd take the card into the office tomorrow morning and use that one.

35

The park was situated two miles across town. I picked up the pace to a powerwalk, repeatedly checking my surroundings. The knot of fear in my stomach was continuously tightening, a constant reminder of the trouble I was in. But I needed to get used to it. That was how it'd be from then on – living my life in constant fear.

I arrived at the park in a little over thirty minutes. An upbeat voice pumped through the air via a Tannoy, encouraging runners approaching the finishing line. Animated crowds of people were cheering them on. The weather had been kind, a crisp autumnal breeze cooling the sun's heat. It was an annual event, with scores of people raising money for charitable causes close to their hearts. But I couldn't find the appetite to savour the jovial atmosphere.

'Mia!' a voice called out, drowning out the roar of supporters lining the edge of the track.

I turned to a red-faced Alex. He was standing with a group of others from the KM Group I didn't know that well.

They were all sporting Grace's T-shirts. Alex beckoned me to come over.

I joined them, faking a slight limp, and thanked them all for their participation.

'All for an excellent cause,' Alex said. Seeing him dressed in Lycra shorts and a T-shirt was odd – a complete contrast to the smart suits he showed up at the office in. 'What happened to you?'

'I tripped down the stairs and pulled a muscle in my leg.'

'Any excuse!' he jested.

'I'm serious.' A wave of heat rushed up my neck, travelling to my face faster than the runners pacing around the track. I never was good at lying.

'Never mind. Kelly will still sponsor you. I'll have a word with her. I have some good news. One of my clients agreed to double his sponsorship if I finished. An extra thousand pounds.'

Sometimes, fate has a way of playing into your hands. And it certainly had the day I joined the KM Group. There was no way we'd have been anywhere near raising the amount we had for Grace's Appeal if it hadn't been for their support and that of their generous clients. But on the flip side, I'd never have met Kat if I hadn't got that job. And I wouldn't be in such dire straits.

Alex continued. 'Elodie and I took him to dinner on Friday night and managed to sell him and his wife two tickets to the ball, too.'

'Wow! That's great. Thank you.'

'Full house, eh? It's going to be a great night.'

Elodie appeared, pushing baby Savannah in a buggy with two young boys holding on to the handle.

'Daddy! Daddy!' the youngest of the two kids yelled.

They let go of the buggy and rushed to Alex, squealing.

He swept them up and sat one on each hip. 'These two monsters are my sons. Meet Mason and Miles.'

'We're not monsters, Daddy,' the older boy stated. 'You're the monster.'

Alex made a face at them and roared. The three of them giggled.

I thought about Charlene Robertson and her two boys – Henry Robertson's two sons. A family unit torn apart. A wave of shame rippled through me.

'We want ice creams,' the older boy said.

'Come on. I'll take you,' Elodie said.

Alex lowered the boys to the ground and kissed his wife. 'I'll catch up with you in a bit.'

'Have you heard about Kat?' I asked when they were gone.

Alex shook his head, frowning.

I updated him.

'Hell! That's dreadful.' He asked questions about the police investigation, which I answered the best I could. 'Are you OK, Mia?' he asked kindly.

'I'll be fine. I hope you don't mind, but I must find my brother.'

'No worries. I'll tell Kelly. You've got my number. Keep me posted.'

I spotted Callum funnelling through the conveyor belt of finishers to collect a medal and a goody bag. When he emerged from the masses, guzzling water from a plastic bottle, I congratulated him with a hug, savouring the comfort of his arms around me, not caring he was hot and sweaty. I was safe with Callum. He pointed at my leg, raising one eyebrow in a questioning arc. 'Did you not fancy it?'

I pushed him away. 'I tripped down the stairs at the hospital.' I relayed Kat's fate. 'The police questioned me last night.'

His jaw dropped. 'What the hell was she involved in for that to happen?'

I shrugged. 'They think it was a break-in gone wrong. Kat's not talking, so we don't know exactly what happened.'

He bombarded me with questions I couldn't answer. He cocked his head sideways. 'Come on. You lived with the girl. The police will be grilling you more, you know. They won't stop until they bleed you dry. So if there's something you're keeping quiet about, you'd better tell me. I might be able to help.'

I stared at his innocent face, wishing I could open up about the tangled mess I'd caught myself up in. But he'd only tell me to go to the police. I could hear his voice trying to persuade me: "You know it's for the best."

I couldn't do that to him. My mess would bring shame on him. On my whole family. No, I had to weather the storm alone. It'd pass. Sunnier days would come again, Mum always told us.

'I don't know a thing. If I did, don't you think I'd tell you?'

I hated myself more than ever. I never lied to my brother.

But that's what Kat had turned me into – a criminal and a serial liar.

36

FundMeToday
GRACE'S APPEAL

£220,400 raised of £300,000 goal
844 donations
Recently donated:
Alice Elder £50
Anonymous £500
Robert Baker £100

We still had nearly eighty thousand pounds to go, I calculated while I took a bus to the hospital. All I wanted was to go home and crawl under my duvet, but I couldn't let Ruby down again. I'd promised I'd join her at the hospital after the run.

I tried to see Kat, but the visiting hours were different

from those in the PICU. The nurse told me to come back later.

Grace was asleep when I arrived at her cot side. The soft fluorescent lighting threw a pale glow over her tiny body struggling for breath.

'She's so innocent,' Ruby whispered, clutching the side of the cot. 'It's so unfair. Why can't she get better?'

'Why don't you go home for a while?' I suggested. 'I'll stay here with her.'

'I feel too bad when I leave her.' Ruby snuffled. 'I left her last night.'

I put my arm around her. 'Oh, Rue.'

'Don't.' She shuffled my arm off her shoulder. 'I'll start crying.'

I didn't know what to say to comfort her because there were no words. I wanted to tell her everything was going to be OK. We were going to get our baby girl to the USA. But I couldn't guarantee that. Nothing was certain. 'At least go and have something to eat. I'll stay here as long as you want. Remember what Mum said. Take care of yourself, and you're better equipped to care for your baby. Especially when she gets home.'

She rolled her eyes but managed a tiny smile. 'I'll go and get some lunch. Have you eaten?'

'Yes,' I lied. I hadn't, and I was hungry, but the thought of food was sickening.

With Ruby gone, I sat by my niece's side, going over everything that had happened in my head. I'd been a good person until I'd met Kat. I'd just made a dreadful, dreadful mistake. A terrible decision I'd pay for as long as I lived. I just didn't want my family to pay for it, too.

Grace stirred. I stiffened in the chair. She let out a whimper. I jumped up and looked at a monitor flashing and beeping.

'Nurse!' I shouted. 'Help.'

Two nurses dashed to the cot from the adjacent bay. Their faces were blank slates, devoid of the overwhelming panic pouring through me. One of them silenced the monitor.

The other one adjusted a wire attached to Grace's chest and said, 'It's OK. A wire came loose. She's fine.'

That was what it must have been like day and night for Ruby. A constant stream of worry that she was too young to bear. I hooked Grace's delicate fingers around my pinkie finger. We had to get her to the USA.

Ruby returned with a wrap and a bag of crisps, talking to a nurse who was wearing a plastic apron. She was a heavyset woman with a large personality.

'I need to carry out a few observations.' She whipped a thermometer from her trolley full of medical equipment, chatting about a Netflix series she was watching with her daughter. After taking Grace's temperature, she asked Ruby, 'Would you like to hold her?'

'Is she up for that?' I asked. 'She looks so frail.'

'The close contact is good for babies.'

'You do it,' Ruby said to me. 'I held her yesterday.'

I pointed to the ventilator and the various drips keeping my niece alive. 'What about all the equipment?'

'We do this all the time,' the nurse said.

'But I'm all dirty.'

She gave a gentle laugh. 'You'll be fine. Wash your hands thoroughly and put this on.' She handed me a plastic apron. 'I need to get someone to help me. I'll be straight back.'

I washed my hands in the small sink on the side wall and returned to the upright armchair, ready to receive my niece.

The nurse came back with a healthcare assistant. 'Ready?' I nodded.

The two nurses worked in perfect harmony, unclipping the leads attached to Grace's body, gathering them and twisting them into a circle. The nurse carefully lifted Grace while the healthcare assistant supported the leads and guided the ventilator tube. Together they delivered Grace into my arms as easily as if they had handed me a bag of shopping.

I cradled my niece and welled up. I couldn't let her down. We had to get this money for her. She had to go to the USA.

I stayed until early evening, encouraging Ruby to keep strong. When I left her, I stopped to see Kat again. Her condition had taken a turn for the worse. Blood tests had indicated she'd developed an infection.

I sat in a chair talking to her, telling her about the fun run and all the good the KM Group were doing for my niece, thanks to her efforts. That was part of the problem. She'd always made me feel guilty – as if I owed her something for everything she'd done to get Grace's Appeal up and running. I wondered if that had always been her plan.

She remained non-responsive. Twenty minutes later, one of the monitors connected to her body beeped. The harsh sound was like a foghorn in the quietness of the ward. A stony-faced nurse appeared, her eyes darting around studying the monitors. She slapped a button on the wall and whipped the blue curtains around the bay. Several nurses and doctors appeared, causing a commotion.

'What's happened?' I asked.

The nurse guided me away, telling me we needed to let

the professionals do their job. She took me to an empty side room opposite with a made-up bed ready for the next incoming patient, from where I could see through to the window of Kat's bay. But I couldn't see her, only a flurry of hospital staff.

After ten minutes or so, the pandemonium died down, and the nurse appeared, suggesting it best I leave.

'Is she going to be OK?'

Her face remained expressionless. 'We're monitoring her.'

I couldn't go straight home. My body was weak and hollow. The lack of food had finally taken effect. I headed to McDonald's a couple of streets away. It wasn't the best choice, but it was cheap, and I needed carbs. I ordered a portion of fries and a cup of hot chocolate and took them to a table at the back of the seating area. While I ate the chips, I scrolled through my phone. It had got to the point where part of me wished there was news of Henry Robertson, so I knew where I stood. The ball was fast approaching, and I had so much to do that week. Perhaps I was never caught on CCTV. Maybe I'd walk away from all the trouble with only my guilty conscience as punishment. It would still be a life sentence.

Four women roughly my age took the table next to me, tucking into their big bags of food before they'd even sat down. They were loud, slurring, arguing about which pub they were going to next. One of them had long blonde hair. She reminded me of Kat on the night she'd strutted up and down her living area in her wig.

The image of Kat's broken body played games with my head the whole distance home. Games I feared I'd never win. I was in so much trouble. And I didn't know how to dig myself out of it. When I swung a right into Mum's road, my phone rang. I stopped and pulled it out of my pocket. My heart skipped a beat. No Caller ID was scrolling across the screen. I couldn't explain why Grace's vulnerable face flashed before my eyes. I leaned against a garden fence for balance, whispering into the evening sky, 'Please let Grace be OK.'

Hesitantly, I answered the call.

The controlled gravity of DI Prince's voice confirmed my suspicion. He was about to divulge news I didn't want to hear. 'I'm sorry to inform you Katherine has passed away,' he said. 'We're now treating this case as a murder investigation.'

37

I negotiated the journey to the police station with my phone lodged between my shoulder and chin, weaving my way amongst the throng of early morning commuters. I was regretting the two large glasses of wine I'd drunk when I'd arrived home last night. Instead of calming me, they had only served a hefty dose of anxiety, which skyrocketed as the minutes turned to hours. I tossed and turned all night like a desperate insomniac at the end of their tether.

Finally, I got hold of Kelly. 'I'm going to the police station now.' The apprehension in my voice was unmistakable. 'Thanks for your understanding.'

'Not at all. Take what time you need.' There was a note of sympathy in her voice. 'This is truly awful. What is this world coming to? Not even safe in your own home. We're all in shock. The police are coming here later.'

'What? To the office?'

'Yes. They want to speak to a few of the staff. See if they can find anything out. I'm not sure what I'll be able to tell them, though, to be quite honest. Kat always kept to herself.

Take the rest of the day off, Mia. This must be incredibly upsetting for you.'

'It's OK. I'll be in after they've finished with me.' There were certain arrangements for the ball Kat had been organising, and I needed to take over. And besides, I needed the money. No work. No pay. Simple as.

The air was oppressive in the interview room. It was smaller than the one I gave my statement in on Saturday, which only added to my claustrophobia. I sat on the cold, rigid chair, alone with my thoughts, my hands beneath my thighs, waiting for what was to come.

Kat. Dead.

I still couldn't believe it. I willed myself to keep a clear head despite the thick fog growing denser around me by the hour. I turned to a knock at the door.

DI Prince and DS Harrow, the same detectives who had interviewed me last time, walked in and sat in the two chairs opposite me. DI Prince dropped a folder on the table, yawning. DS Harrow clicked on her tablet and delivered the same spiel as before. I was there of my own free will.

On the way, I'd considered asking for a lawyer. But I'd only have had to lie to them. No, if the time came to get a lawyer, then it was time to hand myself in. There was the expense to consider, too. Forget it. I didn't have a penny to my name, and neither did my family.

The DI twiddled a pen between his thumb and forefinger. The movement in my peripheral vision was irritating. He took a deep breath and straightened his back, stretching his upper body several inches. 'We're finding it really hard to trace her next of kin. You said Katherine's mum was on the scene, but we can't track her down.'

'I never met her, but I know Kat sometimes went to see her.' I tried to control my nerves that were seeping into my shaky voice. 'It was a while back.' I paused to think. 'Around when I first moved in. That's all I know.'

'We have an address for her in Manchester, but there's no one there. We're going to speak to Katherine's – your – work colleagues later today.'

The DI leant forward and bent his head over his pad. The fluorescent lighting shone off his polished scalp. He read a note, his podgy finger following the line of text. Looking up, he continued his questioning. 'You and Katherine worked together. How was work?'

'Good.'

Silence greeted me as if he was waiting for me to fill in the gaps, but I remained tight-lipped. I was conscious not to appear unhelpful, but I didn't know what else to say.

'Anyone else she used to hang out with there? Staff? Clients?'

'No. No one, really. She was quite reserved at work.'

'Reserved? What do you mean?'

'She got on with her job. I told you before. I'm in a different department, so I didn't have much to do with her in the office.'

'Did Katherine take drugs?'

I gritted my teeth. There was no point lying. They would've smelled weed in the apartment and most likely found the stash she kept in an old biscuit tin on the bookshelf. 'She liked to smoke pot.'

Another silence.

He left it thirty seconds and said, 'Mia, work with me here. Katherine's been murdered. Your friend. Your flatmate. Your work colleague. Whatever she was to you. I can't quite fathom your relationship. What's more, there were signs she was tortured. You aren't exactly offering up much here.'

'I'm telling you as much as I know.' Desperation crept into my voice. 'I'm trying to help. I can't believe this has happened. But I don't know what else to tell you.'

'See, some things aren't making sense to me. They're simply not adding up.'

I held his eye contact, my heart pounding.

'If this was an aggravated burglary, why did we find a large sum of money in Katherine's handbag? Nearly five thousand pounds. Why wasn't it taken?'

My jaw dropped, partly in shock and partly because that was how I thought I should react. I couldn't come across as evasive, or, worse still, suspicious. It must be the proceeds of some of her watch sales, maybe Henry's watch. She could have gone out on Friday night and sold it when I'd stayed at Mum's .

'Were you aware Katherine kept such large sums of money about the place?' DS Harrow asked.

I shook my head. 'No.'

'Tell me, Mia.' Delving into his folder, the DI produced a photograph. He held it in the air, staring at it, frowning as if trying to evoke a reaction from me. He showed it to DS Harrow and raised his eyebrows.

She nodded.

He dropped it on the table. 'Have you ever seen this before?'

He flipped the photo over and pushed it across the table.

My hands slipped from under my thighs and tightened into fists on my lap.

I feared I was going to throw up.

38

I stared at the photo, willing myself to stay calm.

My heart leapt into my throat.

There was no mistaking it.

The photo showed Henry Robertson's watch.

Drawing it closer to me, I squinted at the image. I shook my head and quickly slid it back towards the DI. I couldn't afford to divulge how much my hands were shaking, a visible sign of the fear racing through me. 'No. I've never seen it. Why? Whose is it?'

'This watch was found in a drawer in Katherine's apartment. I'm aware women sometimes wear men's wristwatches. I get that. But this one? No. I don't think so. I might be mistaken, but it's too big and clunky for a woman. Take another look, Mia.' He nudged the photo back towards me.

I studied the photo again. My mind raced. If I said yes, in fact I did recognise it, and Kat often wore it, the line of enquiry would end. But no one else would've seen her wearing it, and I'd be caught out. I blurted out, 'No. As I said, I've never seen it before in my life.'

He drew a long breath, slowly releasing it. 'So, if you're unable to recognise it, it begs the question. Who does it belong to? Try again; are you sure you've never seen it?'

My heart was beating so loudly, I was scared they could hear it. I pushed the photo back in his direction. 'No, I'm sorry. Never.'

'The strange thing is, our team found no fingerprints over it.'

I inwardly breathed a sigh of relief. I wasn't clever enough for all the lies. I never considered that my fingerprints could have still been on it. 'How can that be?'

'It's as if all fingerprints had been wiped clean with the cleaning fluid we found in the same drawer.'

I frowned, feigning confusion. 'I can't help you, I'm afraid. I don't keep my belongings in the lounge. It was all Kat's stuff. It was her apartment. I only rented a room.'

'Strange.' The DI scratched his bald head. 'But we're running some checks to determine who it belongs to. With a watch of this value, we should be able to trace the serial number.' The detective wiggled his pen again, drawing another long breath. 'So you can see our conundrum, Mia. A stash of cash. An incredibly expensive watch. This doesn't appear to be a random attack. We believe it was calculated.'

I raised my eyebrows and shrugged. 'It seems there was more to my landlord than I knew about.'

The detective ignored my comment. 'Did she have a boyfriend?'

I shook my head. 'I don't know for sure, but I don't think so.'

'Girlfriend, perhaps?'

'No. No boyfriend or girlfriend as far as I know.'

Kat was fond of one-night stands. I often went home

alone after an evening out with her. She'd turn up the following morning, declaring a hangover from hell and sharing far too much information about the guy whose bed she'd ended up in. Thankfully she wasn't the type to invite the guys back. I'm not sure I could've stomached waking in the morning to find some creep wandering around the apartment. I guess it was another example of her method of control. Everything was always on her terms. The graphic detail she went into about the pleasures they'd given each other I found revolting. And she knew it. I'd feel my cheeks flaming, but I still listened, nodding, and laughing at the bits she expected me to.

She often told me I needed to lighten up. I was highly strung, she said. But she had, on other occasions, told me I was intelligent and beautiful, and a ton of her friends would've given their right arm to take me home for the night. That's when I started making excuses about going out with her: Ruby needed me; Grace wasn't well; I had a migraine.

'I have another question about a box of wigs we found under Katherine's bed.'

'Sorry?' I said, buying time. I should've known the wigs would be raised at some point.

'We found a selection of wigs.' The DI produced another photo depicting the box of wigs Kat kept beneath her bed. 'Do you know anything about these?'

There was no use denying it. My DNA would've been all over those wigs, especially the blonde one. 'Yes. Kat liked to wear them sometimes when she went out.'

'Why?'

Think, Mia. Think. I had to sound authentic... and convincing. I shrugged. 'To complement her outfit. She liked to pretend to be someone else.'

'Why?'

'She said it was fun. We both used to dress up in them sometimes. Dance about in them. Pretend to be pop stars, that kind of thing,' I faked a laugh as if I was embarrassed to admit that. 'Sometimes she used to go out in them.'

The detective dug further into Kat's life.

His questions seemed to go on for hours. I thought I'd never get out of there.

'Mia. I'd like to remind you we're dealing with a murder investigation. Please think hard. Do you know anything else that could help the investigation?'

I slowly shook my head as if I was still considering his question. 'If I think of anything, I'll call you straight away.'

The DI turned to his colleague. He slammed his folder closed. 'OK. Let's leave it there. Thank you for your help.' He nodded at me. 'We'll be in touch.'

39

Callum drove me to collect my belongings from Kat's flat.

'I was surprised the police said I was allowed back here so quickly,' I said

'It's only a small apartment in the grand scheme of things,' said Callum. 'They would've got straight onto the forensics on Saturday. What's the latest with the ball?' he asked.

'Kelly is still supportive of it going ahead.' I pointed to a parking space in front of Kat's apartment block. 'That'll do.'

Callum squeezed his car into the tight space. 'I never did get around to visiting you here,' he said. 'I'm sorry about that. I should've made the time.'

'There never seemed the opportune moment. Thanks for doing this. I've been dreading coming here again.'

'Don't be silly. I would've insisted if you hadn't asked.' He stared up at the block of apartments. 'How did she afford a place like this on a PA's salary? It's a nice part of town, and the service charge must cost a fortune.'

That was all I needed – for my brother to start interrogating me. So far, I'd managed to dodge his questions. I shrugged. 'I think her family helped her to buy it. So she didn't have much of a mortgage.' I swallowed the lump in the back of my throat that had been constantly there for days. Whatever my relationship with Kat had come to, it was hard to talk about her in the past tense. 'The KM Group pay well, and I guess the rental income from her lodgers helps.'

He switched off the engine. 'I won't be allowed in, so I'll stay here. Call me when you're done, and I'll come and help you bring your stuff down.'

I trudged up the stairs leading to Kat's apartment, carrying a cardboard box. The stairwell was darker than I recalled. I opened the fire door leading onto the landing where a tall, uniformed police officer was standing guarding the door to Kat's apartment. Bright-yellow tape was stretched across the door emblazoned with *Crime Scene. Do Not Enter*. It was surreal that until that week, that flat had been my home.

The officer dug a bunch of keys out of his jacket pocket and opened the door. 'I'll need to come with you,' he said in a grave voice. 'It's normal procedure, so don't be alarmed.'

Hesitantly, I stepped inside.

The officer's shoes echoed behind me.

The apartment was eerily quiet. A stillness hung in the air as if to pay homage to my departed friend. Friend? No, I couldn't think of her in those terms anymore despite her gruesome end. Not after the way she'd treated me, reducing me to a ball of putty that she could stretch and pull into the shape of the human she wanted me to be.

I passed the living room door. The sound system, typically blaring out music or a TV programme, was silent. The whole place smelled different, as if the stale, musty, smell of cannabis was seeping from the walls.

The officer followed me to the bedroom. 'I shouldn't be too long,' I said.

He stood in the doorway watching me. I started packing my belongings into the blue suitcase that had been hauled from the top of the wardrobe during the raid and left open on the floor. Claustrophobia overcame me. It was as if the walls were closing in. I couldn't bear to be there any longer. When the case was full, I packed the remainder of my belongings into the cardboard box and gathered my toiletries from the bathroom. I worked quickly and methodically, not wanting to spend further time there than I had to.

When I'd finished I took the suitcase to the front door, making a point of avoiding Kat's bedroom. The officer carried the box for me. I called Callum.

'I'm all done,' I said, sad for Kat and disillusioned that, apart from the few bits I had at Mum's place, the suitcase and box were all I had to my name.

40

Callum swung the suitcase into the boot of his car. 'If this is all you've got, I can't see you made that place much like home.' It was as if my brother knew more than he was letting on and was testing me.

I climbed into the car and glanced up at Kat's apartment. My tense muscles eased a little. The relief I felt that I'd never have to go back there was immense.

Callum drove me back to Mum's flat. He relayed a story of a car chase he was involved in on the other side of the city last week. Two young kids had been driving a stolen Ford without insurance. I was only half listening. I was contemplating opening up to him about everything that had happened since I'd met Kat. How I needed a confidant – someone to share the trauma engulfing every moment of every day. But every time I found an ounce of bravery and opened my mouth, I thought about how unfair it'd be to compromise his position. He'd have had to report me if he wanted to keep his job.

'Home sweet home.' Callum switched off the engine. He

gazed at me quizzically. 'You know, I haven't even seen you cry.'

I stared out of the window. There was no space for tears. I was too clogged up with crippling guilt and regret. 'I'm pleased to be out of it all, to be honest.'

'Why?'

'Kat was a bit wild.' I turned to him. 'You know, parties. Men.'

'Drugs?'

'What makes you say that?'

'I'm not stupid, Mia. I'm a copper, for Christ's sake. I know you did drugs with her.'

'Rarely.'

'You changed when you moved in with her.'

'Was it that evident?'

He removed the keys from the ignition. 'Not all the time, but yes, sometimes. You seemed spaced out. I guessed you were doing weed.'

'I'm sorry.'

'Don't be sorry. You were experimenting. It's part of growing up. However, I would've thought you'd have matured enough not to get caught up in that kind of stuff. I was about to have a serious word with you before all this kicked off.'

'I was in awe of her, you know. It sounds stupid, but she had me under her spell. I went along with stuff I shouldn't have.'

'Like what?'

'Just stuff.'

We took the box and suitcase up to Mum's flat.

'Coffee?' I asked.

Callum only drank strong black coffee or water.

'Sure.' He sat on a chair at the kitchen table and checked

his phone while I washed the dishes in the sink. Mum must have left in a hurry. Once the kettle was boiled, I fixed a coffee for him and tea for me. I sat, my hands around the hot mug.

'Right, sis.' Callum placed his phone facedown on the table. He took a deep breath. 'Come on. Talk to me.'

I stared at him blankly.

'I know it's been a really horrible tough time for you. But there's something else bothering you.'

I sipped my tea. 'What makes you say that?'

'I'm your big brother. I know these things.'

'Don't you start. You sound as bad as Mum.'

'Come on, Mia. I wasn't born yesterday. Let me in.'

Those last three words melted me, sending my guard crashing down. I blinked. Two tears sprang out of my eyes. My bottom lip quivered. I shuddered, unable to stop shaking. 'I'm so scared, Cal.'

He shuffled his chair across the tiled floor until he was beside me. 'I knew there was something more than you were letting on.' He placed his strong arm around my shoulders. 'Talk to me.'

I drew away from him. I didn't deserve his sympathy. I didn't deserve anyone's sympathy. 'Kat was targeted.'

'Targeted?' He frowned, and his chin dropped. 'What makes you say that?'

I shook my head. 'That came out wrong. Whoever did this to her was coming for me. I'm certain of it.'

His eyes widened, his gaze fixed firmly on me. '*You?*' His eyebrows drew together. 'I don't understand.'

I stifled a sob. 'You must promise you'll never say anything to another living soul about what I'm going to tell you.'

'That much depends,' he replied light-heartedly as if trying to defuse the tension.

'Seriously.'

'You're scaring me, sis.'

The floodgates to the dam of my troubles opened, and I spilt every last detail to my brother. I explained Kat's illicit enterprise and how she'd enticed me into her web of illegal gain. And how she'd groomed, yes, groomed me, under the disguise of obtaining money for Grace's treatment. I finished with what had happened with Henry Robertson: the watch, the money, and the wallet.

Callum sat in silence, his jaw dropping further and further towards the floor.

41

Callum thumped his fist on the table. 'What the hell, Mia?

'I one hundred per cent think they came for the wallet.' My voice was barely a whisper.

'Where is it now?'

I pointed towards the kitchen door.

'In your bedroom? You've got it here? Oh, Mia.'

I didn't dare tell him where I'd hidden it. At the time, Grace's teddy had seemed a logical place to hide the wallet and the smashed pieces of Kat's phone. Now I couldn't believe I'd been so dumb.

He placed his hands on his head and splayed his fingers. 'What the fuck were you thinking?' He clenched his jaw.

I flinched. Callum rarely swore. In fact, he'd never date a girl a second time if she swore, so I knew how angry he was.

'I was wrong. I can't tell you how much I regret what I've done.'

'What makes you so sure that's why they broke into Kat's place?'

The moment I'd found Kat after the break-in flashed

through my thoughts. The bruising. The swelling. The split lip. Her clothes in shreds. 'I found an SD card inside it. I think that's what they probably want. What do I do, Callum?'

'You need to go to the police. Tell them everything.' He was speaking without having processed the enormity of the situation.

I needed to let him calm down.

'I can't.'

'Mia. What happened to this Henry guy was a professional hit. You're not only putting yourself in danger. Think about Mum. Ruby. Grace.'

'I can't. What will Mum say when she finds out her daughter is a thief? And not only that, but I also drugged someone. Hell, Cal. It'd kill her.'

'You've got to face the consequences. At least you'd be safe.'

'And what about the ball? Kelly will cancel it. We can't do that to Grace or Ruby.'

A scowl appeared on his face. He shook his head. 'What a mess you've got yourself into!'

'Don't you think I should at least find out what's on the SD card? See what I'm dealing with?'

'Are you mad? No, Mia. Take it to the police. They're the professionals. Let them deal with it.'

'I'll be put away, Cal. Think about it.' I lowered my head. 'I spiked a man's drink and stole from him. I never reported his death. And I lied to the police about the watch and money.' I fixed my eyes on his. 'I'd go to prison.'

'You've got a clean record. You just got mixed up with the wrong crowd. With a good defence lawyer, you could get well away with a suspended prison sentence or probation.' He didn't sound convincing.

'How could we possibly afford a good lawyer? You know we don't have that kind of money.'

'We'll find a way.' My brother may have been older than me and had a much better job, but at times, he could be so callow.

'And what about you, Cal? What will it do for your career? Think about that. What will your bosses think when they find out your sister's a criminal?'

'Nothing. It'll be OK if you give yourself up now. But it'll be a totally different story if they find out I hid this.'

I dropped my elbows on the table and my head in my hands. 'I feel constantly sick with dread. I can't believe what I've done.'

'Why did you do it?'

I slowly raised my head. 'For Grace, of course. Why else?'

Callum puffed out a large breath. 'What happened to you, Mia? You were always a good girl. Ruby was the one always getting into trouble. Not you.'

He was right. Mum always joked she gave birth to the Devil the day Ruby was born. My sister went from a baby who never slept to a teenager who had more tantrums than a toddler. Mum even had to bribe her to go to school. But I'd always toed the line. What *had* happened to me?

Kat.

Kat was what happened to me.

'How have you managed to keep this to yourself?' Callum asked. 'I knew something was up with you. But never in a million years would I've guessed it could be this bad.'

I digested the possibility of being sent to prison. 'I keep thinking about Grace. I just want her to get better.'

He raised his voice. Another thing he rarely did. 'We all want her to get better. But we fundraise. We do charity fun runs and grow a moustache. Or, like Mum, bake cakes with her friends and sell them during their lunch hours. Have you done this to other blokes?'

'No! I promise you. It was only the once.' I held my hand up to him. 'OK. OK. Leave it now. I feel crap enough as it is.'

He didn't get it. Participating in a 10k fun run or baking a batch of fairy cakes wouldn't get us the funds needed to save our niece's life.

'They must've got rid of this Henry guy's body,' he said.

'Who?'

'It was a professional hit. Whoever did it must've gone back and cleared up. That's the only explanation I can think of for why he hasn't been found.'

'How can they do that?'

'These people know what they're doing, Mia. I've come across them at work. They're ruthless. Evil.'

'What would they have done with the body?'

He shrugged. 'Who knows? Chucked it in the river. Buried it somewhere. Burnt it.'

I cringed, thinking of Henry in that hotel bar on Wednesday night. 'It may never be found,' I said.

'Maybe. But what happens if it is? It'll only be a matter of time before they trace him back to the hotel. I'm surprised they haven't already linked his stay to a credit ca – Oh, sorry! I guess you've got his credit cards.' The sarcasm didn't suit him.

'I was in disguise. I know this sounds awful, but you'd never have guessed it was me.'

'What about your beauty spot?'

I touched the skin beneath my left eye. 'I covered it up with make-up. It's amazing what a good concealer can do.'

'So what was this guy doing at your offices?'

'I don't know, and I can't exactly ask, can I?'

'Go and get it.'

'What, the wallet?'

He stared at me incredulously. 'No, the bloody washing basket.'

Veins bulged at the side of his bright-red face. His eyes flared with fury. It was the angriest I'd ever seen him.

Ignoring his sarcasm, I steadied myself against the edge of the table. I was weak from the constant fear I was living with. But my shoulders were somehow lighter. Opening up to my brother had appeared to shift some of the anxiety I'd been carrying around for the past six days. I reached into my bag and dug out the SD card. 'This is what I found.' I dropped the piece of plastic onto the table. 'It looks like what you might use for your camera.'

He examined the card but didn't touch it. 'You need a smart reader for this.'

'I know. Have you got one?'

He shook his head. 'Not for this size. You can easily get one, though.'

'There's one at work. I wanted to find out what was on it today, but, of course, I didn't go in.'

His gaze rested on me. 'You've got to go to the police with all this, Mia.'

'At the moment, they've nothing to go on.'

'At the moment, maybe. But they will. They're smart, these people.' He stood, his arms ramrod straight on the table. 'Maybe not now. It could take days, weeks, months.' He glared at me. 'But whoever did this to Kat will hunt you down, and you'll end up in the same place as her.'

'I'm not going to the police until I find out what is on this card.'

42

Kelly jumped out at me from her office the following morning as if she'd been waiting for me to arrive. 'I wasn't expecting to see you today.' She rolled up the sleeves of her crisp white shirt.

'I need to keep busy.' I also needed to get paid.

As if reading my thoughts, she said, 'I've asked Alex to include yesterday as compassionate leave for you when he runs payroll. If you need more time off, you must take it. You've been through a traumatic ordeal. Don't underestimate the impact it can all have on you. These things take their toll. There are ways we can help you, you know. I'll get HR to talk to you.'

Kat had always said there was a soft centre to Kelly's nut-hard shell.

'The event organiser for the ball called last night.' Her voice changed as if she was trying to inject some positivity into her tone. 'Only four days to go. Lauren has been helping me with the items Kat was running with. Everything's going to plan.' She reeled off a list of outstanding jobs. 'Where are you staying?'

'Sorry?'

'I guess you're no longer at Kat's flat?'

'I've moved back to my mother's home.' My voice cracked.

'If you need anything, you know where I am. Keep busy, Mia. It's the only way to get through troubled times. When my parents died twenty years ago, I buried myself in my work.' She swept her manicured fingers around the plush reception area. 'And the KM Group was the result.'

I walked through the office. Colleagues greeted me with sympathetic smiles, offering condolences for my flatmate, the lovely Kat. It was concerning how much she'd fooled so many people.

Chucking my bag under my desk, I swapped my trainers for my pumps and switched on my computer. Last night's discussions with Callum had left me cold. I felt oddly disconnected from my body, as if the real Mia was floating above, watching the criminal who Kat had turned me into.

Alex wasn't around. He was probably in his morning meeting with the marketing team. While waiting for the computer to fire up, I opened the stationary cupboard between my desk and the adjacent desk where Shari kept a selection of office stationery and equipment. I rummaged around, searching for the smart card reader I recalled seeing there. Moving aside a stapler, a Sellotape holder, and a hole punch, I came to a wooden desk organiser crammed with odds and ends: paperclips, pens and pencils, staples, scissors, a couple of nail files, and a selection of coloured bulldog clips. There it was. I grabbed the card reader, a small black box with a lead that slotted into the back of the computer. It was exactly what I needed. I put it in my bag.

I didn't know why, but I pulled my phone out of my bag and searched for Henry's wife's Facebook page. She'd posted again, another desperate plea about her husband. And she'd fronted a local police appeal, composed and dignified, and asked for information about her missing husband.

It was unimaginable where Henry's body might have been. Every suggestion from my brother tormented me. I couldn't decide which was worse – buried, burnt, or dumped in the river. They all sounded equally horrific.

Alex disturbed me, arriving at my desk with two cups of tea. I put my phone on charge.

'You know I liked Kat,' he said. 'She always knew the right words to say.'

I nodded but kept quiet, not wanting to get embroiled in a conversation about Kat.

He continued. 'She was a person who was ever present, but you never really knew her, if you get what I mean.' He handed me one of the cups. 'This must all be hard for you. You knew her more than the rest of us did.'

I took the cup, trying to disguise the slight tremble in my hand. 'Thanks.'

He hovered at my desk, suggesting he wanted to talk some more, but I turned to my screen. He took the hint and left me.

I tried to catch up on outstanding issues from my absence yesterday, but my concentration levels were below zero.

It wasn't until late morning, when Alex announced he was off to a meeting, that I had the chance to use the card reader. I slotted the SD card into the opening of the reader, breathing a sigh of relief to hear a click as it slotted into place. It was compatible. Plugging the reader into the USB port on the back of my computer, I waited in anticipation, praying it recognised the device. I didn't want the added complication of installing other drivers. A notification popped up on the screen saying I'd been successful.

I opened File Explorer. The card reader appeared as a removable drive. Cautiously, I peered through the glass partitioning, checking that no one was heading for my desk, and clicked on the contents of the card.

I was in.

43

My heart was drumming as if I was doing something I shouldn't be, which, for all intents and purposes, was the case. I peered through the glass partitioning again. Heads were down, and everybody was busy.

The card contained a master file and six subfiles titled from one to six with two accompanying letters. I opened the master file. A list of names appeared on the screen, numbered from one to eight. Six of the names on that master list appeared to correspond to one of the subfiles judging by the letters of their initials. Scrolling through the list of names, I stopped at the fifth one. It was Billy Brookes, the footballer who I'd met when Alex called me into that meeting last week.

I clicked on the corresponding file, 5BB, half expecting them to be password protected, but they weren't. I skim-read the contents about the twenty-six-year-old football premiership rising star. It appeared Billy had been involved in some betting practices that violated the Football Association's rules on gambling. The file contained copies of newspaper articles outlining the allegations when he'd laid bets on football matches directly related to the club he'd played for during a period of injury. Furthermore, the gambling continued when he'd restarted work to the extent he'd betted on matches he was playing in – a big no-no. True or not, it looked as though he'd wanted a quick fix to the problem, and the KM Group had arranged, for an undisclosed fee, to make it disappear.

I was confused. It was hardly earth-shattering. No one was seriously injured. No one had died. But Billy Brookes must have been on that list for a reason. I scanned the list again but definitely didn't recognise any other names. I tried to piece the puzzle together. Henry was murdered for that SD card. It contained the name of a client of the KM Group. Henry had met Kelly the day he was shot. Was that a coincidence? It seemed unlikely, but I didn't know for sure.

An enthusiastic chorus of "Happy Birthday" filled the office, a frequently heard singsong because Kelly always brought a cake for each staff member's birthday. Organising the birthday cakes was – had been – one of Kat's jobs.

Previously, I would've joined in, but I ignored it and stared at the list of names. I needed to get that information to Callum. He'd know what to do. Without thinking, I pressed the print icon on the master file containing the list of names, followed by Billy Brooke's subfile.

Jumping up, I rushed to the printer on the low filing cabinet between mine and the adjacent desk only a few steps away. The printer sprang into action, moaning and groaning. I anxiously waited until it whirled and ejected a report I'd submitted earlier.

I scanned my surroundings, consciously aware that somebody could approach my desk at any time. My phone beeped, making me jump. It was a message from Ruby in our family

WhatsApp group with a photo of Grace. She was awake but looked drowsy. Ruby had written:

> We got a thousand-pound anonymous
> donation this morning. Any idea who it's
> from?

I replied to say I didn't know. We'd had many anonymous donations. When the first large one had come in, Kat had said she thought it was one of the KM Group clients. People who had more money than they knew what to do with. A clunking sound drew my attention back to the printer. It had stopped mid-cycle. I tugged the piece of paper. It wouldn't budge. Damn! It was jammed. I swore under my breath. I wasn't thinking straight. I never should've printed that stuff at work.

Panicking, I returned to my computer and locked the screen. Alex would be back at any moment. I bolted back to open the top of the printer, trying to prise out the scrunched sheets, part of which were printed with smudged data.

A sudden presence beside me startled me.

Alex was standing by my side.

I stared at him questioningly. 'I thought you were going to a meeting?' That came out wrong. It sounded accusatory.

'I did. It was only a quick one. Want some help?'

'Sure.'

'The bloody thing is always playing up,' he said. 'We must get a new one. Or at least get this one serviced.'

A wave of panic rushed through me. I couldn't afford to

let him see what I'd printed off. Not with Billy Brooke's name on there. 'I can sort it. It did this to me the other day, too.'

'There's a knack to it,' he protested. Reaching to the back of the printer, he opened the rear compartment and tugged the jammed piece of paper. It wasn't shifting. He thumped the rear side. 'Don't ask me why, but this sometimes helps.' He gave it another whack.

I rushed back to my desk, my heart racing. With trembling hands, I unlocked my computer and promptly cancelled the print jobs. I slid a file along the desk and stood it upright against the screen, hiding the SD reader from sight.

'There we are.' Alex pulled out a crinkled wodge of paper. He stepped across to my desk and handed it to me. 'It should be fine now.'

'Thanks.' The printer spat out another piece of paper. I darted over and grabbed it before Alex had the chance.

He returned to his desk, tapping his hand on the top of the printer on the way. 'I'll get onto arranging for this thing to be serviced.'

After folding the piece of paper containing the list of names, I stuffed it into my bag and checked the print queue on my screen to confirm I hadn't inadvertently printed the document twice. The print queue was empty. To make sure, I opened a random document, printed a page, and disconnected the card reader from the computer.

I removed the SD card and returned it to my bag and the card reader to where I'd found it in the filing cabinet. Only then did my heart stop racing.

44

I phoned my brother, but the call went to his voicemail. I didn't get another chance with the SD card because Alex flitted between his office and the desk beside me all morning, and I was too unnerved to try while in his presence. When lunchtime arrived, I planned to get a few items from the pharmacy, but on my way out of the office, Kelly's forthright tone demanded my attention.

I stopped in my tracks, backstepped and entered her office, coughing on the thick smell of her perfume. It was light in there, the floor-to-ceiling windows giving a magnificent view across the city. She tapped an expensive-looking fountain pen on the table. 'I'd like to have a word with you.' Her hand moved to her mouse, and she shut down her screen. She emerged from behind her desk. 'Come on, let's go to lunch.'

Uneasy, I followed her to a French restaurant about ten minutes from the office, tucked away in the basement of an elaborate row of Georgian houses. It was small and chic, with a fancy decor and crystal chandeliers. I was out of my comfort zone.

Kelly was obviously a frequent diner there. The hostess warmly welcomed us, led us to a table, and pulled out a chair, indicating for Kelly to sit.

'It's good to see madame,' she said in a French accent.

Hurrying to the chair opposite and removing it from beneath the table, she nodded at me, gently pushing the chair towards the table when I sat. She removed the folded, white linen napkin from the table, gently shook it out, and laid it over my lap.

Kelly had already done the same with hers. It was all very surreal.

'Can I get you some water?' she asked.

'Still or sparkling?' Kelly asked me.

'I don't mind.'

'A bottle of both,' Kelly said.

The hostess handed us leather-bound menus. 'We'll give you a little time to decide what you'd like to eat, then someone will be over to take your order.'

I peered from side to side, taking in the panelled walls and the plush velvet seating.

'I hope this place is OK for you,' Kelly said.

Before I met Kat, I'd rarely eaten out. Family meals in a restaurant were considered a treat when I was growing up: one course at the local pub, that was saved for special occasions. When I moved in with Kat, she took me to places where the food was beautiful but eye-wateringly expensive. The type of meal that left me wanting to pop into McDonald's on the way home.

'It's great.'

'It's one of the few places where I know we'll be afforded some privacy.'

I forced a smile, taking repeated glances at her face while she perused the menu. There was a vulnerability about her I'd never noticed before. Not in what she said but in how her forefinger glided over the menu choices. I was dying to ask why she'd met with Henry on the day he'd died.

A waiter arrived to take our order. 'I'll have a steak,' Kelly said. 'You?'

I snapped the menu closed. It made a noise louder than I'd expected. The professional-looking couple dressed in suits at the adjacent table turned to stare. Heat crept up my neck. I placed the menu to the side. The prices were staggering. A steak sounded a safe bet. No sloppy sauces to spill down my blouse.

'I'll have what you're having.'

The waiter took our order and rearranged our cutlery, returning with steak knives. Kelly made small talk about the company for a while. She steepled her hands. 'I've been thinking. And you don't need to make a decision straight away. It may be too soon for you. But business is business, and we must carry on.'

I was curious as to what she was about to say.

'I'm going to need a new PA. How would you like to give the role a trial for a few weeks? Feel free to say no. I'd completely understand.'

Her offer to step into Kat's shoes came as a shock. I didn't have the skills or the experience. And it was morbid to be considering doing so. 'What about Lauren?' I asked. 'Doesn't she want the job?'

'Between you and me, because it's not yet been officially announced, but Lauren's pregnant. Naturally, I'm delighted for her. So the answer to your question, for obvious reasons, is no.' She drew a breath and smiled. 'Alex is always singing your praises.'

'That's very kind of him.'

'And, from what I've seen of you, you've impressed me, Mia. Especially how you've dealt with the past few days. Very professional. Very efficient.'

'But I don't have the experience Kat has… had.'

'Experience often comes with bad habits. So, in my eyes, it's not always about experience. Talent, efficiency, and commitment are far more important. Three traits I see in you.'

Me, talented? I'd never heard my name and that word used in the same sentence. In school, I'd always been average.

'We can give it a trial run. I'll provide you with all the training you need. There are plenty of online courses for personal assistants, too. I'd much prefer a blank canvas I can work with. You can stay as a temp at an increased hourly rate, of course, and if we both feel it's working, we can look to make it a permanent position. Give it a go. I'm sure we can make it work.'

I didn't know what to say. Her briskness, coupled with the golden opportunity, knocked me off guard. The offer was appealing. More than anything else, I could give so much more to Grace. I made a quick calculation. Once we'd managed to get the funds together for the treatment, there would be an ever-increasing pressure on finances post-procedure. It was an enticing invitation to a better life for my family. Not that our money worries would disappear. But life would be more manageable.

My thoughts continued to whirl. I'd have my own office and desk and telephone. And a proper salary with the benefits Kat had often bragged about: health insurance, paid annual leave, gym membership, not forgetting the hefty annual bonus paid in December's pay that Kat had used last year to purchase her Mercedes-Benz C-Class Cabriolet.

But I wished it hadn't come off the back of someone else's misfortune. And since discovering what was on that SD card, I wasn't sure I wanted to work there anymore. I needed to stall Kelly and get the ball over and done with before making any rash decisions.

The waiter returned with our food, placing a plate of steak with a helping of spinach and fondant potato on our placemats. The juicy smell was mouthwatering. It was the first time my appetite had been in evidence for a week. I followed her lead, copying how she cut into the steak and ate the accompanying vegetables.

'What about Alex?' I asked.

Kelly sliced another piece from her steak. 'I can deal with Alex. We can get another temp to cover what you were doing until Shari returns from maternity leave. You can help train them.'

Me, train someone? I couldn't believe what I was hearing. At any other time, it would've been music to my ears. I just wished the funeral march would stop playing in my head.

'Have a think about it and let me know.'

'OK.' I berated myself for not showing a little more enthusiasm. Kelly would be expecting it. 'I'd love to give it a go.' I blurted out. 'Thank you for considering me.'

'Not at all. As soon as we get back to the office, I'll speak to Lauren about getting you started.'

· · ·

When I returned to my desk, six missed calls from Callum were waiting on my phone. I called him back. We played phone tag for a while before I finally managed to speak to him.

'Where've you been?' There was an edge to his voice.

'I've been trying to get hold of you. I thought you might be on nights,' I whispered. Alex was still at his desk. 'What's up?'

'Where are you?'

'At work. I'm leaving soon and going to the hospital so Ruby can go home for a bit.'

'I need to see you.'

'Why?'

'I'll meet you in that pub on the road opposite the hospital. The one with benches outside. You know the one?'

'I think so. What's happened?'

The line went dead.

45

I panicked. Callum was going to drag me down to the police station.

I glanced at the desk beside me. Alex was engrossed in reading a document, running his fingers over the short bristles of his buzzcut hairstyle. I grabbed the SD card reader from the filing cabinet and slipped it into my bag. No one was going to miss it for a night. I powered down my computer. 'I need to get going,' I called out to Alex.

'Sure. Thanks for coming in today, Mia. I know it couldn't have been easy for you. But as I've told Kelly, you're a true professional. Are you sure you're going to be OK for Saturday?'

I nodded. 'Kat would've wanted the ball to go ahead.' It's true. Whatever Kat was, she had been genuinely supportive of Grace's Appeal.

I made for the exit, head down. My brother had sent another ripple of unease pulsating through me, so I didn't have the bandwidth to converse with anyone. But Kelly caught me when I passed her door. 'Mia, could I have a quick word, please?'

I walked to her desk.

'Your new office will be ready for you tomorrow,' she said.

She hadn't wasted any time. I gripped the handle of my bag. It wasn't right. I couldn't simply move into Kat's old desk.

'Out of respect, we'll leave Kat's office as is for the time being.' She gave me a straight-lipped smile. 'I've decided to put you in the smaller office at the end of the corridor.'

'Actually, I was thinking the same.'

'You can move your things in there tomorrow. But as I said this morning, if you need more time off, you must take it. I'd completely understand.'

I bit my bottom lip. It was all happening too quickly.

Taking the lift to the ground floor, I clutched the handrail and closed my eyes. I couldn't bear to look at myself in the mirrored walls.

I stepped outside into a haze of people. A cool breeze floated in the air, a sign of autumn on the doorstep. The late-September sun was still out, peeking from between the clouds. But my world was black. A cold, dark cave I desperately wished I'd never crawled into. I dug into my bag for my sunglasses.

I worked up a sweat, eager, yet with a deep sense of dread, to see Callum. I wondered if he'd used his rights as a police officer to search for information on Henry Robertson, but I quickly dismissed the thought. Callum was pure, and whiter than the clouds dancing across the early evening sky. The type of person whose moral compass was always pointing north. And he loved his job. He'd never have done anything to compromise what he'd worked hard to achieve.

He wasn't at the pub when I arrived. It was a typically

British establishment rooted in tradition, with low beams and a curved bar embellished with brass hooks and plaques. It was stuffy in there and noisy from the crowd cheering on a game of football bawling from a giant screen on the far-end wall.

I ordered two Cokes and a packet of cheese and onion crisps and took them outside, grabbing the only empty picnic table in the garden around the side of the building. It was in the shade of a line of apple trees, a perfect retreat from the sun fighting to dodge the clouds. While waiting for Callum to arrive, I checked my phone to see if there were any updates on Henry Robertson. So much had happened since that night, and it was hard to believe a week had almost passed.

I poured my Coke into a glass and took a sip. A starling swooped down and landed beside the packet of crisps, gazing at me as if asking for a bite to eat. 'If I give you one, you'll want more, little fella.' It flew away. I opened the packet and ate a few crisps. They were my favourite flavour, but they tasted of nothing. It was as if my nerves had stripped my taste buds bare.

My phone pinged with a text. It was from Ruby. Grace hadn't had a great day. I typed a reply, conscious I was beginning to sound like a broken record with my repeated messages telling her to keep strong. I clicked on Facebook as Callum marched around the corner of the garden, his face stern. He sat and peered around, checking no one could hear what he was about to say.

'What's happened?' I asked.

He looked around again.

I followed his gaze. 'Just spit it out,' I said.

The table next to us had emptied, and the bustling hum

of conversation from other drinkers and the noise from the traffic would've absorbed what he was about to say.

'You're frightening me.'

He leaned across the table, poked out his chin, and whispered, 'News hasn't broken yet, but I heard a body has been dragged from the river.'

My hand rose to cover my mouth.

'It's a male.' He stared hard at me. 'And he's had a bullet put through his head.'

46

I held my brother's stare, my stomach in my throat. 'Hell! It *was* a professional job,' I whispered.

'Not that professional, it seems. Otherwise, the body would never have been found. And he'd never have let you go the night he chased you.'

'So whoever chased me returned to the hotel room to clean up and remove the body.'

'Unless there were more than one of them.'

'That's why the hotel staff never reported him missing.'

Callum nodded. 'Because they never found him in the first place. You have to go to the police, Mia. You're withholding information that could help them find who did this. It isn't right.'

'We don't know it's definitely him.' My words were futile. Of course it was him. I was grasping at the frail strings of hope that the police were wrong.

Callum dropped his head to the side. 'Come on! How many bodies are dragged from the river in this city every week? It rarely happens. And what are the chances that the body pulled out in the past six months has a bullet through its head?'

I shivered. 'How did they find it?'

'It sounds as though it was a rush job. The body was wrapped in tarpaulin and packed with heavy weights. They believe the rope around the tarpaulin came loose and freed the weights. The body floated to the top.'

The taste of cheese and onion from the crisps burned my throat. 'What will happen now?'

'They'll get the body identified and dredge the river to search for any other clues. They'll want to find any other evidence they can: phone, wallet, keys, that kind of thing.'

'How long will that take?'

'It's not going to happen overnight. They'll have to deploy a professional team of divers.'

'Will they link the body to Henry Robertson?'

He gave me a firm look that told me not to ask such dumb questions.

'How long will it take to identify the body?'

'Not long. It's only been in there a short while, so his body wouldn't have decomposed. I guess his wife will come and identify him.'

I shuddered. 'If it's definitely him.'

'Stop being so bloody stupid.' He peered around him, frowning.

'No one can hear us. It's too busy.'

'I'm sorry. I shouldn't have raised my voice. I'm stressed out.'

'I don't want the police to unravel everything until after the ball.' I dug into my bag. 'I need to show you something.' I found the folded piece of paper in the inside pocket. 'I managed to get into that SD card. And guess what I found?' I unfolded the piece of paper and showed it to him. 'There was what appeared to be a master file with a list of eight names. Then there were six corresponding subfiles, each linked, from what I can make out, to six of the people on the master list. I don't know about the other two.'

Callum took the piece of paper. He perused the names, his eyes darting from side to side. His jaw dropped. 'Oh, hell.' His eyes met mine.

'What?'

'You can't go to the police.'

My head tilted to the side. 'Why?'

He reread the list. 'Whatever have you got yourself involved in here, Mia?'

'I don't know.' My body turned cold with dread. 'I'm scared.'

He swept a scattering of crumbs from the table and laid down the piece of paper. I leaned in until our heads were almost touching.

Callum jabbed his finger at the top of the list. 'I know these two names.'

'Who are they?'

'Police officers.'

'Police?'

He nodded. 'Yep. And they're high-ups.'

I glanced from the list to him. 'What about the others?'

He shrugged. 'I don't recognise them.' He scanned the list again.

I pointed to Billy Brooke's name. 'This guy here is a client of the KM Group.'

'Who is he?'

'A footballer who got into some trouble a few years back. Billy Brookes. Have you heard of him?'

He shook his head. He was passionate about rugby but not a follower of football. 'How do you know him?'

'I don't know him as such. He was at a meeting Alex asked me to join. Kat told me he was super-rich. She was considering targeting him.'

'What was in the subfiles?'

'I only got to see the one connected to the Billy Brookes guy.'

'And?'

I told him what I'd found. We discussed theories, but nothing made sense.

'Kelly has offered me Kat's job.'

He scoffed. 'Talk about jumping in someone's grave.'

'I did think it was a bit soon, but she said things have piled up because Kat was off at the tail end of last week, and she needed to fill the role as quickly as possible. She said she could recruit from an agency but would rather it was me.'

'How do you feel about that?'

'It's the best opportunity I've ever been offered.' I picked at a splinter of wood coming loose from the tabletop. 'It's a shame it's due to such crap circumstances.' I slammed my hands on my temples and dragged my fingers down my face. 'I can't stand this anymore. Perhaps I should go to the police.

He held my gaze. 'No. You can't.'

47

'Why not?' I asked.

'I need time to process it all,' Callum added.

'What do you mean?'

He studied the list as though it was an exam question he didn't know how to answer. He shook it at me. 'This, and the news of the body being found, changes everything. I'm not sure what you should do for the best now. This list of names got this guy killed. It's obvious whoever came into the hotel room last week came for that SD card.'

'So you think Henry was blackmailing the guy who shot him?' I pointed to the list. 'You think he was one of the people on here?'

'Heaven knows.' Callum scanned the list again. 'Who are all these other people?'

'I wish I knew.' I patted my bag. 'I've brought the card reader home to find out what the subfiles contain. It was too risky trying to do it at work. Alex was around most of the day, and I was scared he'd catch me.'

'So what was Henry Robertson doing at your offices on the afternoon he got shot?'

'That's what I've been dying to know, but I obviously can't ask. All I know is what I told you. Kat said he had a meeting booked with Kelly. She chatted to him and set up a fake meeting in the bar of his hotel that night.'

'Where you came into the picture.'

'Correct. I guess the police will find out he went to meet Kelly last Wednesday, and it will come out. He was very flirty, Kat said.'

'Is that a coincidence, do you think?'

'What do you mean? That Kelly is involved in what happened? I did think that this afternoon, but it doesn't seem her style.'

'It's strange there's a KM Group client on there.'

'Do you think Henry was going to expose these people? Could he have been blackmailing them?'

Callum shrugged. 'What did this Henry guy do for a living?'

I recalled Henry and I going to his hotel room that night. 'He said something about a gadget that was going to change the world, but I can't remember what exactly.'

'How the hell did you get involved with such a bunch of crooks?'

'It won't be for much longer. I'll quit after the ball.'

'Sod the ball.'

'No, Callum. It's our one chance to raise big bucks for Grace. By Sunday morning, we could've reached our target. I need to hang on for a few more days. If I quit now, what will Kelly say? Anyway, you're barking up the wrong tree. Kelly's a good person.'

He eyed me sceptically.

'She's been kind to me.'

His expression remained unchanged.

I sighed heavily. 'I can't believe she's involved in something like this.'

'You've always been so gullible, sis.'

I ignored him. It wasn't the time to take offence. 'Do you think they'll find out Henry was staying at that hotel on that night?'

'You have to leave your details to reserve a room in a hotel like that,' Callum said. 'I'm surprised the police haven't already worked out he was there.'

I puffed out a large breath. 'His wife mentioned in a Facebook message that he said he was staying with a friend for the night, but the friend said they knew nothing about it. I wonder why he would've told her that but gone to a hotel.'

'Perhaps he was having an affair.' He stared at me. 'Or wanted to entertain a prostitute.'

'He appeared to love his wife judging from his Facebook page.'

Callum rolled his eyes. 'Give me the card.'

'What do you mean?'

'The SD card, hand it over. We need to find out what's on those other files. I'll see if it fits into my laptop.'

'No way. I don't want you to get involved in this mess.'

'Don't you think I already am?'

'It's my insurance policy.'

He frowned at me.

'If this person comes for me like they went for Kat, I've got something to give them. I'm keeping it.'

'Whatever! You're so naive, Mia. These are the type of

people who, if they come after you, will ensure you'll end up the same way as Kat. Even if you do give them what they want.'

48

My sister was putting on a brave face when I arrived at the hospital. A new patient, a baby girl the same age as Grace, had been rushed into the adjacent bay earlier that evening. Ruby had overheard a doctor discussing the baby's case with the parents. She had a disease Ruby couldn't even pronounce, and her future was grim. Even grimmer than Grace's.

Dark circles ringed Ruby's heavy eyes. 'I'm not coming to the ball on Saturday.' She said it with such defiance.

I stared at her. 'What? Why?'

'I haven't got a dress.'

'I told you I'd sort one for you.'

I'd tried to get her one when I bought mine at the second-hand shop. But they didn't have anything in her size. The owner had suggested I go back there yesterday; she was expecting a large quantity of stock from a massive charity event that had taken place in the city over the weekend. But I'd had more pressing things to sort out.

Ruby pointed to her face. 'Look at the state of me. I can't get up and make a speech in front of all those people.'

'We're making it jointly. And I'm doing most of it. You're her mum, Ruby. You've got to be there.'

'My place is here with her.' She pointed to Grace's cot. 'I mean it. Count me out. I'm not going.'

I clenched my jaw. Usually, I would've been happy to hold the fort for my sister and confront her battles, but today I had enough of my own to fight. But it was no use arguing. As much as I loved my little sister, she was the most stubborn person I'd ever met. When she said no, she meant no. There was never room for even the slightest negotiation.

'Please don't be angry. You'll do a brilliant job without me,' she said. 'Will you read out my part of the speech on my behalf?'

She only had a few lines to deliver, so it wasn't a problem for me to learn her part, but she was meant to be helping me set up the room on Friday. But she wouldn't change her mind. 'Sure.'

'You do understand, don't you? I'm her mother, Mia. If anything happened to her, and I wasn't here, I'd never be able to live with myself.' She pulled her phone out of her pocket. 'Did you see this?'

I glanced at the screen showing Grace's FundMeToday page.

'Your boss donated one thousand pounds for you *not* running in the fun run on Saturday.' She stared at me, her eyes wide. 'That was generous.'

'Wasn't it just!'

It was also unsettling.

I wasn't sure how much I trusted Kelly anymore.

· · ·

Mum was, thankfully, in bed when I arrived home. I went straight to my room and grabbed my laptop. It was years old, a hand-me-down from Callum when he'd bought himself a newer model. I would've bought myself a new one, too, if Grace hadn't come along.

Dropping down onto the bed, I fired up the laptop. I stared at the screen, which whirled and grunted before begrudgingly coming to life. I found the card reader in my bag, managing a smile at the screensaver: a picture of me holding Grace a couple of weeks after her birth. She was so tiny, barely three pounds, and her skin so pale. We couldn't believe how her head fitted into the palm of Callum's hand as if he were holding a baseball.

I traced my finger across Grace's forehead, overcome with sadness. None of us had known how sick she was. We simply thought she was premature and needed time to catch up.

I slotted the card reader into the port at the side of the laptop. There was a spinning hum, but unlike at work, when I'd accessed the port straight away, an error message appeared. The system didn't recognise the device. I thumped the duvet. Nothing was ever easy. Frustrated, I googled what I needed to do next. It was complicated, but I managed to navigate around the system and install the relevant drivers. It was slow, and the laptop was heating up. A swirling noise echoed around the quietness of the room.

At last, the system recognised the card reader, and it appeared as a removable drive. I clicked on it, finally able to view the contents of the card. I opened the list. I needed to be methodical. The two names at the top of the list were who Callum said were police officers, but I couldn't figure out why they didn't have subfiles connected to them. The third name was Bronwyn Harris. It sounded familiar, but I couldn't work out where from. I clicked on the subfile titled 3BH and started reading the contents. I got as far as the third line, learning Bronwyn Harris was accused of domestic abuse against her husband, Peter, when the laptop made a whirling sound. The screen turned blank.

The laptop had run out of battery.

I jumped up, swearing, and threw it on the bed. Dropping down on my hands and knees, I searched for the charging cable under the bed. It was full of rubbish under there: a couple of bags of old clothes, a chocolate wrapper, a selection of stray plastic hangers, and an old pair of trainers. The charging cable wasn't there.

I searched in the wardrobe, dreading the worst.

I must have left it at Kat's place.

49

My new office was nothing on the scale of Kelly's grand one, but the privacy couldn't have come at a better time. There was a desk and a bookcase, which was bare save two potted plants on the top with leaves that trailed midway down the sides.

I sat at the desk and switched on the computer. My phone rang. I looked at my watch. It must've been Callum finishing work. We'd been playing phone tag all night, between me trying to find news of Henry's fate online and him working. From his messages, he wanted to speak to me as desperately as I wanted to speak to him, but as I was about to accept his call, Kelly entered the room dressed in a military-green dress with a long, pleated skirt. It suited her.

I rejected Callum's call and switched my phone to silent.

'What do you think?' she asked, sweeping an arm around the office.

'It's... great,' I said.

'It's a little sparse, but you can put your own touch on it.' She hesitated. 'I know things are tough at the moment, Mia, but as I said yesterday, I firmly believe that throwing yourself into your work can get you through the bad times. Now, let's get started. I've arranged for IT to change your privilege codes to give you the necessary access to carry out your new role. You should be able to get into my diary now so you can manage my meetings and appointments. Your main password should work the same. Any problems, speak to IT.'

'I'll need someone to explain how this all works.'

'Of course. All arranged. Lauren knows our business inside out. She'll be along shortly to show you around the different systems.' Kelly's powerful perfume stuck in my throat. 'At eleven o'clock I've got a potential new client coming in. I'll need you to join us in meeting room A. Much the same as yesterday. You take notes.'

I nodded, trying to keep a clear head and take it all in, but my mind was too preoccupied, racing with images of the police dragging a body from the river.

'Also, Maggie Smith is coming in straight afterwards, so you can stay for that meeting. She's a model we've been working with. She had a run-in with an air hostess on a flight last year and got herself into a bit of bother. Unfortunately for her, a reporter on board took great enjoyment in recording the incident and selling the story to the papers.' Kelly rolled her eyes. 'It's a shame it happened because she's a delightful woman. But luckily, we've managed to turn it all around for her. Big lessons learned. Maggie won't be drinking on aeroplanes again.'

We both turned towards Lauren as she brought in two large cups of tea.

'I'll leave you in Lauren's capable hands,' Kelly said. 'Please print off the minutes from the last meeting we had with Maggie and bring them along to the meeting. Lauren will walk you through client file access, and I'll see you at eleven.' She nodded goodbye and left the room, the pleats of her ankle-length skirt sashaying around her long legs.

I retrieved my laptop from my bag. 'I don't suppose you could help me out?' I asked Lauren. 'I left the charger to my laptop at Kat's place. I wondered if there was a spare hanging about anywhere here?'

Lauren studied the porthole on the laptop. 'I used to have this model before the systems were upgraded. I might possibly be able to help you.' She took a sip of her drink. 'Want me to look now?'

My neck tensed. 'If you wouldn't mind.'

'Give me five.'

While she was gone, I tried Callum's number again, but there was no answer.

Lauren returned, waving a charger in the air. 'This might do the trick.'

'You're a saviour.' I connected the laptop to the charger and plugged it into the wall, trying to conceal my relief when it started charging.

Lauren dragged a chair next to me. 'Let's start with Kelly's diary.' She placed her hand over the mouse. 'Here, let me drive and show you the necessary bits and pieces.'

She took over, wiggling and clicking the mouse, and explaining the ropes of the KM Group. She talked so fast that it was hard to keep up with my note-taking, making my writing ineligible. I wouldn't stand a hope in hell when I returned to these.

'That's strange.' She frowned. 'You don't seem to have access to Kelly's diary. We need to get that sorted for you.' She picked up a pen and wrote a reminder for herself on a Post-it note.

'Did you not want to take this role back on?' I knew the

answer, but I wanted to strike up a conversation with her to see if I could find out more about Kelly.

She bit her bottom lip as if to stop herself from talking, but she couldn't contain the giant smile beaming across her face. 'Can I trust you with a secret?' she asked.

'Sure.' I pressed my forefinger to my lips. 'Mum's the word.'

She patted her flat belly. 'I'm pregnant.'

'Congratulations!'

It was her turn to press her finger against her lips. 'Shh... no one knows apart from Kelly and Alex.'

'When's it due?'

'It's early days. I'm only twelve weeks.' She returned to the screen and took me through what it entailed to be Kelly's PA.

I didn't get a break until mid-afternoon when Kelly left for a personal appointment across town. My head was whirling, my nerves teetering on a razor's edge. I checked the news. Nothing had broken about the discovery of Henry Robertson's body... yet. I searched his wife's Facebook page. Hordes of messages had come flooding in on her recent posts, but she hadn't posted anything new.

I connected the card reader to my laptop. I clicked on the file I'd started reading last night about Bronwyn Harris, who had been accused of domestic abuse against her husband, Peter. But the file wouldn't open. I clicked again, but it looked as if it was corrupted.

I returned to the main list of names. Number four was Richard Nought. I clicked on the subfile 4RN. It opened. My eyes were drawn to the picture to the side of a paragraph of text. The lens was focused on a man, perhaps in his mid-sixties, tangled in a passionate embrace with a less distinguishable younger man with a mop of dark hair. I read the text. The older man, Sir Richard Nought, was a High Court judge. I clicked on the photo to enlarge the image. He was a handsome man with thick, neatly brushed silver hair.

A noise disturbed me. Alex was in the room. He retracted his broad shoulders as if I'd startled him as much as he'd surprised me.

'If I didn't know you better, Mia, I'd think I'd caught you doing something you shouldn't be doing.' He laughed and continued to my desk.

'I'm typing up meeting notes.'

He was getting nearer. 'Can I trouble you with something?'

My heart raced. I glanced at my screen displaying the photo of the two men embracing. 'Sure.' I toggled the screen to the website of a local sandwich delivery company the KM Group used for lunchtime client meetings, which Lauren had been showing me earlier. 'What can I do for you?'

He placed a file on the desk. 'These expense reports you prepared last week.'

He opened the file and enquired about some changes I'd made. He seemed to stay forever, asking question after question. I couldn't get rid of him. It was as if he was doing it on purpose, tormenting me. But I was being paranoid.

When he finally left, I toggled the computer back to the SD card with growing unease. Each file stared back at me like an impossible crossword puzzle while I tried to find the clues as to why and how Henry Robertson was linked to it all.

The unease stayed with me all day, but Kelly kept me busy, which helped to some degree. I was putting my jacket on to leave for the day when my phone rang. It was Callum.

'We need to meet.' His voice was firm. 'Now. Get to my flat as soon as you can.'

50

I raced across the city to Callum's place, which he shared with two friends he used to go to school with. The growing sense of dread pulsing through me was impossible to escape. The streets were busy, workers taking advantage of the fine weather for the time of year and walking instead of jumping on the bus. I was on edge, constantly looking for someone who never appeared, except in my endless anxiety.

The lift was out of order, so I raced up the two flights to the three-bedroom flat with views of a launderette and an independent supermarket below another block of flats opposite. I'd been sad the day Callum moved into that flat. I had missed him but understood why he had to leave Mum's place.

I knocked on the door, gasping to catch my breath.

Callum appeared, casually dressed in grey tracksuit bottoms and a white T-shirt, his feet bare. He opened the door wide. 'At last.'

I coughed at the smell of Lynx aftershave and overused trainers. 'I need some water.' I followed him to the kitchen, which was tidy, given three young guys lived there. I leaned on the doorframe. 'Is anybody else in?'

'Nope. They're both still at work.'

'So, what's so important you called me over here?'

'Go and sit down.'

I didn't like the tone of his voice or the slight stoop of his usually perfectly held shoulders. I entered the living room, a sense of foreboding in each step. The TV was on, blaring out an advert for men's razors. Floor-to-ceiling doors led onto a balcony used to store three mountain bikes and a deckchair one of his flatmates used for when he vaped. It was a relatively large living room for a modern flat but doubled as a dining room. Not that the small table seating four was put to good use. It was covered in unopened junk mail, a box containing a new pair of shoes, and a pair of gaming controllers.

Retrieving my laptop from my bag, I sat on the sofa, a threadbare three-seater that used to belong to one of his flatmate's parents. I positioned the computer on my lap, found the card reader and SD card and set them up, ready to dive into the files again.

Callum arrived with two glasses of water and two cans of Coke.

'Go on, hit me with it,' I said.

I glugged the water, choking as I neared the end of the glass. A picture of Henry I recognised from his wife's Facebook page flashed on the TV screen. I stared at Callum. 'What the hell?'

He slowly nodded. 'I'm afraid so.'

The newsreader's grave voice sent a chill rushing down my spine. 'A body pulled from the river yesterday has been

formally identified as investigative journalist Henry Robertson. Police are investigating the deceased's last known movements and are asking for anyone who saw him last
Wednesday to contact them on the number shown at the
bottom of the screen.'

51

'I thought he was some kind of inventor, not a frickin' investigative journalist. He said he was working on some technology that was going to change the world.' I shook my head vigorously. 'He must've lied.'

The newsreader continued to the next story.

Callum stood holding the back of a dining chair beside me, staring at the floor, his knuckles white and the veins in his hand swollen. He appeared to be in another world, but he nodded. 'Yep. He must've.' He stepped over to the doors, opening one to a gentle breeze and the hum of rush-hour traffic. 'That's why I wanted you to come here.' He returned to the sofa and plonked himself down beside me. 'I know someone working on the case.'

'Who?'

'It doesn't matter. You wouldn't know them. That Henry guy was a loose cannon. I've been looking into him. He threw himself into situations others wouldn't.'

'Like what?'

'Bringing people down. A few years ago, there was a

scandal involving a bunch of builders using sub-par materials to build houses. He called them out. Since then, there's been sex and corruption scandals, and that type of thing.'

'I guess he met his match when he got involved with whoever shot him.'

'It seems so. And I've checked out the two police officers on the list. They're unsavoury characters but very popular. I don't know the full extent of the influence they have up or down the ladder. The team are piecing together Henry's final movements. Apparently, when his office was broken into, a sceptical detective made a flippant comment about it being a cover-up.'

'A cover-up?' I frowned. 'How? What does that mean?'

'They suggested Henry staged the office break-in to cover up for his disappearance. He already had plans to disappear. All this is top secret, of course.'

'Who the hell am I going to tell?'

'They've got nothing to go on at the moment. His computer files were all destroyed during the break-in. Everything was removed from the Cloud, his diary wiped. All they know – at the moment – is he came to the city last Wednesday afternoon.'

I took a deep breath. 'Do you think they'll link him to the hotel room?'

He didn't need to speak. His raised eyebrows and *what-do-you-think*? expression answered what he obviously considered a dumb question.

'I need to give myself in, Cal. It's the right thing to do. Two people are dead.'

'Not because of you.'

With a trembling hand, I opened the can and poured the Coke into the glass. 'Well, one of them partly is. If I hadn't taken that wallet, Kat would still be here.' I crushed the can in my hands.

'It was only a matter of time before she was caught, given what she was doing.'

'Once the ball is over, I have no choice. I have to give myself in. Don't worry. I won't let on that you know a thing about this.'

His forehead was creased with worry. 'I'm concerned about you going to the police before we understand why those two police officers are on that list. Did you find anything more on the SD card?'

I turned to the laptop, briefing him on the files I'd started exploring. 'After the two police officers, the third person was a woman called Bronwyn Harris. I was reading about her last night when my laptop died.' I relayed the domestic abuse allegations against her. 'Then, strangely, the file corrupted when I tried to open it again today.' I clicked the photo I opened in the office before Alex had disturbed me. 'Next was this High Court judge in a tangle with a younger guy.'

Callum adjusted the screen to gain a better view. 'How do you know he's a judge?'

'It says so here.' I pointed to the text. 'I was looking at it earlier, but I got disturbed.'

'You shouldn't have had this open at work.'

'I've got my own office now.'

'Still!' Callum pointed to the screen, tracing his finger along the open document. 'Oh, hell,' he gasped. 'Get this. It appears whoever took this photo intended on using it as damning evidence. I wonder if Henry took it or obtained it somehow.' He nudged me. 'Open the next file.'

I opened the document corresponding to the fifth name on the list to find a photo of a grim-faced man with a younger woman. I read aloud the details about the Scottish politician and his secretary.

'She *was* his secretary,' Callum added. 'Until she turned nasty and threatened to expose the affair when he tried to end it. It appears she was paid fifty grand to back off.'

The next file didn't have a photo, but the document detailed a national newsreader involved in a tax evasion scandal. The following one told of the CEO of a large financial institution who was linked to insider trading and made a killing on the stock market.

I opened the next file, which linked to the eighth person on the list, Charlie Andrews – another footballer like Billy Brookes, but way more famous. Even I'd heard of him.

Callum leaned over the laptop, and we read about Charlie, the product of one of the top premiership club's academies. A young player, a natural, with a boatload of potential and real prospects. A unique talent who was going to take the soccer world by storm. But there was an almighty hiccup. Shortly after he'd signed his professional terms, he'd got caught up in a scandal threatening to derail his route to the top. One night, he was out with a group of friends. They went to a nightclub before staggering to a house party where alcohol, drugs, and young women were in abundance. Reckless behaviour, violating club rules. It all turned ugly. A fight broke out, and subsequently, one of the women claimed Charlie Andrews molested her.

Callum pointed to the screen. 'Have you read this bit?'

I shook my head.

He read aloud, summarising the last section. 'Andrews has always protested his innocence. He claimed he'd been foolish but denied ever laying a hand on anyone. The case was later thrown out because, at the time of the alleged attack, he'd long left the party and was at home in bed. CCTV proved it. But it turns out the CCTV was faked. And look.' He stabbed the screen. 'Faked by the first police officer on the list. I knew he was a bent bastard. I guess the other one is, too. All misdemeanours have been wiped clean.' He nudged my elbow. 'Not the police officers, of course, but I bet all these others are all clients of the KM Group.'

'It seems that way. I can check.'

Callum sniffed loudly. 'Do you know what I think?'

I turned to him.

'This Henry guy was an investigative journalist and had gathered all these stories. He met with Kelly to blackmail her with what he had on the KM Group and all those people. He must've shown her the SD card and left her with an ultimatum before going to the hotel – perhaps to give her time to think about what she was going to do. Then, bang! He's dead. And unlucky Mia got caught up in it all.'

'Don't you think it's strange the two police officers on the list don't have a corresponding file? So why are they on the list?'

'Because they're bent cops. I reckon they've falsified evidence to facilitate the cover-ups.'

'What do you mean?'

'Casting a blind eye on things these people have done. Or actively tampering with evidence. Witness intimidation. That kind of thing.'

I stared at him in horror. 'But they're police officers. How can that happen?'

'Believe me, it happens. You've heard it on the news. There's corruption in the force. There are some real hardcore bad guys.' He paused, clutching his head as if trying to make sense of the hundreds of thoughts whizzing through his mind. 'So, if you give yourself in, you expose the KM Group.'

'Not if, Cal. When.' My voice broke. 'And that *when* is as soon as we've got the money from the ball and Grace's treatment is secure.'

Silence fell as we pondered the ramifications of what we'd uncovered.

'It won't be long before the police figure out he was shot in that hotel room,' he said.

'How, though? It must've been professionally cleaned when they got rid of the body; otherwise the cleaning staff would've noticed when they went in there.'

'They'll place him there somehow. Forensics will find gunshot residue; it sticks to carpets, furniture, and even crevices in the walls. And there's the blood.'

My voice wavered. 'Will they be able to tell I was there?'

He screwed up his face in thought. 'I doubt it. How many people have stayed there since?'

I shrugged.

'Say someone stayed there every night. That's at least seven people. And the cleaners would've been in and out every day. And if it was couples staying, that's fourteen people. Plus, you've got the staff restocking the minibar.'

My phone rang. I dug it out of my bag. 'It's the police.' I rolled my eyes and answered it.

DI Prince gave a curt introduction and got straight to the point. 'I need you to come to the station at your earliest convenience.'

52

DI Prince tapped together the tips of his steepled fingers. 'Thank you for coming in again, Mia.'

A terrible smell lingered in the air as if someone had eaten a meal with too much garlic. I felt sick enough as it was.

DS Harrow stared on, stone-faced. Her long hair was styled in a fishtail braid today that rested over her shoulder like a thick piece of rope. Kat used to wear her hair in different styles like her.

I shifted in the chair and placed my hands under my thighs, thinking of Grace. I willed myself to stay calm. 'Anything I can do to help.' I spoke clearly and confidently as Callum had told me to. 'But I've already told you everything I know.'

'Yes, but there've been further developments we'd like to discuss with you.' DI Prince peered at the file in front of him. 'I'd like you to cast your mind back to the evening of Wednesday last week.'

The knot in my stomach twisted even tighter. I reminded

myself of Callum's pep talk: Act calm, Mia. Speak confidently but not cockily.

DI Prince raised his eyes to level with mine. 'Can you tell me what you recall of Katherine's movements that night?'

I held his gaze and shrugged. 'I'm not sure I can.' I stalled, staring at the table, concentrating, feigning being deep in thought. 'Wednesday last week, you say?'

The DI nodded. 'OK. Let's approach this another way. Why don't you tell me what you got up to that evening, then fill in the blanks for Katherine.'

'I left work and went home.' I needed to think on my feet. There could be CCTV of me leaving work that evening. But they'd be looking at Kat's movements, not mine... or maybe not. Anyway, they could easily check what time I left the office. 'Hang on. No, I didn't. It was the day of an event at the market square. I stopped there after work. Then I went back to Kat's place.'

'And what happened next?'

I paused as if in thought. 'When I got back, Kat wasn't there.' I wondered if they could tell I was lying. 'That's right. I remember because she'd told me at work she was feeling under the weather, and I was surprised she wasn't there.'

'And after that?'

'I got changed and went to my mum's place to drop some bits off for my sister.' I stared at the table. 'Kat was there when I got back. She had a cold or some kind of flu bug.'

'Did she say where she'd been that evening?'

'No.'

'How did she appear, Mia? Apart from feeling unwell, was she agitated at all?'

'Not that I recall. She was on her way to bed.'

DI Prince made a note. 'Then what happened between Wednesday and Saturday?'

I frowned. 'I'm not sure I follow?'

'Are you able to recall Katherine's movements?'

I've already told them that. 'As far as I know, she stayed at home because she wasn't well.' I paused, frowning again. I shook my head. 'I don't recall her leaving the flat, but I can't say for sure she didn't. I wasn't there the whole time.'

DS Harrow removed a photo from a beige folder. The two detectives glanced at each other.

'Have you ever seen this person?' She held the photo facing her for a few seconds as if pausing for effect. Turning it over, she pushed it in my direction.

I had to stop myself gasping at the photo of Henry Robertson smiling at the camera lens. I shook my head. 'No. I've never seen him.'

'His name was Henry Robertson. Do you know if Katherine had a relationship with him?' DI Prince asked.

'No.'

'Did he ever visit the apartment?' DS Harrow asked.

'No. I've already said, I've never seen him before.' I glanced again at the photo. 'Unless he went there when I was out.'

'This man's body was dragged out of the river yesterday.'

'How awful.' I stared from one detective to the other. 'What does that have to do with Kat?'

The DI continued. 'A barman at the Parkside Hotel saw Henry Robertson and Katherine together on the Wednesday evening in question. CCTV, although grainy, corroborates this. But it appears Katherine was in disguise, wearing one of the wigs we found under her bed.'

I tried to keep my expression blank, feigning ignorance.

They thought it was Kat in that hotel bar with Henry.

Not me.

'The barman said they left together. We're trying to contact other people staying at the hotel that night, but we have reason to believe Henry and Katherine went to Henry's room together.'

My heart was racing. It was unbelievable. If there was ever a time I needed to remain calm, it was then. I frowned, glancing from one of them to the other. 'And?'

The DI cleared his throat. 'Our forensics team has confirmed Henry Robertson was shot in that room.'

My face scrunched up. 'You don't think Kat did it? She'd never have done such a thing.'

'No. We don't believe it was her at this stage. It was a professional hit. And a professional cleanup.'

I needed to buy time to digest the conversation. I was withholding evidence, perverting the course of justice. I considered telling them about Henry meeting with Kelly last Wednesday but stopped myself. I said I'd never seen him before. I needed to continue going along with their theory as if I was never a part of it; and hold off commenting further until we'd secured the money for Grace.

'Are you OK, Mia?' the DS asked. 'You're quite pale.'

'I'm fine. It's a lot to take in.'

DI Prince continued, extracting another photo from the folder and pushing it towards me. 'You recall the picture we showed you of this watch.'

I nodded.

'Well, we've managed to trace it. The watch belonged to Henry Robertson.'

The DI dropped his hands flat on the table. 'I'll level with you, Mia. I'm struggling here. What was Kat doing wearing a blonde wig in a hotel bar, meeting a married man, with whom we assume she went back to his room? Said man is shot, and said man's watch miraculously appears in Katherine's possession, along with a considerable sum of cash. Not to mention the wig. Whatever she was involved in subsequently got her beaten to death, and I'm left wondering where the connection is. So, come on, Mia. Help me out here. Tell me what you know.'

My stomach was spinning and so were my thoughts. I needed to play it cool. Grace needed me to play it cool. I shook my head, wide-eyed. 'I'm so sorry. I wish I could help you more. But I've told you everything I know. I rarely saw her at the office. We worked in different parts of the organisation. We sometimes went for work drinks together, but we mainly did our own thing.' I was talking too fast. 'I sometimes went out with her on weekends, but not always.'

'What do you mean by your own thing?'

'My family live close by, so I see a lot of them. Kat went to the gym most nights after work and out a lot with her friends.'

'Which friends?'

'I only know the ones I told you about before.'

More questions came hard and fast like he was pounding balls with a baseball bat. I answered all of them the best I could... according to the story I wanted him to hear. They were clutching at straws. I just needed to hold tight.

The DI called it a day. 'We'll be in touch. As I said before, if there's anything else you think of that could help this investigation, please give us a call.'

53

I left the station in a mess but tried to remain calm. If I turned around, I was certain the DI would be watching me.

Three missed calls from Ruby showed on my phone. I called her.

'Where've you been? You were meant to be here two hours ago,' she said despondently.

I glanced at the time. It was now nearly nine o'clock. So much had happened since I'd left work at five. 'I'm sorry, Rue. I couldn't help it. I had to go back to the police station and answer more questions about Kat.'

'Don't worry. Mum stopped in after her shift. She's still here.' There was something different about her voice, a weighted hollowness.

'What's happened?' I asked.

'I'll tell you when you get here.'

I inwardly groaned. I'd planned to go home. I was running on empty and needed to refuel. And if I didn't get some sleep, I was going to implode. I felt compelled to go to the hospital.

I shivered, breathing in the gentle scent of an approaching autumn breeze. It was refreshing after being holed up in the interview room. I took the road towards the hospital and called Callum to update him, but he didn't answer.

The traffic had died down, and the final remnants of daylight were fading into nightfall. I should've taken a bus. I was exhausted. But I was off the main route and could walk to the hospital in a quarter of the time. People were still standing outside bars, enjoying drinks in the lingering warmth of the Indian summer. I eyed them with envy. That was what I should've been doing.

I took the revolving doors to the main hospital concourse and met Mum at our usual swap-over point by the vending machine in the corridor adjacent to the PICU. 'What's happened?' I asked. 'Ruby didn't sound great when I spoke to her.'

Mum stood. Her face was tense, her voice a splintery whisper. 'It hasn't been a good day.'

I bit my lip, wishing things could've gone our way for once.

'She's settled, though.' Mum sniffled. 'We need to get Ruby home for a while. She needs some rest. She stayed up all night last night. Talk some sense into her, can you? The best time for her to get some decent sleep is while Grace is here in the PICU. Once they move her...' She paused to clap her hands together and glance up at the ceiling. 'By the grace of God, please let it happen soon.' She returned my gaze. 'Once they move her to the children's general ward, she won't stand a chance of a minute's sleep. It'll be far too noisy.'

'Leave it with me.'

She reached into her bag. 'I'll get a drink and wait here. Hopefully, you can persuade her, and I'll drive us home.'

I kissed Mum on the cheek and gelled my hands. The doors to the PICU clunked open and closed. My phone beeped. I took it out of my pocket. There was a missed call and a text from Callum.

Call me. Cal

He'd sent it five minutes ago. I must have lost signal when I was in the lift. I sidestepped into a small alcove housing a water fountain and two plastic chairs. I stabbed his number, eager to find out what he wanted and to brief him on what had happened at the station, but there was no answer. He had to be the most difficult person to get hold of at times. It went with the job.

In the quiet drone of the ward, Ruby was sitting close to Grace's cot, her forehead resting on the rail. The arrival of the ventilator had brought a different dimension to the bay, the soft hum a constant reminder of its presence. Tubes gently rose and fell on Grace's chest with each strenuous breath she took.

A nurse was replacing one of Grace's drip bags, working delicately yet with accuracy and speed. I laid a hand on my sister's shoulder.

She turned around. Her face was a grey picture of pain and exhaustion, much like how I felt. 'I can't believe this is happening. We have to get her to America, Mia. We have to. What can I do to make this happen?'

I pulled up a chair beside her, our gazes fixed with steely intensity on the child we both loved so much.

'I'm working on it,' I whispered. 'We're all working on it.'

'I sent our MP an email. I was speaking to another mum in the parents' room last night. She said she constantly complains to her MP about the lack of support for her daughter. Sometimes it works to get things moving in the right direction.'

I raised an eyebrow. 'What did you say?'

'I told her the truth.' She lowered her voice to the slightest of whispers. 'My daughter is going to die if she doesn't get the help she needs. She's got kids. I googled it. Nine and six, and she's four months pregnant. I asked her what she'd do if it were her baby.'

'How did she answer?'

'I haven't had a reply yet.'

'Don't hold out any hope. I'm on it, Rue. I promise you, I am.' She'd never know how true those words were. 'You need to come home for the night, though. I insist.'

She nodded. 'I know. The consultant said the same.' She rearranged Grace's blanket. 'She's got nurses constantly watching over her here.'

The fearful grief of leaving Grace was overwhelming for us all.

Ruby cried as we exited the ward. 'Every time I say goodbye to her, even if it's to go to the loo, I can't help thinking I could be saying goodbye for the last time,' she said. The ward doors thumped closed.

'Negative thoughts get you nowhere.' Mum took her arm. 'Come on. Let's go home.'

We hurried to Mum's car. She turned the key in the ignition, muttering a prayer, hoping it'd start. She always did. The vehicle, a fifteen-year-old Renault Clio, was clinging to life like the flame of a candle on a birthday cake. She forked out a fortune for the never-ending repairs, and she needed a new car; but a nurse's pay barely covered the essentials, especially since Grace's arrival in our lives.

She puffed out a large breath of relief when the engine started. She drove out of the car park. 'What shall we have for dinner?' She glanced in the rearview mirror. 'Girls, get off those phones. I asked what you wanted for dinner.'

Ruby continued typing on her phone. She'd set up an Instagram account to track Grace's illness, hoping it'd help attract donations to the FundMeToday page. It had worked to a certain extent. Several people had donated the odd ten or twenty pounds off the back of it, but her followers were mainly parents with their own sick children with sky-scraping funds of their own to raise. She showed me the screen. 'We got another fifty pounds today.'

I smiled my encouragement, restraining my thoughts from turning to words: *fifty pounds wouldn't even cover the cost of getting to the airport.* Three hundred thousand pounds! It had seemed such a mountain to climb when we'd started out, and I couldn't quite believe how far we'd got, especially given the backbreaking weight I'd been carrying on my shoulders.

'Girls!' Mum raised her voice. 'I asked what you wanted for dinner.'

'I was thinking pizza.' I nudged my sister.

Ruby nodded absently, her gaze fixed on the screen. 'Whatever.'

'I'll jump out at the store,' I said.

After stopping at the shops, I led us up the staircase to the place I now called home again. It was a relief to be there, a comfort amid the madness I was living through. The corridor was in darkness, save for a single LED light casting shadows across the facades of the surrounding six flats. As we approached Mum's door, I abruptly stopped, flaying my laden arms outwards to stop Mum and my sister from going further.

Ruby knocked into my back. 'What the hell?' she barked.

'Shh,' I whispered urgently, staring at the wide-open front door.

54

My heart hammered. It couldn't be a coincidence.

The consequences of the situation didn't register with Mum. She pushed past me. 'I didn't leave it open. Mia, you were the last one out this morning. It must've been you. How careless. How many times have I told you kids? You must double-check you've locked up when you go out.'

I tugged her coat. 'Shh,' I repeated. 'I think someone has broken in.'

'What makes you say that?' Mum said.

'Call the police,' Ruby demanded. 'Quick.'

I grabbed Mum's wrist, trying to prevent her from digging her hand into her coat pocket for her phone. 'Stop, Mum.' Given my recent encounters with the law, the ramifications of involving the police were beyond fathomable. 'Don't call the police.'

'Why?' Mum's eyes were wide and tense. 'Someone could be inside.'

I edged closer to the door. 'Call Callum.'

Mum yanked the collar of my jacket, dragging me backwards. 'You're not going in there, Mia. I'm calling the police.'

'I said no. No police.' I raised my voice loud enough for Mum and Ruby to exchange shocked expressions.

Mum's jaw twisted to the side – a sure sign she didn't have a clue what I was thinking.

'You're scaring me,' Ruby said.

'Call Callum,' I repeated.

The unease in my voice fixed a frown on Mum's face. 'If you say so, but I don't understand—'

'Just do it, Mum.'

Ruby badgered me to tell her what was going on.

Mum connected with Callum. 'Someone's broken into the flat. We need you here.'

My brother's voice muffled through the mouthpiece. 'Is Mia there?'

'Yes.' Mum sounded as if she was about to burst into tears. 'Put her on.'

Mum handed me her phone.

Callum barked orders. 'Don't go in. Stay where you are. No. Forget that. Go to Mum's car. I'll meet you there.' His order was assertive. 'I'll be there as quickly as I can.' The line went dead.

Mum stood with her hand held out to the side, holding her phone. 'Why don't we call the police?'

'Callum is the police.' I yanked Mum's arm. 'You heard what he said. Let's get downstairs.'

We quietly retreated towards the stairwell. I wondered if the intruder was the same guy who'd murdered Henry and Kat, if it was even the same person. I wanted to run and hide and deliver my family to safety, but it was hard to know what safety looked like. Visions of how my life was going to be if I didn't hand myself in – forever hunted down until the inevitable happened – tormented me. But if I handed myself in and exposed what was on the SD card, I'd never get Grace's money. I could even end up meeting the same fate as Henry and Kat. And there was a chance my family could, too.

We bundled into Mum's car, me in the front, Ruby in the back.

Mum wrapped her arms around her body, clutching the sleeves of her coat. 'Should I drive us somewhere?'

She peered at me, but Ruby answered her.

'No. You heard Callum. Stay here.'

Mum wouldn't take her eyes off me. 'What are you not telling us, Mia? I know it's something. You've been highly agitated. Your flatmate was murdered. Now someone has broken into our home. We don't need this kind of trouble on our doorstep.'

I didn't know how to answer her. But I couldn't pull the dark wool of my troubles over her eyes for much longer. 'Let's wait for Callum to get here.' I switched on the radio and turned up the volume.

Ten minutes passed before Callum's police car arrived. Ten minutes of Mum bombarding me with questions like the detectives at the station had. There wasn't a vacant space, so he parked behind Mum's Renault and jumped out. I wound down my window.

Callum poked his head into the car. 'Are you all OK?'

'No,' Mum piped up. 'I want to know what's going on.' She pointed at me. 'There's something this one isn't telling us.'

'Wait here,' he ordered, speeding off before I could object.

We waited for what seemed like an eternity for my phone to ring. It jolted me from my trance. Callum's number flashed on the screen.

'You can come up. It's a bit of a mess. I'm not sure if anything's been taken.'

Mum stood in the middle of the ransacked living room, her eyes wide in shock.

Callum shot me a look before helping Mum and Ruby hunt around to assess the damage. I slipped away and headed straight for Ruby's room. I needed to get there before she had the chance. Grace's teddy bear was still on the bookshelf. I grabbed it and unzipped the back. The taste of bile filled my mouth. Henry's wallet and Kat's smashed-up phone were still in there. I stuffed them into my jacket pocket.

Ruby appeared, startling me. 'What are you doing?' She took the teddy from me, frowning.

'I was starting to tidy up.' I pointed to the teddy. 'I found it on the floor and was putting it back on the shelf.'

'Look at the mess in here.' Ruby was close to tears. 'It doesn't make sense. It was as if whoever did this was searching for something.' She picked up a couple of soft toys from the floor.

I took her arm. 'Let's go and make sure Mum's OK.'

'Funny,' Mum said when we returned to the lounge. 'I can't see that anything's gone.'

'I can't see anything missing, either,' Ruby agreed. 'But I remember watching a programme once. We could be trying to find something months later and only then realise it's gone.'

'We have to call the police. Get a crime reference number, at least,' Mum said.

'No,' I answered forcefully.

'Why on earth not?' Mum raised her voice. Something

she rarely did. She was one of those people who were difficult to anger. 'I don't understand. Our home has been broken into.'

Callum tried to placate her. 'Mum, Mia's right. There's no point. What will happen? An officer will turn up, log it and, trust me, it'll go onto the huge pile of other burglaries and crimes that remain unsolved. And in any case, I am the police.'

'This is serious. There's every point.' Mum was shaking. It upset me. 'Will someone *please* tell me what's going on?'

I couldn't stand the disappointment, confusion, and fear pasted over her face.

The time had come.

Resolute, I spoke. 'Let's all sit down.' I looked at my brother. 'We need to come clean... I need to come clean.'

55

'What the hell have you done, Mia?' Mum cried.

We sat around the small kitchen table, and I confessed to my family the series of horrific events I'd been through. How Kat had coerced me into her criminal activities and my reasons for agreeing. The hideous episode in room four-nine-three of the Parkside Hotel. The events surrounding Kat's death. What I'd discovered on the SD card in the wallet sitting on the table before us. And how it appeared to be linked to my boss and the KM Group.

My heart ached for Mum.

'So why haven't you told all this to the police?' she asked.

Callum explained. 'The thing is, I can't be sure how far-reaching the involvement is of the police officers on the list. They have their fingers in so many pies. They're the type who are everyone's mate. Even the seniors seem to suck up to them. I don't know who to trust.'

'I'm going to hand myself in when the ball is over,' I said. 'Once we've secured the funds for Grace's treatment.'

'You're not safe.' Mum folded her arms. 'You have to go to the police now. They'll be able to protect you.'

'Let's at least hold off until after the ball,' Ruby argued, seemingly ignoring the severity of the situation. 'Think about it. If she goes to the police now, it'll all blow up, and the ball won't happen.' The desperation in her voice for what that meant for Grace rang loud and clear. 'We won't get the money.' She banged her hands on the table. 'This would all have been for nothing.'

'No,' Mum insisted. 'This is wrong. I haven't brought you all up to be like this. Callum, tell the two of them. You've got to agree with me. Surely?'

Callum sat with his legs spread apart, one hand on each knee. 'You aren't listening to me, Mum. Before I saw that list, I was vehement Mia should go to the police. Hell, I would've driven her there myself. But now, no.'

Mum sat back in her chair. 'Why? I don't understand.'

Exasperated at not being listened to, my brother spelled it out again. 'Bent cops are implicated in all of this, and I'm not sure who I can trust in the force anymore.' He dropped his elbows to rest on his knees and clasped his hands together. 'I'm working on an idea.'

The three of us stared at him.

'How we can expose the KM Group and all those on the list.' He fixed his gaze on me.

There was something about the way he was staring at me that unnerved me even more.

'What's more, I may be able to keep your name out of it. We all need you here, sis. Not behind bars. You'll just have to come to terms with the part you played in this utter mess.'

'You don't understand, Cal. I can't live like this anymore,' I protested. 'Constantly looking over my shoulder, waiting for the next thing to happen. Especially not now you're all involved.'

I shook my head. You thought you were a good human being, and then one day, in a moment of madness, you made a terrible decision and realised you weren't.

I lowered my head in shame and relief – shame for what I'd done, but relief that at least my brother understood the motivation behind my crime.

'You're not a bad person, Mia. You're the kindest person I know.'

'Thanks!' said Mum and Ruby in unison.

Callum rolled his eyes. 'You know what I mean. This was all born out of desperation and an evil woman. You're a victim here, Mia. Kat played on your vulnerability. You've been stupid, yes, but you're a victim all the same. She saw how desperate you were. How much you love Grace and want to help her. She used that to get inside your head.' He puffed out a large breath. 'If you give me the SD card, I'll get it to the right person. I've got a way of doing it anonymously, and I'm sure I can trust the person to do the right thing.'

'I don't like the sound of this,' Mum said. 'I don't like it at all.'

Callum turned to her. 'You don't have to like it, Mum. You have to trust me.'

Ruby gesticulated. 'The ball has to go ahead.'

'I don't want you going back to that place tomorrow, Mia,' Mum said. 'Or ever again, for that matter. You need to find another job.'

Callum tried to reassure her. 'Mum. It's fine. Think about it. What would it look like if two young women at the same company were murdered? The police would be all over that place like a virus. Whoever was responsible for Kat's death wouldn't want that.'

'I've got to go back, Mum,' I said. 'Kelly and I are going to Moorlands tomorrow to ensure everything is ready for Saturday. Nothing is going to happen in the office. Nothing will happen at the ball. We get Grace's money. That's our priority. Then I'll go to the police.'

Ruby chimed in. 'Sounds like a plan.' Her thoughts were focused on getting Grace the help she deserved. Naturally, everything else was secondary for her.

I understood.

Callum asserted himself, standing, towering over the three of us. He held out a hand to me. 'Give me the SD card, and I'll sort it.'

'How?'

'As I said, I'm going to expose it all anonymously. I'll make this all go away. I promise.'

If only I could have genuinely believed that'd be the case.

56

When I arrived at the office the following morning, Kelly relentlessly added tasks to my to-do list. I was quickly learning why Kat had rarely taken a lunch break.

She leaned on my desk, rolling out her commands like an army officer barking orders. 'Please join me in room C at nine-thirty. I have a client coming in for a meeting, and I'll need you to take notes.' She glanced at her Apple watch. 'I'll have to meet you at Moorlands later as I have a couple of personal appointments I must keep beforehand. Remind me what time we're due to be there.'

'Two o'clock.' My voice dipped. I no longer felt safe in her company.

'That should give me plenty of time. I can drive us back here afterwards.'

I turned to my computer and checked my inbox. IT had sent an email informing me they had fixed all outstanding access problems and that I should contact them with any further issues. That meant I should be able to access Kelly's diary. I clicked on it, desperate to find out what time she'd met Henry Robertson last Wednesday.

But there wasn't a meeting scheduled that day.

All that was showing for that afternoon was an entry titled *personal*. I squinted at the screen, wondering if that referred to her meeting with Henry. I scanned the other entries. The sections between noon and two p.m. today were blocked out and titled the same – *personal*.

My jaw tensed. Maybe Kelly had changed the title for that two-hour block in case the police started poking around. She would've known they'd be asking questions when they'd discovered Henry was in the office on the day he'd died.

I couldn't concentrate. A deep-rooted unease kept my eyes constantly darting towards the door as if I was waiting for more trouble to enter without knocking.

I kept thinking about what the following days would bring. If Callum's idea went to plan, and I didn't find myself back at the police station, I'd be jobless again. The thought filled me with dread. I was unemployed for periods between temping jobs before I'd joined the KM Group, and I'd hated it. Days that began at midday and ended when there was nothing left worth watching on the TV. Loafing on the sofa doing diddly-squat was a guilt-free, pleasurable ride as a teenager, but it no longer afforded the same appeal.

It wasn't until Kelly left to attend her personal appointment around noon that I could breathe properly. I was typing up the notes from the meeting earlier when Alex appeared, waving a wad of papers.

A wide grin stretched across his face. 'Guess what, Mia?' He didn't wait for a reply. 'I've secured an incredible addition for the silent auction.' He rested his hands on my desk and leaned towards me. The pleasant smell of his aftershave wafted over me. 'I've been working on one of my clients who has a villa in Sicily. Six bedrooms. Nice place, Sicily. You been there?'

I shook my head. I'd never even been abroad before. It was the most envious I'd ever been at school when friends described their summer trips to Disney and sunny Spain. The only holiday we'd ever taken was a miserable week in a filthy apartment on the Welsh coast. Both Callum and Ruby came down with the flu. It rained every day. The heating packed up, and Mum had concluded, "What's the bloody point?"

'Two weeks, as well!' Alex continued. 'We should see some generous bids coming in for this one. A good few grand.'

I allowed myself to genuinely smile for the first time in days. 'Thanks, Alex. You've been so supportive.'

'Don't suppose you have a stapler around here, do you?' He peered around my desk.

I opened my drawer and quickly found him one.

'What's up, Mia? You've not been the same since you started working for Kelly. Is she pushing you too hard?'

'It's more to do with Kat.'

'Of course. Of course. That was insensitive of me. Have you heard any more from the police?'

I shook my head.

The office phone rang. I reached to pick it up.

He dropped the papers on my desk. 'These are the details of the villa you might want to do something with before tomorrow night. Blow the images up for the display, perhaps?'

'How kind. I really don't know what we would've done without you all. Ruby is so grateful. We all are.' I answered the phone and found my corporate voice. 'Kelly Meyer's office. How can I help you?'

'Could I speak to Miss Meyers, please?' a European-sounding – Spanish, perhaps? – woman asked. She rolled her r's like the Spanish woman who lived in the flat above Mum.

'Kelly isn't here at the moment. Can I ask who's calling?'

'I'm from the Chiropractic Clinic. I've left a couple of messages on Miss Meyers' mobile, but she hasn't replied. This is the only other number I have for her. She left her scarf here last week, and she hasn't arranged another appointment, so I thought she might want to come and collect it.'

'No worries. I'll let her know.' Then it occurred to me. It was the clinic on the way to the bus stop where I needed to catch a bus to Moorlands. The venue was on the outskirts of town, and it would take too long to walk there. 'Are you in the building at the end of the High Street?' I asked.

'That's right,' she replied.

'I'll be passing by in about half an hour. I'll pick it up for her.'

The Chiropractic Clinic was housed on the ground floor of a double-fronted Victorian house. I held on to the metal railing and pulled myself up the steps from the High Street, reading the advertisements displayed in the blacked-out window for the ailments they claimed they could treat: headaches, whiplash, slipped discs, trapped and pinched nerves, and various back, shoulder, arm, and neck pains.

I stepped inside. No one was around. The white-painted wooden floor creaked as I walked over to the small reception desk and pressed the bell. A pinging sound echoed around the room. I checked the time on my phone, hoping someone would quickly show up. The bus was due in under three minutes.

A woman dressed in a white tunic and trousers appeared, her grey hair tucked in a tight bun at the nape of her neck. 'Can I help you?'

I could tell by her accent she was the woman I'd spoken to on the phone. 'You called earlier. I'm here to pick up Kelly Meyers' scarf.'

'Ah, yes. Let me get it for you.'

'I need to catch a bus in three minutes.' I pointed to the door. 'From outside.'

'Sure. I'll hurry.'

The woman disappeared. I knocked my knuckles together, glancing around the clinical-looking room. True to her word, she reappeared in a flash and handed over a red silk scarf. I placed it in my bag.

'Is she back at work?'

'Sorry?' I asked.

'Miss Meyers. She wasn't well at her appointment last week. It was a bad fall.'

'Fall?'

'Yes, she passed out, so I suggested she stay here for a while.'

I was confused. Kat told me Kelly had met Henry at the office around that time last week.

The woman continued. 'As we haven't heard from her, I wanted to check she was OK.'

'Yes. She's fine, thank you. I must dash.'

'Give Miss Meyers our regards.'

I rushed outside. The bus doors were folding shut. I ran, hoping to catch the driver's attention, but my foot caught an uneven paving slab, sending me flying. A young guy caught my fall. I regained my balance and thanked him. The bus rumbled away.

I swore repeatedly. The next bus wasn't due for half an hour. I had no option but to walk. I typed the address of Moorlands into Google Maps on my phone for directions and broke into a jog, regretting not switching my pumps for my trainers.

The afternoon sun was still so warm for a late September day. I hoped the weather would hold for Saturday. People were happier when the weather was warmer. Kat had told me that. It made them drink more, which in turn made them splash more cash.

I jogged most of the way, slowing to a fast walk to abate the sweat dripping down my back. The fumes of the Friday afternoon traffic caught my breath as the conversation with the Spanish woman played on my mind.

Despite what Kat had said, it didn't sound like Kelly could've met with Henry Robertson on the day he'd died.

But I couldn't work out why Kat would've lied to me.

57

Navigating a shortcut, I arrived twenty minutes late at Moorlands.

Kelly was waiting for me on a sofa in the reception area. She stood and straightened the creases from the legs of her tight-fitting trouser suit.

'I'm sorry I'm late. Did you get my text? I missed the bus.' I dug into my bag. 'Your chiropractor called.' I handed her the scarf. 'You left this there last week. They've been trying to get hold of you.'

Kelly took the scarf and quickly wound it around her neck, effortlessly making it look stylish. 'Yes, yes. I've been meaning to call them back. It slipped my mind. Thank you.'

'They said you had a fall last week.'

The muscles in her face tensed up. 'How inappropriate! What happened to client confidentiality?'

'I'm sorry.'

'Not your fault.'

I wanted to ask her if she had returned to the office that

day but couldn't think of a reply if she asked me why I wanted to know.

She held an arm towards a set of double doors. 'Let's get going. They're waiting for us.'

I followed her to the Eddison Suite, where she opened the door into the grand ballroom. It took my breath away. It was so different with all the decorations adorning it like a massive bowl of jewels.

Thirty tables, each seating ten guests, surrounded three sides of the large ballroom floor in a U shape, fronting a stage laced with fairy lights. Each table was covered with a navy tablecloth and set with gold cutlery and cream linen serviettes folded lengthways and held in navy napkin rings. A display of clear balloons containing pieces of gold and navy confetti with Grace scribed across them made for a sophisticated centrepiece. My eyes welled up. Whatever Kat was, and Kelly, they'd done my family proud. They'd stepped in to help as if Grace was one of their own. It was the kid thing, Kat had said. Kelly had lost a baby, and she was an aunty to Alex's three kids, making her sympathetic to the cause.

People darted around, arranging the final touches to the elaborate tables dressed for royalty.

Kelly pointed to two giant screens at the back of the stage. 'That's where we'll show the slides from the presentation on one screen and a running total of the fundraising page on the other. People will be able to see donations as they come in.'

'Won't that make them feel uncomfortable?'

'No time to worry about people's feelings, Mia. We're on a mission. We have to get in people's faces and make them donate more. If they see the money ticking over, they'll get caught up in the moment and join in. Don't forget, these are people with money. We simply need to make them spend it.'

It seemed grotesque, but if it got Grace where she needed to be, I wasn't arguing. 'Thanks, Kelly. Thanks for everything you've done for my family.'

'I like to help where I can. Especially for such a worthy cause.' She stroked the ends of her red scarf. 'It can't be easy for you all. Come and see the silent auction.'

However, and whyever, she'd got involved with Henry Robertson, she'd helped me and my family.

She led me to the room where the roulette wheels and poker tables had been set up. 'Get a few drinks in them and get them in here!' She laughed. It suited her. She had attractive straight teeth. She didn't laugh often. She was always too focused on her work.

Taking my arm, she led me to the room next door, where the silent auction had been set up. Rows of tables held plastic displays detailing all the items included in the auction: an exclusive private dining experience for six at a three-star Michelin restaurant in London; a two-week stay at a top hotel in Hawaii; a meal for two with a surprise celebrity couple; a week in a mountain cabin in the French Alps, with a private chef included. The list went on and on. Experiences I could've only dreamed of enjoying. It was all highly impressive.

'Who's the celebrity couple?' I asked.

'It's a surprise.' She winked at me. 'You'll be astonished at how much keeping the intrigue will increase bids. I didn't study psychology at university for nothing!' She revealed the names of the couple, a man and a woman in showbusiness, but they were unfamiliar to me.

We returned to the main hall where Susan Trice, the event organiser, was teetering towards us in her high heels, carrying a plastic box. Her face was bright red as if she'd run a race. 'I hope you're pleased with everything.'

Kelly nodded. 'We most certainly are. You look harassed. Is there anything we can do to help?'

Susan paused as if wondering if she should delegate tasks to the woman paying her bill. She tapped her manicured nails on the top of the plastic box. 'That'd be great.' Snapping the lid off the box, she offered it to Kelly. 'Here are the place cards. If one of you could dish out these, it'd help considerably. I'm still working on the silent auction display. You've got some incredible items there.'

'We have indeed,' Kelly said.

'That villa in Sicily looks incredible.'

'It sure does! I might have to bid on it myself.' Kelly took the box from Susan and passed it to me. 'You start with these, Mia, and I'll help with the display.'

Susan dug into the box and pulled out a piece of paper. 'This is the table plan. The cards are organised in groups of ten by table. Once one of my team becomes free, I'll send them to help you.'

When they disappeared, I reached into my bag for my phone. I snapped a few shots of the room and sent them to our family's WhatsApp group chat with a brief message.

What do you think? Impressive, eh?

Hopefully, it'd brighten Ruby's day – as much as it could be brightened at the moment.

I took the box to the table nearest the stage, labelled table number one on the seating plan, and hooked my bag over the back of one of the padded chairs. In the fuzz of my exhaustion, the chair looked so inviting. I imagined sitting on the soft cushioning, crossing my arms on the table and resting my head. Twenty minutes, that was all I needed.

An exploding noise cut through my thoughts. I spun around, expecting someone with a gun. But it was only a plate someone had dropped on the floor.

I was constantly on a knife's edge, waiting for the next catastrophe to unfold.

I left the box on a chair and studied the seating plan Kat had organised with Kelly because they knew all the clients. My family were seated at the table alongside Kelly, who was coming alone. Kat had told me Kelly didn't have a partner. She was happily married to her work. Kat had been due to sit at that table, too, but her place card had been removed and exchanged for a person's who I didn't know. I laid the glittery gold cards alongside the napkins on each dinner plate. I moved to table two, positioned behind table one.

Alex and his wife were the top guests on table two. I found their cards, Alex and Elodie, and arranged them beside their napkins.

But when I reached for the following two cards, my jaw dropped.

They belonged to Richard Nought, the High Court judge named on the SD card, and Mary Nought, who I assumed was his wife. My eyes jumped to the third name, but I didn't recognise it. But I did the fourth name: Bronwyn Harris.

Kelly appeared by my side.

'That was quick,' I said.

'She was fussing about nothing. Come on, shake a leg. We need to get back to the office. Let me help you.'

I handed her the place cards for tables six to ten and a copy of the seating plan. When she went off, I scanned the other people on table two, picking up three names I recognised from the SD card. I swallowed hard. Surely, they were all Alex's clients.

58

I couldn't control the thoughts racing through my mind.

I needed to speak to my brother.

The afternoon traffic hampered our journey back to the office, much to Kelly's annoyance. She turned on the radio to a news channel giving a market update on financial centres worldwide. 'Blast these bloody drivers. I swear some of them head straight at you on purpose.' Pulling up to a set of road-works, she tapped her fingers on the steering wheel as if it could make the lights turn green faster.

A news summary came on the radio. Towards the end of the segment, the presenter gave a brief update on the lack of progress in apprehending Kat's killer. Word from a reporter suggested it could be gangland related.

Kelly and I glanced at each other.

'What utter nonsense. Kat wasn't that kind of person.' She shrugged. 'Unless she got herself involved in something dubi-ous. But she wasn't like that.'

Little did she know about her former PA.

The presenter moved on to an update on the shooting of

Henry Robertson. It was as if they'd deliberately put the two incidents back to back to torment me. I squirmed in my seat, the leather squeaking. Heat rose up my neck. I opened the window, stuck having to listen.

'What terrible, terrible news,' Kelly said. 'What is the world coming to? The poor wife, the poor children.' She sighed heavily. 'How can you ever get over something like that? It's beyond belief.'

Either she was innocent of any involvement or wrongdoing, or she deserved to be handed an Oscar there and then.

When we got back to the office, she asked me to dig out some notes for a client she was meeting tomorrow. But first, I searched the client database for Henry Robertson. There was no file for him anywhere. While I was at it, I searched for the people on the list of names on the SD card. The nausea swimming through my veins was unbearable as one by one, my suspicions were confirmed. Apart from the police officers, they were all Alex's clients.

I paused, clutching the side of the desk. I had to get it straight in my mind. Henry Robertson had possessed the names of a group of Alex's clients. He was killed for that list, and so was Kat. Henry visited the KM Group offices on the day he'd died. He was meant to meet with Kelly. She wasn't there. Alex must've met with him instead. My gut instinct told me Henry blackmailed Alex, which was what had got him murdered.

The question was, how was Kelly connected to it all?

If she was at all.

Kelly appeared at my door, startling me. 'Do you have those meeting notes?' she asked abruptly.

'I'm just printing them off. I'll bring them straight to you.' I was surprised she didn't read them online, but

Lauren had told me Kelly always liked a hard copy of meeting notes.

After taking the relevant papers to her, I sat at my desk, staring at the screen. I had to know if Kelly came back to the office last Wednesday. Then I remembered the system for monitoring people entering and leaving the office Lauren had shown to me. Staff logged in and out with their personal KM Group cards, and visitors were given guest passes. I had access to the system as my role now involved allocating visitor passes when Lauren was out of the office or at lunch.

I referred to the notes I'd taken when Lauren was training me. They were practically ineligible as she'd talked so fast that I'd found it hard to keep up. Following the scribbles I'd made on accessing the system, I figured out how to log on and find the entries for last Wednesday.

But it was strange. No visitor passes were issued that day. So either Kat had lied to me, and Henry never came to the office, or details of the pass he was issued with had been wiped off the system. It had to be the latter. Definitely the latter. I recalled seeing a KM Group lanyard in Henry's hotel room. So, someone had erased all traces of Henry entering the building.

I studied Kelly's movements from last Wednesday. She'd left the office at noon to attend her appointment, but, according to the system, she didn't return until Thursday morning. Perhaps there was an error in the system that didn't clock her coming back on Wednesday, but that seemed unlikely.

Alex appeared at my office door, asking about a report I'd been working on with him a few weeks ago. He approached my desk. The sweet, resinous waft of his aftershave, which I used to like, was suddenly unappealing.

I couldn't reply to his question, simply because I didn't know the answer without studying the figures. 'Can you give me half an hour, and I'll get back to you?' I wanted him gone.

He nodded. 'Send me the answers via email.'

Perhaps Kelly called Alex to tell him about the fall she'd had at the clinic and asked him to cover for her in the meeting with Henry.

The question was: how could I turn the situation to my advantage – to Grace's advantage – before I handed myself in?

59

Mum was still not back from work when I arrived home, which was a relief. Stress was bleeding through me, slowing me down.

I poured a glass of wine, hoping it'd calm me, but even a second glass did nothing to settle my nerves. Finding a plate of leftover cottage pie, I heated it in the microwave. But when I removed the zapped offering, it looked like something you'd feed to a dog. The smell didn't help. But I had to stay strong, so I forced down a few forkfuls while I scrolled through Facebook on my phone.

I found Charlene Robertson's page. She'd posted a picture of Henry and her on their wedding day with a few accompanying lines explaining Henry's body had been found. She asked for privacy for the foreseeable future, so she and her children could deal with the tragedy that had ripped their lives apart.

The sadness in her written tone brought tears to my eyes. I couldn't read anymore. There was no room for tears. Standing, I scraped the remaining cottage pie into the bin. I found

Callum's number to update him on my latest findings, only to get his voicemail.

I dug out the speech for Saturday night. As Ruby wasn't going to be at the ball, I needed to pick up her section, which wasn't something I could do off the cuff. I wasn't smart enough. I paced up and down the hallway while practising it. I'd planned to learn it by heart, but an hour later, I was no further forward. I kept forgetting words, which interrupted my flow. When the rattle of Mum's car pulling into the small car park behind the block of flats announced she was home, I ran to my room and quickly jumped under the covers. When she came into my room, I pretended to be asleep.

But, as it had been for the past eight nights, it was gone three a.m. by the time I finally dropped off, only to be plagued by nightmares of Charlene Robertson chasing me down a dark alleyway. I ran towards the end, where a bright light shone on a fork in the road, which branched off in two directions. One was labelled right, and the other wrong. I knew which one I had to follow, but no matter how hard I tried to run, I couldn't reach it.

In the morning, I waited for Mum to leave for work. When the front door closed, it took all my effort to crawl out of bed. I shuffled to the bathroom and looked in the mirror. My face was pale, my skin sallow, and a foreboding sense of unease gripped my entire body. I considered calling in sick. I was utterly drained. But Alex was taking me to Moorlands that afternoon to ensure all the computer equipment was working and for me to run through the speech ahead of tomorrow night.

·   ·   ·

Alex wasn't there when I got to the office, which was odd. He was usually in before me. I checked my email. Sometimes he took his boys to school. But by noon, he still hadn't arrived.

'Where's Alex today?' I asked Kelly when I joined a meeting with her.

'He's taken a day's leave.'

At such short notice? That was most unlike him.

I panicked. 'He was meant to be helping me set up the screens for my speech.'

'He said to tell you he'll meet you at Moorlands tomorrow at five-thirty, and he'll go through it all.'

I crossed my arms. 'That's leaving it a bit last-minute, isn't it?'

She could detect the panic in my voice. 'I'm sure it'll be fine, Mia. Don't stress.'

I excused myself and rushed to the toilet, where I only just about made it to throw up the remains of the slice of toast I'd managed to force down that morning. I couldn't stop retching. I wasn't sure if I was coming down with something or the stress had got too much.

Luckily, Lauren found me a quarter of an hour later. She arranged for a taxi to take me home. I glanced over my shoulder when I left the office, my shoulders dropping a few inches, knowing I'd never step foot in that place again.

When I got home, I no longer felt sick. I tried to nap but couldn't sleep. Getting up, I paced the flat, practising the speech. By the evening, I was hanging like a wilted flower. I swallowed two of Mum's sleeping tablets she sometimes took when she came off a stint of night shifts to help her get back into a routine. If I didn't get a full night's sleep, I feared a breakdown. I was clinging on to make it to Saturday night.

One more day and it would all be over.

60

FundMeToday
GRACE'S APPEAL

£231,395 raised of £300,000 goal
992 donations
Latest 3 donations:
Simon Porter £1000
Kimberley Jackson £5
Robin Hall £50

I woke up on Saturday morning and checked Grace's Appeal on my phone, pleased to see the generous donation from Simon Porter, a client of Kelly's. I'd seen an expense report of Kelly's with a receipt from when she'd taken him out to dinner. We still had such a long way to go, but the silent auction and casino funds were still to come in, and Kelly believed more of the company's richest clients were going to donate.

Mum brought me a cup of tea. She perched on the edge of my bed. Her face was full of worry. It broke my heart. My mess was affecting her badly, too.

'We finally get to talk. Anyone would think you were trying to ignore me, Mia Hamilton.'

I sat up, flattening the covers, and took the cup from her.

'Your brother isn't answering my calls either.'

'You know what he's like when he's on nights, Mum. I've been playing phone tag with him, too.'

'I've been worried sick about you. What's happening?'

I remained remarkably calm as if the full night's sleep had given me the push to make it over the final hurdle. 'I've told you. Tomorrow morning, when we know the final funds are in and we've got the money we need for Grace, I'm going to hand myself in.'

Her shoulders dropped. 'I'm glad you've come to your senses.'

'I can't live like this anymore.'

'You never know, if you help the police, they might be more lenient with you.' Her voice wavered. 'I wish you'd never taken that job.'

'So do I, Mum. So do I.' I sighed heavily. 'But then we'd never have got all the money for Grace's Appeal.'

'You never know,' Mum said.

We visited Ruby and Grace. It was a sombre visit. Grace hadn't improved since I was last there. We returned home on a downer to get ready to go to the ball. It was a surreal hour while we applied our make-up and helped each other into our dresses, both of us knowing that the following day I'd most probably be at the police station. She ran her fingers along the diamante beading to the waist of my red ballgown.

'You look stunning.' Her face twitched as she strained to contain her tears.

Mum drove us to Moorlands. Before my troubles started, we'd planned to catch a bus there and a cab home so she could enjoy the wine, but she was no longer in the mood for a drink. The conversation was stilted, both of us knowing it could well be the last evening we spent together for a long while.

The orchestra was warming up when we arrived, playing an upbeat piece of classical music. Susan and her team were swarming around, buzzing between tables and putting last-minute touches to the decor. Disco balls that weren't there on Thursday when I'd visited, hung from the ceiling above the dance floor. The mirrored surfaces reflected beams of light around the room like dancing stars. LED candles scattered around the thirty tables flickered, and the stage was lit with thousands of fairy lights. It was stunning. Ruby would've loved it. I recorded a short video and sent it to her.

Alex marched towards us, waving his hands to catch our attention. He was impeccably dressed in black tie with, unusually, a black shirt. All in black, it accentuated his olive skin and gave him a sinister appearance, like a boss from the Russian Mafia, not one from a UK boutique public relations company. 'I'm sorry I didn't make it yesterday. Something came up.'

I bet it did.

'What do you think?' He pointed to the screen displaying a live feed of Grace's FundMeToday page beside the photo we'd chosen of her propped up in her hospital cot half-heartedly smiling. 'It's a great photo,' he said.

I was on edge. A donation had hit the pot since I'd last looked in the car: Linda DuBois £3000. 'Wow! What a generous amount. Who's Linda DuBois?' I asked, but Alex had wandered off to the stage. I tried to calculate how much we had left to raise to meet our target. But my brain couldn't cope with the simple calculation.

Kelly made an entrance dressed in a sophisticated black crepe gown embellished with a large crystal flower on the shoulder. I could tell from the fabric and cut it was a designer dress. It hugged her perfect figure.

She thrust a cocktail into my hand. 'Have this. It'll help with the nerves. Have you not heard of the tennis player? Linda Dubois?'

I shook my head. Tennis wasn't my bag. I took a sip of the drink. My eyes watered. 'Wow, what's in that?'

'Is it strong?' She took a sip of her own drink. 'Goodness, I see what you mean.' She laughed. 'Linda is an absolute darling. American. One of my favourite clients. I told her about the cause, and she's generously donated.'

I fiddled with the diamante beading of my dress. I must've dropped a few kilograms in the past week because the waist had been a little on the tight side when I'd bought the dress. I kept catching my shoe, which made me even more anxious I was going to trip up. That couldn't happen. I was uncomfortable in every regard.

Kelly acknowledged Mum with a nod and a smile. 'I take it you're Mia's Mum. You're so alike. I'm Kelly. Pleased to meet you.'

Mum glanced around. 'It's all so impressive.' Her voice was clipped.

'It's a remarkable achievement,' Kelly said. 'Please excuse me. I need to speak to a few people.'

When Callum arrived, looking dapper in his suit, I collared him for an update on what he'd done with the SD card.

'I'm still working on it,' he said.

I stared at him. Something told me he wasn't telling me the truth.

Alex returned from the stage before I had the chance to quiz my brother. I hated being beholden to that man who I believed had something to do with Henry's and Kat's deaths, and the suffering of Henry's wife and kids. But the difficulty was, I didn't know that for sure. Due to the effort he'd put into helping my family, it was hard to believe he was responsible for such atrocities. But as Callum had told me soon after he'd joined the police, certain individuals are perfect masters of their disguise.

It would only come to light when I handed myself in tomorrow.

Getting Grace what she needed had to remain my focus.

'I'll get some photos and send them to Ruby,' Mum said.

Alex took my arm. 'I've sorted the technical side of things. The presentation is working like a dream. Let's get you up there and make sure the sound is good. We need it spot on. Susan is going to turn the pages.' He called out her name, beckoning for the woman who had done such a magnificent job with the venue, to join us.

Susan appeared, dressed in a smart trouser suit. She smiled at me.

'You nod at her when you're ready,' Alex said.

I took to the stage, full of dread knowing I soon had to deliver a speech to three hundred people. It was a big deal. I'd never got even close to doing anything on such a scale. With a trembling hand, I placed the piece of paper containing the speech on the tempered glass podium beside the screens.

Alex politely asked the orchestra to pause. He could be such a charmer. 'OK. Let's have a run-through.' A voice calling his name. 'Hang on. Elodie's here.' He beckoned his wife over.

Elodie's midnight-blue strapless dress was a perfect match for her dark hair. She gracefully removed a cream shawl draped over her shoulders and adjusted her sapphire choker necklace.

Alex kissed her cheek and introduced her to those around us. 'Mia's about to run through her speech.' He turned to me. 'I'll count down from five, and you go. Five... four...'

The screen beside me flashed. Alex stopped counting. 'See that, Mia?'

I glanced at the screen showing a one-hundred-pound donation from a Mr Bolton, whoever he was.

'The money's coming in. OK. Ready?' Alex said. 'Five, four, three, two, one.'

Get the first sentence out and everything will flow, Kelly had told me.

Gritting my teeth, I glanced at Grace's face on the big screen and began the practice run of my speech.

61

The evening went off with a bang, with Kelly introducing Grace's cause. I was doing my best to stay composed despite my stress levels, but the fear inside me was growing by the minute. I felt like I was in the lull before a storm, a tornado sure to end my life as I knew it. Others appeared to be enjoying themselves, though – everyone except me and my family – but we were doing a good job concealing our inner torment.

Waitresses were clearing away the starters – a choice of melon with Parma ham or wild mushroom pâté. "Simple, tasty and cost-effective," Kat had said when choosing the menu. Every time I thought back to our relationship, it pained me to realise how much she'd controlled every aspect of it.

I was seated between Mum and Lauren, who were both drinking orange juice. The white wine was of quality, but I couldn't enjoy it. I needed a cigarette. There were a couple in my bag from when I'd gone out with Kat weeks ago. I couldn't stop thinking about them. I left the table and wandered outside, where a small group of guests were huddled, smoking and vaping.

I asked one of the smokers for a light. He patted his jacket pockets, produced a lighter, and lit my cigarette. I took a long, deep drag.

'Great event, eh?' he said. 'Poor kid.'

He reeled off a story about his brother who'd had leukaemia as a child, but I wasn't listening. My eyes were fixed on a posh car in the car park. But it wasn't the car that had caught my attention, but the guy who'd climbed out to get something from the back seat.

Was it the person who'd shot Henry Robertson, that bala-clava guy?

I was going crazy. I shook my head and took another puff of the cigarette. The guy returned to the driver's seat.

The orchestra was playing background music to accom-pany the meal when I returned to the ballroom. It was loud enough to create an atmosphere but low enough not to drown out the guests' conversation, which amplified as the wine flowed. The table behind us – Alex's table – was particu-larly noisy. Elodie was talking to a man I'd never seen before, her beautiful, long hair glowing in the light.

Disappointingly, there hadn't been much movement in Grace's Appeal. I wasn't sure how advantageous it was to shove it in people's faces. Perhaps it was too much having a dying kid's face on display while you're drinking a glass of wine and stuffing your face with pâté and posh bread rolls.

I mentioned my thoughts to Kelly, but she disagreed.

She leaned across Lauren and spoke to me encouragingly. 'I've been to loads of these charity events. They all start slowly, but by the time people have a few drinks inside them, bam, the floodgates open. Try not to worry.'

I smiled at her awkwardly.

'And,' she continued, 'If your speech doesn't get them putting their hands in their pockets, they must be heartless.' She winked. 'I'll be having words.'

A fleeting thought passed through my mind wondering if she was a little tipsy herself, but no, it was simply her forthright manner. I could imagine her mingling around the venue and bullying people by the end of the night.

Another raucous bellow of laughter emanated from Alex's table. I turned around. He was sitting between his wife and the handsome High Court judge with silver hair from the SD card. Beside him sat his wife, whose name, Mary, I remembered from when I'd distributed the place cards. Alex appeared awkward, as though the judge was stealing his space. He looked small, like a puppy dog sitting next to his master.

Then it struck me.

The photo of the judge in an uncompromising position with the younger chap on the SD card flashed through my mind.

It was Alex in that photo with the judge!

That couldn't be right. The younger guy had long hair. Perhaps Alex used to have long hair. I tried to decipher the ramifications of that being true. I took my phone from my bag and found the photo.

Kelly leaned over Lauren and prodded my shoulder. 'Mia.'

I jumped. 'I won't be a sec.' I shook my phone. 'I need to take this call.'

I rushed to the toilets, desperate to confirm my suspicions. Locking myself in a cubicle, I expanded the image and squinted at the screen. It was Alex, alright. I hadn't recognised him before. The beardless guy with long hair had deceived me, but the high cheekbones now gave it away.

I needed to talk to my brother.

When I returned to the table, Callum wasn't there. I glanced around the large room. But with the number of people milling around, it was hard to spot him. Perhaps he'd gone to the toilet. Anxiously, I checked the running total on the screen. I clenched my jaw. There was still such a long way to go.

Guests were growing rowdier as the waitresses replenished wine glasses. My gaze continually drifted to the screen, but the total donated wasn't advancing fast enough. Amounts were emerging in dribs and drabs from winners of the silent auction, but by nine o'clock, there was still more than fifty thousand pounds to go.

I glanced at the table behind me, catching Alex and the judge exchange a look. My suspicions were confirmed. They were lovers.

My phone pinged with a text from Ruby.

> How's it going? There hasn't been much movement on the FundMeToday page? I'm going out of my mind here. Please tell me it's going to happen...

The message ended with several emojis displaying a cocktail of negative emotions: sad, confusion, fear, frustration, nervousness, and guilt.

It could have been the effect of the cocktail mixed with the wine, but I felt as if a bolt of energy had pulsated through me. I had to curb the alcohol. For Grace's sake, I had to have my wits about me. But the confidence it gave me made me feel I had nothing left to lose.

I had to take control of the situation.

Callum still had the SD card, and I had a plan.

62

I sought out Alex at the table behind me. Standing, I weaved my way around the back of his table until I reached his side. There was no doubt the alcohol had gone to my head. I could've kicked myself. I shouldn't have underestimated the strength of that cocktail.

Alex spoke before I had a chance to. 'Ah, Mia. Let me introduce you to some of my clients.'

Fuelled by anger and alcohol, I bent over and whispered in his ear, 'Can I have a word, please?'

'What about?'

'Not in here.'

He eyed me suspiciously but got up, brushed down his dinner suit, straightened his bow tie, and followed me out of the ballroom into the main hallway with the staircase. 'What's this all about, Mia?' he asked me, agitated.

'I need to talk to you.'

'Go ahead.'

'In private.'

'This all sounds rather serious.'

'It is.'

'Come to the cloakroom.' He nodded along the hallway. 'There'll be no one there now.'

I marched across the soft-pile carpet and out of the room. At the end of the hallway, he branched off to where Mum and I had dropped off our coats when we'd arrived. He entered the room. I followed him.

It was dark in there and smelled of coats and perfume. I found the light switch. The room was small. A long, white, empty table fronted lines of hanging racks full of coats and furs.

Alex stood with his hands on his slim hips. 'What's this all about, Mia? Enlighten me!'

I took a deep breath and found my courage. 'How are your guests enjoying themselves?'

Alex cocked his head to the side, frowning. 'They're having a great time.'

I reminded myself Ruby needed me. Grace needed me. 'How deep are their pockets?'

'Sorry?'

'I know.'

He crossed his arms, scrunching up his features as if to say he didn't have a clue what I was on about. 'You're going to have to be more specific.'

'The guests on your table. What have *they* been up to? What have *you* been up to?'

'What are you on about, Mia?'

'The list, Alex. The list on the SD card that was in Henry Robertson's possession.'

He stiffened at the mention of Henry's name.

I couldn't believe the courage that had overcome me. But

thoughts of Grace and how far I'd come drove me forward. 'And the photo. The photo of you ensnared in that rather delicate position with the person you're sitting next to tonight. And no, I'm not talking about your wife.'

He puffed out his chest and grabbed my forearm. His face drew so close to me that I could smell salmon and wine on his breath.

'You need to be careful what you're saying. You've no idea what you're getting yourself into.'

'Oh, I think I do.'

'What are you after, Mia?'

I couldn't believe I was having that conversation with the same smart, generous Alex who I'd worked with for the past six months.

'I want to hear it from you. Did you murder Henry Robertson and Kat?'

He eyeballed me. It was unnerving. My heart was racing faster than ever.

'You didn't pull the trigger or rough up Kat, but you arranged it, didn't you?'

Alex remained silent.

'I know, Alex. I know. Henry was blackmailing you with what was on the SD card, wasn't he?'

He glared at me, his expression unhinged. 'Tell me exactly what you want, Mia.'

'I want that fundraising number reached. Then I'll hand you back the SD card that got Henry Robertson and Kat killed.'

He burst out laughing, cackling like a tyrant who had got one over on one of his pawns. Releasing my arm, he pushed me away with such force that I stumbled.

'I'm serious!' I cried out.

'Don't take me for a fool, Mia Hamilton. I already have the SD card. Your brother gave it to me.'

63

'You're lying!'

'You silly, silly girl. If you know what's good for you...' Alex paused, forming his fingers into a fake gun and pretending to shoot me. But despite his bravado, his voice had a hint of fear. 'If you know what's good for you... and your family... you'll shut that mouth of yours. I mean it, Mia. Forget about all this. You don't want to end up the same way as Kat.' He spewed his venom before exiting the room.

The room spun. I grasped my stomach which was churning with nausea. I needed to calm down. I backed against the wall to compose myself, trying to understand why Callum would've handed over the SD card to Alex. If I wasn't wrong, there had been something fearful about Alex's demeanour.

I didn't know how, but I returned to the ballroom. Callum was back from wherever he'd disappeared to. I sat at the table, trying to catch his attention, incredulous that my own brother had betrayed me so cruelly. He was deep in conversation with one of the guys from the marketing department of the KM Group.

The main course had been served, some duck dish Kat had chosen, or stuffed aubergine for the vegans. I didn't like duck. There was something wrong with eating the creature I took Grace to feed in the park. So I'd gone for the aubergine, which, despite being well-presented, I couldn't face. I picked at the salad on the side of the plate, my gaze on Callum, while Lauren jabbered quietly to me about morning sickness.

Heads turned to a collective roar from the table behind, where a man offered another guest a high-five. The screen for Grace's Appeal on the stage displayed a five-thousand-pound donation from Charlie Andrews, the footballer on the SD card. A cheer erupted from the group.

Another text arrived from Ruby:

How's it going?

I couldn't reply.

Eventually, I caught Callum's eye. Stone-faced, I nodded towards the entrance. He got the message.

I excused myself. 'I'm just going to the toilet.'

'Don't be long,' Kelly said. 'I think it might be best to make your speech while the guests are having dessert, not afterwards. People are already wandering towards the casino. We need to keep them in here.'

I met Callum at the main door.

'Are you drunk?' he asked.

I wasn't drunk, just bolder. 'Not in here,' I hissed.

We exited the rear of the venue in silence.

'What's all this about?' he asked, shivering.

'Follow me.'

We came across the entrance to a maze, where I stopped. The orchestra music filtered through the building. It was dark, but once my eyes became accustomed to it, the moonlight brought my brother's concerned features into view.

He stood with his hands in his pockets. 'Are you going to tell me what's happened?'

'I need you to tell me exactly what you've done.' I raised my voice. 'Because I'm having real difficulty processing this right now!'

He removed his hands from his pockets. 'Be quiet, Mia. Calm down and explain! Because I don't know what the hell you're going on about.'

My jaw was tight. 'You gave Alex the SD card. Why?'

His faced dropped. 'How do you know?'

'Alex told me.'

His head fell backwards.

'Why? Why did you give it to him?'

He lifted his head to face me, took a deep breath, and forcefully but slowly breathed it out. 'Because, Mia, these are dangerous people. Very dangerous people. Look what happened to Henry Robertson, to Kat. You don't cross these people. Ever.'

'I don't understand.' My shoulders lifted. I held out my hands. 'You just waltzed up to Alex and gave it to him.'

He was talking faster than usual. 'It's not Alex who's wholly behind Henry's and Kat's deaths. It's Judge Nought.'

My jaw dropped. 'How?'

'Henry met with Alex last week because Kelly wasn't

around. As we thought, Henry tried to blackmail Alex and everyone on the list.'

'Why didn't you tell me?'

'I wanted to keep you out of it. I told Alex that Kat had planted the SD card on you, told you to look after the wallet, and that you were ignorant to everything that had gone on.'

'And he believed you?'

'I think so.' He didn't sound entirely convinced.

'What aren't you telling me?'

He didn't answer.

'How did you know Alex to give it to him?' I asked.

He ran his hand through his hair.

I shoved him like Alex had shoved me earlier. 'What are you keeping from me?'

He laced his hands and plonked them on his head.

I shoved him again. 'Callum?'

He let his arms drop by his sides in submission. 'Because I've become ensnared in this shitshow of an operation.'

I gasped. 'What?'

'One of those two police officers on the list did me a favour a few months back. I messed up – misplaced a piece of evidence. It was a stupid mistake, but bad. Real bad. He made the situation go away. Then they had me.'

'Callum!'

My brother was the last person I thought I'd discover wasn't whiter than white.

'So, what happened? How did you find out I gave him the card?' he asked.

'I confronted him.'

'You did what?'

'I was desperate, Callum. We are desperate.' I glanced around, double-checking no one could overhear us.

'What did you say to him?' he asked.

'I told him he could have the SD card if Grace's target was met.'

He spun around three-sixty and stamped his foot on the ground. 'Christ, Mia!'

'He laughed in my face. Said you'd already given it to him.'

'You don't understand the trouble you're in. Those people are dangerous. Why didn't you speak to me before hatching this stupid idea?'

'Because you would've said no!' I cried.

'No shit.'

'What do we do, Callum? I don't think we're going to reach our target. Grace is not going to make it.' I was hyperventilating out of frustration, anger, and my own stupidity. The alcohol I'd consumed wasn't helping.

He placed his hands on my shoulders. 'Calm down. I'll speak to Alex and try to reason with him, say you didn't know what you were doing – it was all out of concern for your niece.'

'Or should we now just go to the police? For heaven's sake, you are the police. You need to make this all go away.'

'I wish it were that simple.'

I glanced at my watch. 'I've got to get back. How the hell am I meant to make a speech in this state?'

He turned me one-eighty and gently pushed me back to the building. 'Calm down and think of Grace.'

We headed back to our table in silence. Desserts had been served. Everyone had chosen the tiramisu. I'd opted for the mini cheese board. Lauren made small talk. I wasn't listening.

Kelly waved for my attention. 'Now's the time to get up and speak. Go on, chop, chop.'

I walked to the stage. The big screen displayed the first slide of the presentation. The presentation Alex had generously helped me prepare. It was unfathomable that he was caught up in all the mess I was in. What a Jekyll and Hyde character!

Elodie caught my eye, staring directly at me and clapping in rapid short bursts. She smiled in encouragement. The poor woman. She had no idea her dirty, cheating rat of a husband was having an affair with the man sitting on his other side. Or maybe she did. I'd read stories about open relationships. But I didn't believe that was the case with them.

Susan handed me the microphone and gave me an encouraging pat on the shoulder. 'Don't forget to nod when you want me to flick to the next slide.'

My body was shaking. I was in deep water, clinging to a dinghy for dear life. Despite how the evening had ended up, I should've been better prepared to give the speech. As I was about to begin, I saw Alex look at his phone in my peripheral vision. He stood and wormed his way around the tables and out of the room with the phone to his ear.

I cleared my throat. 'Ladies and gentlemen. First of all, thank you for coming this evening and for the amount of generosity you have already shown. My baby niece, Grace, is my world...'

64

The presentation lasted close to ten minutes.

I don't know how I stood on the stage and told our story, but the photos of Grace and the supporting slides spoke for themselves. I noticed Alex return to his table early on while I delivered my words, but apart from that, the ten minutes passed in a nerve-wracking blur, and I was relieved when it was over.

When I left the stage, a generous round of applause from the supportive crowd welcomed me back to my seat.

'Well, if that doesn't get these buggers putting their hands in their pockets, I don't know what will,' Kelly said. 'Grace will be proud of you when she's older and sees a recording of that. Well done.'

She wouldn't be proud of what else I'd done, though!

'Thank you,' was all I could manage. What I wanted to say was what a scumbag her brother was. But maybe I'd get to do that another time. First, I needed to work out how involved she was.

'The results of the silent auction are coming up. You'll like this. It's always interesting to see how much people are willing to pay for items.'

I turned. Alex stood, glared at me, and walked away from his table.

Spurred on by my confidence in addressing such a large audience, I had no alternative. I needed to speak to him again. Somehow, I needed to rectify all the mess. 'Excuse me.' I stood.

Kelly smiled. 'Off again, Mia. Anyone would think you don't like my company.'

'I'm sorry, I need to go to the toilet. Nerves.' I faked a giggle. 'I won't be long.'

Callum was talking on his phone. He appeared uncomfortable. I guessed he was speaking to Ruby. At least it allowed me to get away unnoticed. I didn't want to drag him into more trouble than I already had.

Maybe Kelly had drunk too much, or perhaps she was just being her confident self because when I reached the door, she was on the stage, standing next to the master of ceremonies. He invited her to take the microphone. I briefly stopped at the door.

'Please remain seated while we conclude the silent auction, everyone. Following Mia's wonderful speech, I'd like to relieve you of more of your hard-earned money for such a worthy cause. And I shall be offering lots of creative ways in which you can donate.'

A ripple of laughter emanated from the floor.

I peeped my head around the door. Alex was heading along the corridor towards the cloakroom, where we'd had our previous confrontation. I left Kelly talking to the audience and followed him.

I needed to make it right.

But when I got there, he'd vanished.

I searched from room to room but couldn't find him. At the end of the narrow dark passage, light was seeping through a conference room door left ajar. I hurried towards it. I looked inside. Alex was alone, leaning on the long table, his back to me.

I deliberated my next move. My pulse was racing. The best thing would be to confront him and desperately plead my case to get Grace her treatment.

The decision was taken for me. A fist unceremoniously punched me in the back. I flew into the oak-panelled-walled room, stumbling towards the open floor-to-ceiling patio doors that led to a courtyard and gardens beyond.

I swore out loud and turned.

The judge closed the meeting room door and spoke, his arrogant tone spilling with confidence. 'Mia. My dear. You've got yourself in way over your head, you silly child.'

I glared at Alex. He held my stare, silent.

The judge continued. It became as clear as day who pulled the strings in their relationship. He spoke with clarity as if he was addressing his court. 'Henry Robertson was out to blackmail us. We couldn't have that. No one blackmails us, Mia. And certainly not me. It's all rather fortuitous that Alex managed to step in and save the day.' He caressed Alex's shoulder.

It made me want to throw up. Their wives were waiting for them in that ballroom.

'Kat told me Henry was meant to meet Kelly on the day he was shot,' I said. I had to know if Kelly was a part of this. 'Did that happen?'

'Leave my sister out of this,' Alex said.

The judge cackled. 'Correct, but fortunately for us, Kelly

had her accident and asked Alex to cover for her. And, well, as regards Kat, we knew of her little enterprise. We know the guy who she offloaded her stolen goods to. We thought it was her who took the wallet. It never crossed our minds it was you, little Miss Innocent Mia, who stepped up to help in Kat's hour of need.'

I kept quiet, unsure how to react.

'You shouldn't have threatened us, you know,' the judge said. 'We would've turned a blind eye.' The faintest smirk twisted his lips. 'Maybe not. You're a loose end, Mia. I hate loose ends.' He stared at Alex. 'Don't you?'

'So you hired a professional to do your dirty work.'

The judge bellowed with laughter. 'My nephew, a professional? Hardly. I don't think his CV would impress. Not with our friend Mr Robertson's body bobbing up and down the Thames. I always knew it was a mistake getting family involved. It's time to find a replacement.'

'Murderer.' It was an inane thing to say, but foolishly emboldened, I couldn't stop the word from leaving my lips.

'Me? No! I'd never kill anyone.' The judge wrung his hands for effect. 'I've got my nephew here who takes care of such matters for me.'

I spun around. I hadn't heard the door open and another person enter. But there was no mistaking who that person was. I recognised those eyes instantly. He was the callous killer who had shot Henry Robertson. The guy I'd seen getting in and out of the posh car in the car park when I was having a cigarette earlier.

Balaclava Man.

65

I skipped introductions and bolted out of the double doors, running across the courtyard and towards the gardens, pleased I'd opted for pumps tonight instead of heels.

'Get her!' A booming voice sounded behind me. Sir Richard had lost his humour in a heartbeat.

Running blindly, I fled as fast as I could. A whirlwind of memories from the night I was chased from the Parkside Hotel room spun through my mind. The same panic and adrenaline, the chaotic mix of fear, shot through my body.

In a daze, I found myself at the entrance to the maze where I'd spoken to Callum earlier in the evening. I didn't know why. Perhaps it was the nearest place I thought I could hide until the nightmare was over.

I looked behind me, deliberating. Someone was standing by the building, urgently scanning the grounds. I could only guess who. I carried on, wondering if I should've gone back for my brother. Of course not. Callum would've told me not to be such an idiot. I needed to get the hell out of there.

The decision was made for me. Someone was heading for

me. Whether they could see me or not, I couldn't tell, but I couldn't risk crossing their path.

I darted into the labyrinth of twelve-foot-high hedges. Small box lighting barely illuminated the way. The enormity of the structure dwarfed me. The narrow shingle paths twisted precariously, making a terrible grating sound underfoot.

Foolishly or not, I believed the deeper I got lost in the maze, the better. I was whimpering, terrified. The temperature had dropped, but I was sweating. I glanced over my shoulder at each turn, expecting to see a gun pointing in my direction.

The mixture of straight edges and curves provided ample opportunity to hide or to be found. Stumbling into the coarse branches, I momentarily lost my balance. I stopped, stockstill, terrified someone was in pursuit. But I couldn't hear anything beyond my loud and laboured breathing.

Control your breathing, Mia! Calm yourself down! my inner voice yelled at me.

I broke into a jog. After each corner, I looked behind me. I was alone.

Around the next corner, the ground lighting ended, adding to my trepidation. But so did the noisy shingle that changed to a grass path. And while I couldn't be heard moving, neither could the person hunting me down. In the darkness, a pale glow of moonlight allowed me to gradually and covertly carry on. But I'd lost my bearings – and all my energy.

Completely disorientated, I cowered into one of the bushes to stay out of sight and remain there until morning if need be. My breath was shallow and ragged with fear.

The last ten days flashed through my mind.

I was a nobody the night I'd walked into the Parkside Hotel.

Then I became a criminal being chased by a hitman.

I feared for my brother, for Grace, and my family and what I'd brought to their doorstep. A crunching sound signalled approaching footsteps. The bushes rustled. I placed a hand to my mouth, stifling a cry. Someone was there. Or had I imagined it? But another deliberate crunch of dead leaves told me it wasn't an animal bedding down for the night or a nocturnal friend searching for their supper.

My heartbeat blasted in my ears, a frantic barrage I feared could help whoever was there seeking me out. The footsteps moved slowly, quietly, as if trying to avoid detection.

Was that it? Was that my destiny? The place where I was going to die?

Please no. I thought of my brother, wondering where he was – what had become of him? I drew back deeper into the bushes, recoiling into a hunched position, crouching on my haunches. My terror had hit new heights.

I sensed footsteps growing louder, slicing through the eerie silence, and the shadow of a figure stretched across the ground right in front of me.

They stopped and turned towards me.

66

I refused to be taken like that, passive, curled up like a frightened child.

With all my strength, I mustered a scream and launched myself at the silhouetted figure, catching them in the midriff and skittling them onto the ground. I continued running, taking a corner that led to a lit fountain that dominated a circular section of grass. I ducked behind a stone bench on the perimeter, shaking uncontrollably.

He saw me as soon as he turned the corner.

'Help!' I screamed. It was futile, but I carried on. 'Someone help me! Please!'

Purposely, he stomped towards me. His hand entered his inside jacket pocket and removed a gun. He levelled it at me.

'Mia!' It was my brother's voice.

Callum launched himself, slamming into the balaclava guy. The two of them fell to the ground. But not before the balaclava guy got a shot away. That same unmistakable cracking sound I'd heard in that hotel room on the night Henry Robertson was murdered.

I was dazed, as if I'd been punched in the stomach by a heavy, sickening blow. I pressed my hands over the entry wound. A warm wetness seeped through the material of my ballgown.

'Mia, No!'

Callum and the hitman wrestled on the ground. My brother desperately tried to free the gun.

They were both trying to get the better of each other, but gradually, Callum managed to lower the gun between the two of them. Two shots sounded. Or was it one? Both men stopped grappling, and silence fell like a heavy weight.

'Callum!' I called, but it came out a whisper. 'Callum?'

One of them started to stand. At first, I couldn't make out which one. He was hurt. Badly hurt. Struggling to his feet, he stumbled in my direction.

My chest tightened in shock. 'Callum!'

My brother stared at me with a curious, blank expression. He looked as confused as I felt.

'Mia! I—' His voice faded. His body slumped forward. In slow motion, he fell to the ground with a heavy thud.

'No. No. No!' I desperately tried to cradle my big brother in my arms. But the pain burning through me wouldn't allow me to.

It couldn't be happening. With all my strength, I managed to turn him over. His sightless eyes stared at me. 'Don't leave me!' Sobbing, I pulled him to me until we were one. I couldn't let him go. 'Help!' I screamed. 'Someone help us!' My frantic voice lingered, weaving through the heavy air. I glanced around.

Another bolt of fear shot through me. The judge's hitman lying on the ground. He was still.

With all my strength, I raised myself to my knees and

slowly managed to get to my feet. But I couldn't straighten my back. I remained bent over, clutching my stomach. Putting as much pressure as I could on the entry wound, I struggled across to the body.

There was no doubt.

He was dead.

67

All-consuming panic set in. Mum! I needed to get to my mother. She'd help us.

Still holding my abdomen, I scrambled in Callum's pocket for his phone. There was no signal. I fumbled to find the torch, shining it over my body. I lifted my hand that was covering the wound. The blood blended in well with my scarlet ballgown.

A current of pain caught me off guard like a giant wave of trouble I never saw coming. It ripped through me with each step, but I couldn't stop. I had to get help. Perhaps I could save Callum. I stumbled forward, finding my way back to where small spotlights illuminated the ground. I followed the faint hum emanating from the hall. Blood dropped to the ground like breadcrumbs. A Hansel and Gretel trail leading them to my brother.

My vision blurred. I staggered around the corners and bends of the twelve-foot-high hedges. A godforsaken journey that seemed to last a lifetime. Finally, I spotted the grandeur of Moorlands. Through gritted teeth, I laboured on.

Whatever I'd got involved in, I couldn't die. It wasn't my time.

By luck or by determination, I wound up back at the building. Soon I'd reach Mum. But once inside, a profound weakness overcame me, along with a dreaded sense I was falling. A numbness spread across my body.

But I had to keep going.

I was close.

The hallway was empty. Everyone must have been in the Eddison Suite, from where Kelly's demanding voice rallying support was echoing along the hallway.

'Come on, everyone.' Her voice was distorted, coming in waves like I was underwater, falling, drowning. 'We're still twenty-six thousand pounds short of our target. Grace is depending on you. We don't have long before we start getting kicked out of here.'

I didn't know how, but I made it to the ballroom door.

Kelly caught sight of me. 'There she is, Mia! Come here and remind this lovely audience why we need to relieve them of their hard-earned cash.'

My legs gave way. I fell to the floor. It was cold, so very cold… like I imagined death to be. 'Mum!' My voice was a faint whisper.

I glanced at the large screen.

The numbers were slowly ticking towards the target.

Too slowly. We weren't going to make it.

Perhaps more would come in tomorrow.

But right then, I needed to sleep.

68

My world was black. I couldn't move, couldn't see. I was trapped in a cage, and the doors were bolted. It was suffocating, debilitating. I wanted to scream, but every time I tried, my mouth wouldn't open, and my breath caught in my throat.

But I wasn't in pain. And I could smell. When certain senses failed you, others intensified. I understood that. The odours were sharp and tangy – the sterile cleaning products, the ever-present stench of antiseptic, the anguish and hopelessness. And I could hear. Chairs scraped. Machines beeped. Monitors alarmed. People sobbed. Voices drifted through the shadows, distant at first. Ricochets of sounds I couldn't make out. Then they strengthened as if someone had raised the volume.

'We need to tell her,' a woman said.

I thought it was Mum, but I couldn't be sure.

'As soon as she wakes up.' That was Ruby. Most definitely Ruby.

I could detect the vulnerability in her voice. But if she was there, she wasn't in the USA. That wasn't good. She should have been on her way to the States by now. But who knew how long I'd been there? It could've been days, weeks, months. They could've already been and come back. I tried to open my mouth. I had to know about Grace, the money, and whether we had made it. I had to know if she was still alive.

'Could I have a word?' someone said. It was male. Callum. My brother. It sounded like my beautiful brother was there.

Memories weaved their way through the confusion. The sound of death as his body had dropped to the floor. Or had that been a dream? Oh, please let him be OK. Please, I begged the darkness.

'Sure,' Mum replied. It was definitely Mum's voice.

'The police are here,' the voice continued. 'They'd like to speak to you.' I'd been wrong. It wasn't Callum. The voice was too feminine, too clinical, too cold.

Don't do it, I wanted to shout out. *Don't speak to the police. Make sure Grace is safe first.* But the words wouldn't come. My failing body, trapping my words, wouldn't allow them to leave my lips.

I listened, desperate to hear my brother's voice. Please speak, Callum. But I couldn't hear him. I was shutting down. I could only manage short bursts of awareness. But I was getting better every day. I had to. I'd come so far, I had to make it out of there alive.

69

Two years later

The discordant clang of the door grates on me. It's a sound that will stay with me for the rest of my life. As will the stale smell of confinement ever present in the air.

I'm sitting on the bottom bunk in a cross-legged position, staring into nothingness, when Lexi walks into the compact cell. A tall, broad-shouldered woman, she scared me when she arrived last week. But, although it's early days, she appears to be a much better cellmate than Reba, her predecessor, whose loose tongue, bulky arms, and close connections to similar inmates, had scared the living hell out of me.

'That doctor is well creepy. You ever seen her?' Lexi picks up a plastic cup from the small desk in the corner of the cell and fills it with water. She gulps it down before climbing to the top bunk and lying down.

'Only on my first day,' I say. 'Luckily, I've never had to since.'

'Don't get ill, is my advice.'

I stretch out my crossed legs. My head hits the lumpy pillow. I stare at the bulge Lexi's heavy body has made in the mattress springs above.

It's the downtime in the cell that I've never got used to. The feeling of being caged like an animal is claustrophobic. It's why I look forward to the exercise sessions in the yard so much. I've thrown myself into prison life as advised in one of my earlier counselling sessions, embracing the work assignments and making the most of the educational programmes for when I'm released.

Released – less than four weeks away now. It doesn't seem possible I've been here eight months.

There's movement from the bunk above. Lexi's head appears, dangling like it's in the stocks. 'So are ya gonna tell me what you're in here for before you leave?' She's already told me why she ended up here and the drug dealers she's been involved with since her late teens.

I hesitate. I scooted around the topic when she asked me a few days ago. I couldn't see what value could be gained from confiding in a new cellmate so close to my imminent release. So I'm unsure what makes me spill my story to this virtual stranger. 'I seduced a man and stole his wallet. And then it got complicated.' I relay my story from when I first met Kat to when I woke up in the hospital bed with a tube stuck down my throat. 'I got done for several things – spiking the guy's drink, theft, as well as perverting the course of justice.'

She descends from her bed and drops on the end of my bunk, her jaw dropped to her chest.

'I got a five-year sentence,' I continue.

'But you're getting out soon?'

I nod. 'They're releasing me on licence.'

Her large dark eyes bulge. 'Bloody hell, luv! Talk about unlucky.'

'You can say that again.'

'Your brother sounds like he was a top bloke.'

'He was. The best.' Tears sting my eyes. They always do when I speak about Callum.

'Bet ya mum's cut up.'

I nod. 'We all miss him terribly. I thought I heard him when I was in the coma, but I was wrong. It's his birthday the day I get released.'

'I'm sorry for what you've been through.' She gently hits my foot. 'What happened to the rest of them?'

'The balaclava guy died at the scene. And the judge and Alex got the life sentences the bastards both deserved.'

'You'd have thought the bloody judge would've used someone more professional than his bloody nephew to carry out his dirty work,' she says. 'What about your old boss?'

I tell her how Kelly worked hard to reestablish the KM Group brand after the story blew up. But not even someone with her years of experience could get the company back on track. So she closed it down and started a new company, taking only her favourite clients with her. 'She paid for a top lawyer for me. He put together a great case, highlighting my mitigating circumstances and how I became involved with Kat. Kelly's promised me a job when I get out of this hellhole.'

'That's lucky for you,' Lexi says.

I nod. 'It gives me hope. She's a good woman.'

'Hell knows what I'm gonna do for work when I eventually get out of here.'

I make sympathetic noises. Lexi asks me about Grace. I

explain how Kelly has also taken Grace under her wing as if she's the daughter she lost and has found again. At first, Mum said, 'That woman can stuff her money,' and she refused to have anything to do with her. Mum gave Ruby a hard time when Ruby tried to persuade her that Kelly was innocent of Alex's wrongdoings with his clients. Her solicitor proved as much in court. But Kelly's actions spoke far louder than her words, and she slowly turned Mum around.

I can't believe how much I'm opening up to Lexi. But it feels good.

'At least your niece got what she needed. Is she alright now?' Lexi asks.

I nod. 'The professionals thought she'd relapsed last year. Kelly committed to funding another round of treatment for her.'

Lexi tilts her head to the side. 'Wow! She sounds like a real top chick!'

'Grace was actually alright, so Kelly put the money in trust so if Grace ever needs further treatment, the funds are there for her.'

'What about your sister?'

I tell her that Ruby still looks after Grace, and with Kelly's help, she has set up a small charity that helps babies who need life-saving treatment abroad.

'Good lass! It was all alright in the end, then,' Lexi says.

'Except for Callum. I sometimes feel as if I pulled the trigger of that gun myself.'

Lexi puffs out a long, hard breath. 'You can't think like that. You just got involved with the wrong person. You're still so young, girl. You need to move on. You've got the right people around you now. Just keep your head down. A few more weeks, and you'll be out of here, and you can rebuild your life.'

I shrug, forcing a smile. 'I will. But I'll never forgive myself for the mistake I made.'

'We all make mistakes. It's how we learn from them that counts.'

70

I give a wry smile to the prison officer as the door clunks closed behind me. I inhale deeply. Lexi is right. It does smell different out here. There's a chill in the air, but it's a good chill. Good air.

'Mia!' Ruby runs towards me and throws her arms around my lank body. 'I thought you'd lost weight when I last saw you.' She steps backwards. 'Look at you. You're a bag of bones.' She loops her arm through mine. 'Let's get you home. Mum's got a big lunch waiting.' Her whole demeanour is different, more mature. She's had her braces removed, and her face has filled out. A light-pink-tinted gloss coats her lips. My baby sister has grown up.

'You didn't tell me you'd passed your test,' I say when we get in Mum's car. It's a new one she bought with savings Callum had.

Ruby drives out the prison car park.

'I didn't even know you were learning,' I say.

'I wanted to surprise you. Mum and Grace can't wait for

you to get home.' She pulls out of the T-junction like she's been driving for years.

'I need you to do something for me before we go home.'

'What?'

'Take me to Callum's grave.'

'We thought you might want to go. Call Mum. Tell her we'll pick her up and we'll all go together.'

'Sounds like a plan.'

She updates me on life since she last visited a few weeks ago. 'Come on, cheer up,' she says. 'You're free at last.'

I stare out of the window. 'I don't feel free.' I turn to her. 'The guilt is suffocating.'

'You know you can't spend the rest of your life beating yourself up about Callum's death. He would've hated that.'

'It was my fault,' I say flatly.

'Mia, it was that bastard who was holding the gun's fault. Our brother saved your life. And he would've done the same thing again and again. You know that.'

My eyes well up with plump tears.

'Mia. You need to move on. For your sake. For Callum's sake.'

71

'What was he like?' Grace asks, staring up at me with innocent wonder.

Ruby butts in. 'Just like you. Fierce, determined, and very brave.'

Grace turns to stare at Callum's grave and leans her back into my legs. Like Ruby, she's filled out. Her face is fuller, and a thin layer of fat now covers her bones. Ruby never brought her along when she visited me in prison, so this is the first time I've seen her in the flesh without an NG tube.

I point to the bunch of daffodils in her hand. 'Go and lay them on his grave.'

'That's it,' Grace says, her voice a gentle whisper lost in the spring air, as she places the flowers by the gravestone.

It's a Blue Pearl granite gravestone. The best money could buy. Kelly insisted on it.

Mum links her arm through mine. She's aged even more these past few years. But who can blame her for the lines of grief and worry that have deepened along her brow. 'I'm so pleased you're finally home. I've missed you so much.' Her voice falters. She sweeps a hand towards my brother's grave. 'Just like I miss him so much.'

'Me, too,' Ruby says. But she doesn't cry. She won't shed a tear in front of Grace. She has to remain strong for her daughter and for Mum, she told me during one of the prison visits she made to see me.

Grace shivers. 'I'm cold.'

Mum jumps up. 'Come on, let's get going.'

'I want to stay here a while,' I say.

Mum takes Grace's hand. 'You and I can sit in the car and wait for these two. Hurry along.'

'She doesn't stop fussing!' Ruby says when Mum and Grace are leaving through the graveyard gates.

'Only because she cares.' I sigh deeply. 'She's been through so much.'

Ruby slips her arm through mine. 'We all have, but we all need to move on. Especially you. You've got us. Kelly's offering you a lifeline with a good job.' She points upwards towards the sky. 'I can just hear him now, shouting down: "Let this be a new start for you. Go live your best life. For me. Make me proud."'

I take a deep lungful of fresh spring air and smile at my sister. 'I will.'

Please turn the page to get your free copy of my novella, Choices.

YOUR FREE GIFT

Warning signs presented themselves from the start. Flashing like the neon displays in Piccadilly Circus, they couldn't have advertised things more clearly. But Abbie was too troubled to see clearly. Too damaged to see the dangers Tony Sharpe brought into her life. Until the day he pushed her too far.

Visit ajcampbellauthor.com to get your copy

PLEASE LEAVE A REVIEW

As for all authors, reviews are the key to raising awareness of my work. If you have enjoyed this book, please do consider leaving a review on Amazon and Goodreads to help others find it too.

All my novels undergo a rigorous editing process, but sometimes mistakes do happen. If you have spotted an error, please contact me at aj@ajcampbellauthor.com, so I can promptly get it corrected.
Thank you for choosing to read my books.
AJ x

ACKNOWLEDGMENTS

It takes more than an author to write a book. I'm blessed to have a wonderful team supporting my work. Firstly, thank you to my savvy beta readers. Mr C, Christine Henderson, John Black, Dawn Harland, Sally Riordan, and Phyllis Fried, your observations and suggestions have helped to make this story so much better. Thank you for your time and continued dedication to my work.

Thank you to my brilliant editor, Louise Walters, for helping to make this book the best it can be. And thank you, Tim Barber, for working patiently with me to produce the perfect cover.

Thank you to my ARC team and all the fantastic book bloggers and media people who support my work! Most of you have been by my side since my debut novel. I am so lucky to have you.

Thank you, Mr C and my boys, for your support while I write my stories. I love you more than words can say.

And, last but not least, thank you to all my wonderful readers. Without you, I couldn't continue writing and publishing my books. I hope you enjoyed Mia's story.

BOOKS BY AJ CAMPBELL

Leave Well Alone

Don't Come Looking

Search No Further

The Phone Call

The Wrong Key

Her Missing Husband

My Perfect Marriage

Did I Kill My Husband?

The Mistake

First-Time Mother

I hope you enjoyed reading my ninth published book *The Mistake* as much as I adored writing it. If you haven't read my other novels, check them out on the following pages.

FIRST-TIME MOTHER

My baby is missing. Everyone thinks it's my fault.

I'm so scared carrying my delicate newborn, **Lola**, home from the hospital. It wasn't an easy birth and she is so small. Seeing her gorgeous little face look up at me I swear I'll *never* let anyone hurt her. But maybe I should have been protecting her from myself...

My wonderful husband **Max** reassures me that the blackouts I'm having are normal: I'm sleep-deprived, and I just need help.

Until my baby girl goes missing.

I'm distraught. How is it possible? How could her crib be lying empty?

They think the pressure of being a mother has broken me.

And there's just so much I don't remember, I have to wonder if they could be right? After all, I have done some terrible things in my life... but I'd never, ever hurt my baby girl.

I'm certain someone close to me is setting me up. **And they don't know how far I'll go to bring my baby home again.**

THE WRONG KEY

A mother's love.
A daughter's life.
A race against time.

London-based Steph Knight faces the challenge of a lifetime
when she's sent to New York to cover for a colleague involved
in a tragic car accident.

Recently divorced, Steph sees it as an opportunity for a fresh
start and to spend time with her teenage daughter, Ellie, a
talented musician, before she leaves for university.

Soon after arriving, Steph crosses paths with Edward, a
corporate lawyer, who introduces Ellie to Jack, a bioethics
student enjoying his summer break. As both relationships
intensify, Steph begins to uncover a web of corruption within
her company that seemingly reaches right to the top.

Feeling increasingly threatened, she has no idea who she can

trust. Not even the men they've fallen for are beyond
suspicion.

And then the unthinkable happens.

Steph receives a menacing text message. Ellie has been
kidnapped.

The clock is ticking. Ellie's life is in danger.
And so is Steph's.

Terrified, far from home, and with no one to trust, Steph
must draw on her inner strength to save her daughter... even
if it kills her.

THE PHONE CALL

SHORTLISTED FOR THE ADULT PRIZE FOR FICTION: THE SELFIE BOOK AWARDS 2022

A single phone call can destroy your life.

Joey Clarke was just fifteen when his dad died, leaving him to raise his much younger siblings as his mum dealt with the trauma of bereavement and her failing health.

Ten years on, Joey's only pleasure is spending time with his friend Becca, the love of his life. It's the one escape from his dead-end job, his ever-increasing debts and the fear that enforcement agents will knock on his front door any day.

So when a phone call brings Joey the chance to ease the burdens of his life, he grabs the opportunity, even though he knows things are not entirely as they should be. He justifies it to himself as a way to get back on his feet. But when he finds himself party to a crime linked to Becca, he panics.

As catastrophic events unfold, Joey becomes further embroiled in a web of secrets, lies and deceit. He is now faced with the impossible. Should he confess to the police? Tell Becca? Or should he keep quiet and say nothing?

So, when the next job comes in, Joey wants out. But this time he's in way too deep to say no...

HER MISSING HUSBAND

People don't just disappear.
Someone must know something.

Lori once lived the perfect life with her husband Howie and their teenage daughter Molly – until the day Howie went to work and never came home.

Unable to cope, Lori left her job as an investigative journalist and fled the city. Now a successful author, she lives in rural isolation with her beloved dogs.

But Lori's ordered, solitary life is about to be turned upside down.

Because Frankie Evans, the man she helped convict for the murder of a local woman shortly after Howie disappeared, has just walked out of prison a free man.

And Frankie wants to meet Lori.

Because he has news of her missing husband that he says she needs to hear...

LEAVE WELL ALONE

**A broken family. Skeletons in the closet. Lives in danger.
How far would you go to protect your family?**

When Eva's brother Ben announces he has found their
mother, Eva is determined to have nothing to do with the
woman who abandoned them eighteen years ago to a
traumatic childhood in foster care. Eva is happy now, in a
loving relationship with rich and dependable Jim, and she is
pregnant.

Nothing can change Eva's mind. Her eyes are firmly on the
future. But when her baby is born with a serious hereditary
illness, she is forced to confront both her mother and her
past. Eva begins to find forgiveness.

But as old secrets and layers of deceit emerge, she makes a
shocking discovery, leaving her fearing for her baby's, Jim's,
and her own life.

DON'T COME LOOKING

Would you refuse your best friend's plea for help?

Marc O'Sullivan has disappeared. His wife Sasha is frantic, and Eva is baffled. They were blissfully married with three kids.
The perfect couple... or so everybody thought.

Sasha begs Eva to help her find Marc. But he has given a written statement at the police station where Eva works. It's on record – when his family report him missing, Marc does not want to be found. But why?

Ultimately, friendship and loyalty override Eva's professional integrity, and she is compelled to use her resources to delve into Marc's life, even if it means breaking the police code of conduct and jeopardising her career.

As each day passes, the mystery deepens. Murky goings-on from Marc and Sasha's neighbours heighten the tension.

What dark secrets are they hiding? And what drove Marc's inexplicable actions in the weeks leading up to his disappearance? Behaviour so out of character that Eva struggles to tell Sasha about it.

Will Eva uncover the truth before it's too late and lives are destroyed forever?

MY PERFECT MARRIAGE

It feels like all the air has been knocked out of me. My best friend is dead, killed at her own daughter's birthday party.

All I want to do is run into my husband's loving arms. But he's in handcuffs, covered in her blood. His voice quivers, almost sobbing as officers put him in the police car. 'You don't think I did this, do you? I was trying to save her.'

At first, I'm sure he couldn't have done it. The man I love wouldn't hurt anyone. But as I try to prove that he didn't murder Lucy, secrets begin unravelling...

It starts with the messages between the two of them. Initially, they seem innocent enough. But the more I look, the more I become convinced they were having an affair. Then I find out about his divorce lawyer...

Suddenly my whole life feels like a lie. If he was hiding his plan to leave me for Lucy, can I believe his protests that he is innocent? And if he really did murder his lover, what else is he capable of?

DID I KILL MY HUSBAND?

The police officer's voice is steady as he tells me the news. 'Your husband is in hospital.' My heart pounds. I think about my children, safely tucked up in bed. What will happen to us if he loses his life? And more importantly... do the police know where I really was tonight?

Everybody thinks Michael and I are the perfect couple. But everybody is wrong.

Because my dear, lovely husband was at the heart of a scandal at the school where he teaches. He was cleared of any wrongdoing. At first I believed him. Now, I'm sure he's been hiding something terrible.

But I can't tell the police a thing. Because my husband isn't the only one with secrets.

So, as I stand here knowing I have to tell my children that Michael is fighting for his life, I ask myself: what would be worse? For my husband, the much-loved local teacher, to die? Or for him to live, and for all his lies to come home again?

In the end, the choice is easy. I know what I have to do...

I'll tell the police that I would never, ever hurt my husband. But will they believe me?

ABOUT THE AUTHOR

AJ CAMPBELL is an Amazon USA top 30 bestselling author of ten psychological suspense thrillers and promises stories full of twists, turns and torment.

AJ draws inspiration for her stories from seemingly unbelievable situations in which ordinary people find themselves. She creates compelling characters that resonate with her readers. AJ lives in the UK on the Essex / Hertfordshire border with her husband, sons, and cocker spaniel, Max. She is a dog lover, Netflix junkie, and a wine and Asian food enthusiast. And, either reading, watching TV or writing, AJ enjoys nothing more than getting stuck into a twisty story!